ALSO BY MARGOT LIVESEY

Learning by Heart

Homework

Criminals

The Missing World

Eva Moves the Furniture

Banishing Verona

The House on Fortune Street

The Flight of Gemma Hardy

M E R CURY

MARGOT LIVESEY

A NOVEL

SCEPTRE

First published in Great Britain in 2016 by Sceptre
An imprint of Hodder & Stoughton
An Hachette UK company

This trade paperback edition published in 2017

1

Copyright © 2016 by Margot Livesey

A CIP catalogue record for this title is available from the British Library

Trade Paperback ISBN 978 1 473 65784 7
Ebook ISBN 978 1 473 65785 4

Printed and bound by CPI Group (UK) Ltd, Croydon, CR0 4YY

Hodder & Stoughton policy is to use papers that are natural, renewable
and recyclable products and made from wood grown in sustainable
forests. The logging and manufacturing processes are expected to
conform to the environmental regulations of the country of origin.

Hodder & Stoughton Ltd
Carmelite House
50 Victoria Embankment
London EC4Y 0DZ

www.hodder.co.uk

FOR KATE, ANNA, ALASTAIR,
KIRSTY, AND EMMA, WITH LOVE.

M
E R
CURY

PART ONE
DONALD

1

MY MOTHER CALLED ME after a favorite uncle, who was in turn called after a Scottish king. Donald III was sixty when he first ascended the throne in 1093. He went on to reign twice, briefly and disastrously. As a child I hated my name—other children sang "Donald, where's y'er troosers?" in the playground—but as an adult I have come to appreciate being named after a valiant late bloomer: a man who seized the day. Of course most Americans, when I introduce myself, are thinking not about Scottish history but about a cartoon duck. They are surprised when I tell them that a Scot invented penicillin and that James VI, for whom the Bible was so gloriously translated, was a keen amateur dentist. I used to believe that in my modest fashion, I was contributing to the spread of Scottish values: thrift, industry, integrity. I have my own business, a full-service optometrist's, in a town outside Boston. More than most people, I have tested the hypothesis that the eye is the window to the soul.

Give us a child until the age of seven and he is ours for life, the Jesuits famously claimed, so perhaps it was my first ten years in Scotland that inoculated me against American optimism. I am pleased by an average day, and I know I am neither great nor awesome. What's more, I don't believe other people are either, although I am too polite to say so. Before I started my business, I practiced as a surgeon, which taught me precision and humility.

It was my mother who brought us to the States. In 1981 she was offered a two-year position in the Boston office of her advertising company. My father, a manager for British Rail in the days when there still was a British Rail, was happy to have an adventure. On the plane over, while my little sister, Frances, made her dolls cups of tea, the three of us studied a map of America and made a list of places we wanted to see. We rented a house on Avon Hill in Cambridge. I attended a nearby school where I gradually made friends but my real friend was Robert, whose parents ran a flower shop in Edinburgh, round the corner from the house I still regarded as home. Every week I wrote to him on a blue aerogram, and every week I received a reply to my previous aerogram. Despite the stingy American holidays, my parents worked hard at our list, and from each place we visited—Washington, DC; Yosemite; the Berkshires; New York; Montreal—I sent Robert a postcard.

During our second Christmas I sent him a card from Key West, and it was there, beside the hotel swimming pool, that my parents announced that we were not going back to Scotland. In June, when the tenants left, our house would be sold. I had already written my Christmas thank-you letter to Robert—we'd exchanged model airplanes—and week after week, as I put off breaking the news, my aerograms grew briefer. I was suddenly aware that he would never see the Frog Pond on Boston Common, where my mother had taught us to skate, or the famous glass flowers that I had tried so hard to describe; that my new friends—Dean, David, Jim, Gerry—would never be more than names to him.

At Easter Robert wrote that he and his family had spent a week in a caravan near Montrose. They had played cricket with the family in the next caravan, and he and his brother had slept in their own wee tent. "It was fab," he wrote, "though Ian thrashes around in his sleep like a maniac." I didn't answer. I planned to, almost daily, but I could not bring myself to write even "Dear Robert." After three more letters, which I didn't open, he stopped writing, and when we went back to pack up our house, he was visiting cousins on the Isle of Wight. In the years that followed, my parents returned for a fortnight every August, but I chose to go to summer camp; a brief visit was worse than none. When I returned to Edinburgh at the age of eighteen, to study medicine, one of the first things I did was to go to the flower shop. Over the door hung a sign: Bunty's Bakery. They moved, the woman said vaguely. The new owners of his house were equally unhelpful. During eight years in that small city I never glimpsed him, even from afar. I still have all his aerograms in a shoebox that, although I have no plans to reread them, it would grieve me sharply to lose.

Fran was six when we moved. Within a year, her memories of Scotland had faded; she was a robust American. She has always been on easier terms with life than I have. My mother claims I didn't smile until I was nearly eight months old, and then was miserly with my new skill. "You'd look at your father and me playing peek-a-boo," she said, "as if we'd lost our minds." Even now I sometimes have to remind myself to tighten my cheek muscles, raise the corners of my mouth. I would fit in well in one of those countries—Iceland, say, or Latvia—where people seldom smile. Which is not to say I don't have a sense of humor. I enjoy puns, and have a weakness for silly jokes and slapstick. One of the things that drew me to Viv—you will not see much evidence of it in this narrative—was that she made me laugh. She is the only person I know well who calls me Don. We have been married for nine years and have two children, aged ten and eight. At the wedding reception Viv, already six months pregnant with Trina, carried Marcus instead of a bouquet. Our parents were, at that time, all four, still alive.

The year before Marcus was born, I qualified as an ophthalmologist in Massachusetts. But four years later, when Trina was fourteen months old, I gave up practicing surgery, and we moved out of Boston to be closer to my parents. One unexpected consequence of the move was that Viv, who had loved horses as a teenager, began to ride more often. Her old friend Claudia lived nearby and ran a stable that belonged to her great-aunt. One day, as she knelt to tie Trina's shoes, Viv announced that Claudia had suggested they run Windy Hill together. I knew at once, from the way she focused on the laces, that she had already agreed. One of the things I first admired about Viv was her impulsiveness. She was born saying, "Yes." And I was born saying "Let me figure that out."

The three of us, Viv, Claudia, and I, met with Claudia's accountant, who made it clear that even in a good season, Viv would earn a small fraction of her current salary working in mutual funds. While the accountant went over the numbers, Viv and Claudia exchanged the kind of look that might have passed between members of Shackleton's expedition as he described the challenges ahead. What did they care about horrendous odds? They were bound for glory.

But after the accountant had packed up her spreadsheets, and Claudia had gone home to the house she shared with her great aunt, Viv turned to me. "You have to say, Don, if you don't want me to do this. It was never part of our deal for you to earn all the money."

She had spent most of our second date describing Nutmeg, the horse she rode as a girl in Ann Arbor. What I recall even now, more than a decade later, are not so much the details—his chestnut coat and four white socks, how he whinnied at the sight of her—but the wistfulness with which she recounted them. When I asked if she still rode, she said, "Just enough to know how bad I've gotten." We had both had previous relationships, but this was the only one Viv cared to describe. You could say I'd been duly warned.

So, even as she offered to refuse Claudia, I knew that to accept her offer would change a certain balance between us. Instead I reminded her of her favorite quotation from Margaret Fuller: "Men for the sake of getting a living forget to live." Her earning less, I said, was fine with me. I was happy to support our household. And for several years that was true. I enjoyed my work, enjoyed my egalitarian marriage. I learned to speed around the huge American supermarket; my cooking improved; I bought a vacuum cleaner and found a person to use it. In Brazil, Alice had designed commercial spaces; in Massachusetts she cleaned houses with surprising cheer. My life, despite frequent emergencies, fit me like a well-made suit.

Most of the emergencies then had to do with my parents. My father had Parkinson's, and my mother and I wanted to keep him at home for as long as possible. I arranged for Alice to clean and cook for them, and several days a week I brought Marcus and Trina over after school. I had been a dreamy child, but I became an adult without a minute to spare. As a boy in Edinburgh I had loved visiting the orrery at the Chamber Street Museum. At the turn of a switch each of the planets would begin spinning on its own axis, at the same time orbiting the sun. That was what my life, and the life of my family, was like in the years when everything worked. Unlike the planets, Viv and I touched often.

When Viv and I visited Edinburgh the spring she was pregnant with Marcus, I took her to see the orrery. It had been moved to the ground floor of the museum, and the mechanism that spun the planets had been disconnected. Standing beside the glass sphere with its painted constellations, I had done my best to describe the various orbits.

None of us shared Viv's passion for horses. I was neutral, Marcus hostile, and Trina, who loved most animals, had fallen off a pony when she was four and remained wary. I tried to make up for my lack of enthusiasm by being a good listener. But there is listening, and listening. When my patients talk during an exam, I respond appropriately even when 90 percent of my attention is focused on the cornea, the iris, the lens. And that, I fear, is how I listened when Viv first told me about a horse named Mercury.

We were in the kitchen. I was doing the dishes after a not-bad lamb curry—Marcus and Trina are adventurous eaters—and Viv was leaning against the counter, eating a peach in greedy mouthfuls. It was early September, and the peaches would soon be gone. Nearby in his cage, Nabokov, my father's African grey parrot, was also eating a peach; I had cut his into wedges and removed the poisonous pit. As I rinsed plates, as Viv talked, I was thinking about the woman who had come into my office that morning, so upset she could barely speak; the undertaker had forgotten her father's glasses.

"Mercury," I repeated, the schoolboy's trick for feigning attention. "Commonly known as quicksilver. Also the smallest planet."

"Quicksilver," Viv said. "That would suit him."

His owner, she went on, was the mother of their worst student. When Hilary phoned, Viv had been sure it was to say that her daughter was quitting—but no, she had inherited a horse and wanted to board him at Windy Hill. Mercury had arrived that day. Five years old, a dapple-gray Thoroughbred, the most beautiful animal Viv had ever seen.

"I'm hungry," cried Nabokov, eyeing her peach. "I'm starving."

I took advantage of his interruption to tell Viv about the dead man's glasses. "His daughter was beside herself. We gave her a display pair. I only hope they fit him."

"I can't imagine Dad without his glasses," Viv said. "Mom either."

Even after all my years in the States, the word *mom*, so similar to the British *mum*, still strikes me as a simpleminded palindrome. Our children are resigned to my calling Viv by name, another palindrome, or saying "your mother" like some stern Victorian parent. I tell them they're growing up in a bilingual household. We used to make lists of words that are different in funny ways: *vest* and *waistcoat*, *pants* and *trousers*, *sidewalk* and *pavement*, *sick* and *ill*. I explained that "I quite like him" in Scottish means you don't, and in American means you do.

But I don't blame our two languages for the chasm that opened between Viv and me, so much as Mercury and my poor listening skills—and also, only now as I write this, my father's death. The road to his final exit was paved with so many losses, so many diminutions, that his end should have been a relief. But the psyche is capable of endless surprises; perhaps that's why it was named after a nymph. Looking back over the months following his departure, I can see that I lost track of certain things. So that September evening I failed to notice Viv's excitement.

She was eating a peach, she was talking about a horse, she looked just like herself, her hair, fair when we first met now closer to brown, hanging down her back like a girl's. I did not understand that grief has many guises. It can make a man oblivious to his wife's needs, or susceptible to a hazel-eyed woman, or a thief of keys and codes, or an outright liar. It can obscure the direction of his moral compass. Or utterly change that direction.

I was saying that Viv's father had nice glasses when we heard a sound unusual on our small street: the wail of a siren, growing rapidly louder.

"Something's wrong," said Viv. She dropped her peach stone, I dried my hands, we hurried out into the street. Two fire engines, lights flashing, were parked outside the yellow house five doors down. Dirty smoke billowed from the doors and windows, but there were no flames.

Other people, strangers and neighbors we knew, were making their way towards the fire, drawn by whatever draws our species to disaster. Someone tugged my sleeve, and I saw that Marcus and Trina had followed us. "Will the house burn down?" said Trina.

"No," I said. "The firemen will save it." I bent down and picked her up, more for my sake than for her safety.

A policeman stepped from between two cars and told the small crowd to stand back. "Does anyone know how many people live here?" he asked.

"There's three apartments," a man called out. "The guy at the top works nights at the post office."

Someone else added that the woman on the ground floor worked at a health club.

The house was less than a hundred yards from ours, but I had never seen anyone enter or leave. Even after blizzards, when everyone else appeared with shovels and snow blowers, no one emerged from the yellow house; their stretch of pavement was cleared, or sometimes ignored, by a service. We watched while two firemen forced the front door. Another climbed a ladder, checking windows. Trina started coughing—the smoke had an acrid odor—and I remember thinking we should not be exposing our children to this scene. What if someone jumped from a window, or was carried out unconscious? But neither Viv nor I could tear ourselves away. There were still no flames.

Finally a fireman stepped out of the building, waving his arms above his head: all clear. People began to return home. Viv was talking to a neighbor; Marcus was chatting to our babysitter. Suddenly Trina exclaimed, "Look, Dad."

Following her gesture, I made out the dark shape of a cat in the downstairs window. "It's trapped," she said, her voice rising. "It can't get out."

I tried to tell her that the cat was fine, it lived indoors, but Trina wriggled out of my arms. We made our way over to the policeman. "Excuse me, Officer," I said. "There's a cat at the window."

"You have to rescue it," said Trina.

Now that we were closer, the cat did have a desperate look, its body pressed against the glass. The policeman took in the situation, looking from me, to Trina, to the house.

"Hey, Tim," he called, "can you get that cat out? Don't want to stress its nine lives."

A fireman, presumably Tim, loped towards the building and disappeared inside. A minute later he appeared behind the cat, and a minute after that he was back in the street, holding the cat, gray and squirming, in his gloved hands. "Now what?" he said as he approached.

"We'll take—," Trina started to say.

On the word *take*, there was a noise like a huge inhalation of breath. Suddenly our faces were lit not by the lights of the engines but by flames leaping from the windows on the first floor, the second, the third.

IN THE WEEKS THAT followed, the fire became a local scandal. How was it possible, with fire engines standing by, that the house had been gutted? The woman who came to retrieve the cat two days later said she had lost everything.

"I'm sorry," I said. We were standing in the hall of my unburned home.

"Fuck it." She pushed her hands deeper into the pockets of her turquoise tracksuit. "Maybe it's time to head west. At least I still have my wheels."

"And Fred," said Trina. After two days of hiding under our sofa, resisting Trina's entreaties, the cat was weaving around his owner's legs.

"That's right," said the woman. "I still have my damned cat." She picked him up and buried her face in his neck. "West," I discovered, as we walked to her car, meant her hometown of Pittsfield.

I USED TO WONDER if there was anything that I loved as much as Viv loved her horses—I mean, besides the handful of people for whom I would step in front of a speeding train. At university I smoked grass and took enough coke (once) and Ecstasy (twice) to know that, for me, drugs are not the doors of perception. I play tennis, I garden until it gets too hot, I read, mostly Scottish history, but for the last four years both hobbies and friends have taken second place to my father. I suppose my equivalent to horses is eyes, those pearls, those vile jellies. From the moment we studied them at university, I was fascinated by the intricate mechanism, by the emotions we attribute to the eyes of others, the visions we claim for our own. When I first saw a painting by Josef Albers, I stared and stared at the yellow square within the green square. How had he persuaded the colors to shift and tremble at their margins?

In childhood I was blessed with excellent vision. Then, within a few months of my eighteenth birthday, I quite suddenly found myself squinting at street signs and blackboards. Now I wear a pair of elegant progressives that I reach for first thing in the morning and part from last thing at night; I scarcely recognize myself without them. Viv, so far, has 20/20 vision in both eyes. One of these days, I used to tell her, you'll grow up.

I was in my second year of training as an ophthalmologist at Edinburgh University when my father was diagnosed with Parkinson's. As soon as my mother phoned to break the news, the several incidents I had noticed, and ignored, at Christmas came together in an irrefutable declaration: the way my father dragged his foot through the snow on our Christmas walk, the way he delegated pouring the wine and carving the turkey, the odd jerks of head or hand.

Parkinson's is an idiopathic condition, which means it has no known cause, although smoking, infuriatingly, lowers the risk. There is, as yet, no cure. Often it progresses slowly for years, but my father, once diagnosed, grew rapidly worse, as if the illness had only been waiting to be acknowledged. On the phone my mother's voice was frightened, and when I visited at Easter I was shocked by the changes only a few months had brought. That summer I moved back to the States.

As a manager at the MBTA in Boston, my father was ambitious for his life, not his job. He did not seem to mind that he had never been promoted beyond area manager. He liked to travel, to tend his garden, to kayak and fish; in winter he took tai chi lessons and, intermittently, studied Japanese. He went walking in the Adirondacks and wrote haiku in the manner of Basho. Illness brought out the best in him. He followed a strict diet, did his exercises, and campaigned for better health care. He asked often how he could make my mother's life easier. More recently, he submitted with good grace to the presence of caregivers.

One evening, the second autumn after I moved back, he summoned my mother and me to his study. When we were settled with our drinks, he announced that he was planning to file for a no-fault divorce.

"I'd still want to see you, Peggy," he said earnestly, "but you'd be free to find another husband, one who can make you supper and put in the storm windows. I might linger for years, especially if you keep taking such good care of me."

My mother was wearing a blue cardigan that matched her eyes and well-cut jeans; she was at that time fifty-two, lively, sociable, passionate about her job. Gently she set down her glass. "Edward, did I upset you? I know sometimes I'm cranky, but I never mean to make you feel you're a nuisance. You're not. I'm glad we get to spend so much time together."

My father laughed, and Nabokov, nearby in his cage, gave a gruff imitation. "I'm a huge nuisance," he said. "Elephantine. Actually I find it reassuring when you're cranky. Makes me feel less of a charity case. No, I've been thinking about this for a while. You're in the prime of life. You deserve a companion who can do the things you enjoy."

As my mother walked towards him, I left the room and drove

home to my fit and lovely partner, who, unbeknownst to me, was pregnant with Marcus. Would she have made that offer to me? Or I to her? The answer, I thought then, was yes, and yes.

I met Viv the spring after I returned to Boston, when she sat down beside me on the subway and opened her copy of the *New Yorker* to the article I was reading in mine. Later she confessed she had already read it but hoped the coincidence might draw my attention—which, along with her elegant profile and crooked left pinkie (an accident with Nutmeg), it did. As the train emerged onto the bridge over the Charles River, we both paused in our reading to look at the gray water, and I asked what she thought of the article. Until that very morning I had been carrying a torch for Ruth, my girlfriend of four years, who was still in Edinburgh, studying to be an anesthesiologist. We had talked often but vaguely about her coming to Boston. Walking home after I got off the train, with Viv's phone number written in the margin of my magazine, I had finally understood that Ruth would never move to the States.

I lived then on the pleasingly named Linnaean Street, where, more than two decades earlier, Fran and I had gone to school. We both recalled our teacher telling us about the famous taxonomist, a brilliant man who believed that the swallows in Sweden wintered at the bottom of frozen ponds. The forsythia was just coming into bloom, and as I neared my apartment, I picked up a bright red cardinal's feather. I slipped it into the letter I wrote to Ruth that weekend. Only after the envelope disappeared into the mailbox did I realize that I now faced a modern dilemma: namely, how to avoid e-mail until my letter arrived. I could not bear the childishness of being caught in an excuse—computer problems, a hospital emergency—or the mendacity of writing as if nothing had changed. So, as with Robert, I hid. I deleted

Ruth's e-mails unread, her phone messages unheard, until they dwindled and then ceased.

Viv, as I've mentioned, at that time worked in mutual funds. I liked that her job was so different from mine, and I liked that she knew so much about current events. My patients were not, for the most part, affected by changes in weather and regime, but in her world a storm in the Indian Ocean, or a new president in Chile, could change everything. She followed international politics in a way that only a few of my American friends did, and she was reassuringly left-wing, believing not only in the obvious causes—gay marriage, women's rights, abolition of the death penalty, gun control, recycling, universal health care—but in the more obscure ones like proportional representation, job sharing, and death with dignity. She had grown up in Ann Arbor, where her mother still lived, and had seldom met a Republican. One of the things she envied about my profession was that I met all kinds of people. "And you make them better," she said. "We try," I said, "but sometimes it's too late, or we make mistakes." Viv nodded, and said fund managers made mistakes too. She tried never to forget that money always represented something precious: a house, a goat, a violin. Later that night she took me to a club, where we flung ourselves around on the dance floor. Need I say I was equally charmed by her high-mindedness and her exuberance.

After qualifying as an ophthalmologist in Massachusetts, I practiced for two years. I found surgery deeply satisfying, but when Trina was born, and my father's condition worsened, I needed a job with shorter, more predictable hours. My sister worked as a publicist for a music company in Nashville, and was as helpful as a person living a thousand miles away can be, phoning frequently and visiting when she could, but the brunt of my father's care fell to my mother and to me. Viv and I moved to our town outside Boston. I started my business, and Viv joined Claudia at the stables.

Since our father's death, Fran and I have been much less in touch, so it was a pleasant surprise when, the Sunday after the fire, she phoned. Viv talked to her for twenty minutes before handing me the phone.

"How's it going?" Fran said. "Viv seems really excited about this new horse. It's nice to hear her being enthusiastic again."

As I said, there is listening and listening. At the time Fran's "again" did not register. Viv's job in our marriage was to be the enthusiast. Over the years she has taken lessons in boxing, salsa, and more recently, Pilates. She had learned to make a gâteau Saint-Honoré. She campaigned for Clinton, Gore, and Obama. She protested the start of the Iraq war and the threatened closure of our Montessori school. Her ability to enter wholeheartedly into a cause or an activity is one of the many things I admire about her. Or, I should say, used to admire.

2

THE DAY AFTER FRAN'S phone call, Merrie greeted me at the office with the news that our UPS delivery was late, and my first patient was already waiting. Her glasses were pushed up on her forehead, and she spoke in the extra-calm voice she uses on busy days. I can claim no special intelligence in hiring Merrie; she was the receptionist for the business that previously occupied these premises, a dermatologist's, and when I took over the lease, she phoned to ask if I needed help. "I know zilch about optometry," she said, "but I can talk to anyone, and I'm a whiz on computers." Both of which turned out to be true. She is also tall, a serious runner, a devout Catholic, and the single mother of three daughters, two of whom share her coffee-colored complexion while the third, the youngest, is much darker. She has never mentioned a father, singular or plural. On the rare occasions when she steps out from behind her desk to give me advice, I pay attention.

Besides Merrie and myself there is Leah, who is trained in optometry, and Jo, who is in her twenties and still taking classes. Merrie had urged me to hire Jo. "We need some young blood around here," she said, and she was right. Jo is good with our older patients, talking them into more flattering frames, urging them to give progressives a chance. The four of us get on famously and rarely meet outside the office.

My first patient was seated in a corner of the waiting room, wearing the uniform of the local Catholic school, reading a magazine. The older girls roll up their skirts and loosen their ties, but this girl's skirt was knee length, her tie neatly knotted. She did not look up as I said, "Good morning. I'm Dr. Stevenson." It was her mother, in her own short skirt, who gave me a girlish smile and said that Diane was having trouble seeing the blackboard.

"No, I'm not," said Diane quietly.

While she continued to gaze at the magazine, her mother said they'd moved to our town in June. Diane had always been a good student, but her new teachers were complaining that she never volunteered in class, and sometimes confused assignments.

In my office Diane read the first two charts and then guessed wildly, mistaking P for X, N for O. At last, not turning on the light, I sat down beside the chair.

"What is it?" she said. "What's the matter?"

"Stand up," I said. "Close your eyes and walk towards the door."

Arms outstretched, she took a couple of hesitant steps then stopped. I urged her on, and she shuffled forward until her hand touched the door.

"What's the matter?" she said again. "Am I going blind?"

"No"—I reached for the light—"but you are shortsighted, and no amount of willpower will change that. If you don't wear glasses, you'll miss most of what's going on around you. You may have an accident, or cause one. Let me show you how things will look."

Diane returned to the chair. "Can't I have contact lenses?"

"When you're older," I said. "Within a week you'll barely notice your glasses."

We bargained our way to a prescription. Back in the waiting room, her mother thanked me. Her voice went up at the end of her sentences in a way I couldn't place until later, when Viv told me that she had grown up in Canada. While we waited for Merrie to finish a phone call, I asked Diane if she knew my friend Steve Abrahams, the biology teacher at her school.

She nodded. They were doing a cool project on soil. Her mother chimed in that Diane preferred micro-organisms to people.

So my first meeting with Hilary ended, neither of us knowing the part we already played in each other's lives.

IN THE MONTHS FOLLOWING my father's death, I missed him in every way imaginable. I also found myself, as I had not since Marcus was born, with odd stretches of time, sometimes as long as half an hour, when I had no immediate task, and in those empty intervals I also missed surgery. The week after I saw Diane, I met with a patient to discuss his cataract operation. As I held out my model eye, twelve times life-size, and explained how the new lens would be folded to fit through a small incision in the sclera and then unfolded behind the pupil, I wished that I were the one sliding the lens into place.

I put the feeling away to examine later and drove to Windy Hill. In the decades since she inherited the farm, Claudia's great-aunt had sold off most of the land, but the stables were still surrounded by fields and woods. The nearest neighbor, half a mile away, was a fancy farm stand and nursery. As I drove up the hill to the barn, several of the horses grazing in the paddocks on either side raised their heads. I recognized Dow Jones, the bay Viv used to ride in competitions. I parked in my usual spot beside the row of horse trailers. In the large field half a dozen riders were circling under Claudia's instruction.

"Shoulders back, Louie," I heard her call.

I was searching for the slouching rider when a flash of white caught my peripheral vision. During my years with Viv, I have, inadvertently, learned a good deal about *Equus caballus*. Horses have been domesticated for over six thousand years. They appear in early cave paintings at Lascaux and Pech Merle. The wealthy King Croesus had a soothsayer who described the horse as a warrior and a foreigner, and another king, I forget his name, was buried surrounded by a dozen stuffed horses. Until the twentieth century, horses fought on many battlefields and were part of most people's daily lives. They have the largest eyes of any land mammal and are blessed with both binocular and monocular vision. Historically horses are divided by a kind of class system. Hardworking horses—cart horses and plow horses—are described as cold-blooded. Racehorses, Thoroughbreds, and Arabians are hot-blooded. Those in between—the warm-blooded horses—are bred to combine the best of the other two.

Mercury, true to his name, was unmistakably hot-blooded. The lines of his body, the arch of his neck, the rise and fall of his stride, were, I agreed with Viv reluctantly, beautiful. I was so absorbed in watching him that I paid no heed to his rider until, nearing the fence, she waved. Then I recognized Diane's mother. Turning back to the circling ponies, I saw that the girl on the brown pony, not quite trotting, was my patient, minus her carefully chosen glasses.

Besides the indoor arena, the stables consist of a large barn that houses most of the stalls, a tack room, a feed room, and the office, and a smaller building that houses additional stalls and storerooms. Inside the barn I made my way to the office, a modest room furnished with various castoffs. My mother donated the red curtains and the table and chairs. I contributed two filing cabinets that Merrie wanted to replace and a coffeemaker. That afternoon Marcus and Trina were working at opposite ends of the table: Marcus on homework, Trina on an elaborate drawing.

"Hi, Daddy," they said.

"How was your patient?" added Marcus. He has Viv's fair coloring, but his high forehead, straight eyebrows, and slightly blocky nose are, according to my mother, a direct throwback to my namesake: Uncle Donald. He is an ardent swimmer and almost always smells faintly of chlorine.

"My patient was all right," I said. "He liked knowing about his surgery. Some people do, some people don't."

"Which are you?" Trina reached for another crayon. Small for her age, pale-skinned and dark-haired, she is the barometer of our household, monitoring approaching storms, pleading for calm weather. She can work on a single picture for an hour.

"I like to know about things in advance," I said, "but I tend to worry. What about you?"

"I don't like surprises," she declared. "And I don't want anyone to cut me open."

"Surprises, yes," said Marcus. "Definitely no cutting."

Like many children, mine are deeply interested in bodily functions: how long they can hold their breath, or stand on one foot, whether they can walk in a straight line with their eyes closed, where sweat comes from. When Marcus broke his leg on the playground last May, they were both fascinated by the X-ray showing the thin dark line across the tibia. And when my father, in a last vain effort to control his illness, had an operation that involved cauterizing areas of the brain, Trina drew a picture of him, his head haloed in sparks.

"Where's Viv?" I asked.

"With the horses," said Marcus, unhelpfully.

She was not in the feed room or the tack room. She was not in the first row of stalls. At last I heard her voice coming from a stall in the second row. She was talking to Charlie, one of the stable girls, who was grooming the school's oldest pony, the stalwart Samson. I rode him once, and it was like riding a carousel; whatever I did, he followed the horse in front. Now I patted his whiskery nose and joked that they were getting him ready for the rodeo.

"Poor Samson," said Viv. "You don't give him enough credit."

"We're putting him on a diet," Charlie added. "He's going to be our most improved pony." A slender girl with a loud laugh, she had been working at Windy Hill for nearly three years and was Viv's favorite among the stable girls.

I explained that I wanted a quick word with Diane Blake before I took the children home. Viv said her lesson ended at five. How did I know her?

"She's one of my patients. Her mother was riding that gray horse you told me about."

"Mercury. Isn't he amazing?"

"He's fantastic," said Charlie, her voice as dazzled as Viv's.

Back in the office I asked Trina and Marcus if we could wait for ten minutes. While they returned to their projects, I studied the calendar on the wall. Each day displayed a list of lessons, deliveries, vet's and farrier's visits, which stable girls were on duty. Merrie kept a similar calendar in my office. Of course there were surprises—Marcus's leg, a horse struck by colic—but for the most part, I thought, as I sat in that cozy room with my industrious children, we knew what we were doing next week, next month, next year.

The lesson ended. From nearby came the stamp of hooves as the riders dismounted. When I stepped out of the office, half a dozen girls were milling around the lockers that had been installed last year, after a student's purse went missing. Claudia had argued against them. "I worry they make the stables seem less safe," she said. "Like a dog wearing a muzzle." But Viv had prevailed, and within a week everyone took the lockers for granted.

Diane was not among the girls. Maybe she's outside, Claudia suggested, and there she was, leaning on the fence that bordered the field, pretending to watch her mother, although, without her glasses, I knew that horse and rider were a blur. I greeted her and asked why she wasn't wearing them.

"I thought I only had to wear them at school."

"Don't you want to see what's going on the rest of the time? Wouldn't you like to see your mum riding?"

She responded to my question with one of her own: her teacher had posed the old ethical dilemma about who to save when a museum catches fire, your grandmother or a Rembrandt. "Most people said Grandma," said Diane, "but I said the painting because it will give thousands of people pleasure. Which is the total opposite of Grandma."

As she spoke, Mercury broke into a trot; Hilary lurched perilously and grabbed the saddle. Maybe it was just as well that Diane couldn't see what her mother was doing. "Do you like Rembrandt?" I asked.

She shrugged. "Mom and I saw a painting by him in New York, of a guy on a gray horse. He looks as if he's going on an important errand. I liked that painting, and I bet I could get to like others."

Later, when Viv showed me a copy of the painting, I agreed

with her description. Dusk is falling, and the young man, the Polish rider, gazes intently at the viewer as if he is on his way to save someone he loves. But that afternoon, before I could question her further, Trina appeared; she had finished her drawing and wanted to go home. As I drove down the hill, it came to me that the test I had set Diane in my office was one my father had set me. When we lived in Edinburgh, our next-door neighbor had been blind. My mother instructed me to say, "Hello, Valerie, it's Donald," when I met her in the street. But sometimes I simply walked past her or, on bolder days, ran. One afternoon my mother caught me in this cruel game. After supper my parents sat me down. My mother said Valerie had come to the hospital when I was born, and until her eyesight failed, she often babysat for me. My father said he had once asked her what was the worst thing about being blind.

"And do you know her answer?" he said. "Never knowing who's there."

Then he had blindfolded me, led me out into the street, and told me to walk to the corner.

3

I MET VIV, AS I have said, the spring after I returned to Boston. With most of my previous girlfriends, we had been friends before we became lovers. With Viv, I at last understood the expression "falling in love." We slept together on our second date, and I felt as if I were tumbling off a high wall, a wall I had built, brick by brick, out of self-control and hard work. But suddenly I didn't care about control; all I wanted was to be entwined with this woman. I was enthralled by her intelligence, her ambition, her gift, like that of Donald III, for seizing the day, her American confidence that all would be well, and if it wasn't, it could be fixed. When, eight months later, she told me she was pregnant, I picked her up and carried her around the room. At last, I thought, I would feel at home in America. And Viv and I, I was certain, would be good parents. We agreed on the importance of rules and routines—plenty of books, not too much sugar or television—and on public education. When her friend Lucy sent her son to private school, Viv had begged her to reconsider. So our quarrel about private school for Marcus was notable as both our first major disagreement about the children and my first experience of Viv abandoning a deeply held belief.

A couple of weeks after Mercury's arrival, we were having supper at a Mexican restaurant when Viv announced that

Greenfield School had an open house in early November. "It's on a Thursday," she said, "so we can all go." Her tone suggested some long-agreed plan.

I set down my beer. Why on earth, I asked, would we want to visit Greenfield? If we needed an outing with the children, we could go to Louisa May Alcott's house, or Drumlin Farm.

Viv set down her own beer and clasped her hands, pleating her crooked finger in with the others. "Don," she said, "I've been talking about this for months. The middle school is a disaster."

As she listed the problems—broken computers, too few textbooks, large classes, wacked-out teachers—I realized it was true: since soon after Marcus broke his leg, she had been complaining about the school. But I had heard her complaints as a to-do list: the things we would, as committed parents, work to change.

"These are the crucial years," she went on, "when the pathways in the brain are formed."

She spoke as if she was quoting someone, and I was sure I knew who. The morning after we moved into our house, Anne had knocked on the door with a tray of cinnamon rolls. She, her husband, and two daughters lived across the street; she worked part-time as an architect. Last year the older daughter had bitten another girl. Anne had enrolled her at Greenfield and begun fervently promoting the school.

"If you're worried about Marcus's pathways," I said, "why not help him study rain forests and follow his chess tournament?"

Twice in the last week Viv had arrived home too late to help with homework. Now, as the server brought our enchiladas, she ignored my criticism. No amount of help at home, she said, smiling firmly, could compensate for a bad school. When I repeated the arguments she had made to Lucy, her smile vanished. She accused me of being stingy. We Scots, as I have already remarked, have a long and honorable tradition of thrift, but the word *stingy* made me grasp my knife like a scalpel.

"Viv, you're talking about spending what would be a year's salary for many people on a child's education."

"Please, Don." She reached across the table. "I know it's a lot of money, but let's take a look at Greenfield. Marcus is my son. I want the best for him."

Marcus was my son too; I would have given him my kidneys, my lungs. Let me think about it, I said.

Recognizing a major victory, Viv changed the subject. Mercury was already gaining weight, she said. He preferred a snaffle bit, not too thin. I ate, I nodded. I was still bristling at her charge of meanness. Had she forgotten that my going to the office, day in, day out, was what kept us afloat, and allowed her to ride her beautiful horse?

I WISH I DID not have to bring Jack into this story, but without him there would be no story. Until three years ago, when retinitis pigmentosa rendered him legally blind, he was my patient. The last time I checked, the vision in his good eye was 10/200; what is visible to a normal person at two hundred feet, he can only see at ten. He can make out the burners on his stove, and sort white socks from dark ones. His bad eye detects only the brightest lights. I have had to break grim tidings to many people, but telling Jack, a man my age, a man in love with books—he teaches classics at the university—that nothing could be done about his failing vision was particularly hard.

I was tiptoeing around the subject when he interrupted.

"Forgive me, Doc," he said, "but the short version is, I'm going blind. Farewell the daylight world, farewell the winged chariot, aka Apollo."

He was my last patient of the day, and we had walked together to the nearest bar, where we drank Scotch and he told
me how Odysseus finally, by guile and strength, gets rid of the
suitors. As he spoke, he kept his vivid blue eyes fixed on my
face. Even knowing what I did, it was hard to believe how little
he could see. A few weeks later I invited him to dinner, and a
few weeks after that, at his insistence, I took him to meet my
father, who was still living at home. They had enjoyed a lively
conversation about the Adirondacks, where each had hiked in
better days. Jack was one of the few people I had kept in touch
with during the awful last year of my father's life. His apartment
was on the edge of the campus, and it was easy to drop in on
the way to and from the children's various lessons. The week
after Viv and I argued about private school, I stopped by while
Marcus was swimming.

"Screw tops," Jack said, opening the bottle I'd brought.
"God's gift to the blind."

He poured two glasses of merlot and led the way to the sofa.
I asked about his book. That summer he had begun to write
about blindness, his own and the wider history of the condition.

"I'm working on a topic near to my heart," he said cheer-
fully. "Namely what I find most annoying about sighted people.
Number one is people asking if I want to touch their faces. To
which the answer is, Christ, no. Stay away from me with your
Helen Keller fantasies. The couple of times I tried it, I could
only make out major features: noses, eyebrows. Cheers."

"Cheers." I clinked my glass to his. "Maybe it only works if
you've been blind from birth."

"Maybe it only works if you're a kinky person who likes to feel
faces. Another thing that drives me crazy"—he was warming to
his subject—"is when I ask someone where I am, and instead of

telling me, they say, 'Where do you want to be?' As if they could transport me by magic carpet. Let me show you something."

Jack's apartment consists of three large rooms. The bedroom and the living room open off the hall, and the kitchen, which is large enough to eat in, opens off the living room. He got up and, carrying his almost full wineglass, stepped around the coffee table, crossed the room, skirted his desk, and disappeared into the kitchen. He came back again without spilling a drop.

"Okay," he said. "Close your eyes. You do it."

I closed my eyes, picked up the glass, took two steps, and stopped. That evening in Edinburgh when my father blindfolded me, I had come to a standstill after three or four steps. I tried to turn around, banged into a parked car, called for help. Now, still with my eyes closed, I said, "I can't."

"Give me your glass."

With a glass in each hand, Jack took only a couple of steps before he too stopped. "One glass, yes. Two glasses, no. I need one hand free to 'see.' "

We had talked on several occasions about facial vision, that sense that allows the blind to detect obstacles. Now I suggested he keep a record of how soon he sensed an obstacle, whether size or surroundings made a difference.

"The library at the Perkins school must have the latest research," I said. "Speaking of schools, I wanted to ask you about Greenfield. Viv has a bee in her bonnet about Marcus going there."

Jack frowned. "That doesn't sound like Viv. Did something rattle her?"

I brushed his question aside. "Not that I know of," I said. "Can you tell me anything about the school?"

He began to list its virtues: a great classics department, a first-rate library, a music teacher who was a terrific jazz trumpeter, school trips to Tanglewood and Storm King. "But," he said, "I can't imagine spending thirty grand a year to send a kid there."

Neither, I said, could I.

MY LIFE, FIRST AS an ophthalmologist, now as an optometrist is one of close quarters, peering into eyes, studying charts and lenses. Most days at lunchtime I go for a brisk walk, as much for the luxury of gazing at birds and buildings as for the exercise. The day after my drink with Jack, I was striding down our main street when I caught sight of a couple seated in the window of a Thai restaurant. Something about their attitudes—the woman with one hand outstretched; the man watching her—drew my attention.

In Edinburgh Robert and I used to play a game that involved staring at a person and seeing how long it took for them to notice. The answer was usually less than a minute. I stopped staring, walked to the traffic light, crossed the street, and headed back on the far side. From a distance my mother's expression was hard to decipher, but her posture conveyed the same information: she liked this man.

Only a few weeks before Viv had remarked, not for the first time, how great it would be if Peggy met someone; I had agreed. But as I retraced my steps to the office, a small part of me was drifting loose. Dead leaves fluttered across the street, and suddenly I was back with my girlfriend Ruth on an autumn day in Scotland. We had walked along the Firth of Forth to the Hawes Inn in South Queensferry. As we sat by the fire, drinking beer, I had told her about Robert Louis Stevenson. He had come here to drink when he was a mediocre law student. Later, he had set a crucial scene in his novel *Kidnapped* at the Inn.

In a far corner of the office parking lot, someone had abandoned two beer bottles. As I carried them over to recycling, it came to me that I had deleted Ruth's messages not only because I dreaded her anger but also because I was afraid that suddenly, at the eleventh hour, she would offer to come to Boston. Even before I met Viv, my patience with our long-distance relationship was utterly gone, drained, like the bottles, to the last drop.

THAT EVENING I DID not mention seeing my mother to Viv. Instead we talked about whether Marcus was ready for the advanced diving class, and which of us should undertake the delicate task of asking our neighbors not to park so close to our driveway. And the following evening, when my mother came over, I again said nothing. At supper she described her art history course. They were studying William Morris and his attempts to create a utopian community.

"Hands up who'd like to live in a commune," my mother said.

Trina said she liked summer camp, but only for two weeks, and Viv said her dormitory at Yale had made her want to spend a decade in solitary confinement. I volunteered that I'd enjoyed the summer I picked grapes in France, sharing a house with half a dozen other pickers.

"What about you, Peggy?" said Marcus. "Would you like to share your house with lots of people?" He and my mother took each other seriously.

"I wouldn't like to share my present house," she said, "but I like the idea of friends living nearby. Maybe a big house divided into condos so that you could have privacy and company."

You mean assisted living, Viv suggested, and my mother's eyes flashed. "Absolutely not. Those are segregated communities, our version of putting the elderly on an ice floe. I mean people of all ages, living together and learning from each other. That's one of the utopian beliefs: everyone has something to teach."

"You could give Ping-Pong lessons," said Marcus.

"And you could teach people to swim."

After she left and the children were in bed, Viv said, "Peggy's on the move. Did you notice her earrings? And she's gotten highlights. She'll be off on the Orient Express soon."

Here was my chance; but still I said nothing. I could not bear the prospect of Viv's delighted exclamations. Instead I asked if she had fed Nabokov.

Jack told me once that the word *secret* has the same root as *separate*. I think of that now as I parse out this history of how our family ceased to be Viv's sun. We both kept secrets, and our secrets kept us separate.

4

THE OTHER FRIEND I see regularly is Steve, the biology teacher at Diane's school. He and I were friends at high school in Cambridge, lost touch for over a decade, and reconnected when his second wife came to my office in search of new glasses. The week after I saw my mother in the restaurant, he and I met at the local park to play tennis. Steve, not afraid of his own ambition, wore tennis whites. I, pretending not to care, wore dark shorts and a red T-shirt. As we changed ends, I asked if his mother had enjoyed her cruise.

"Not as much as she's enjoyed complaining about it since she got back." He described her vicissitudes with food and fellow passengers, and then, as I'd hoped, asked about my mother. She had helped him campaign for the school board.

"She's enjoying her course on the pre-Raphaelites," I said. "And I think she might have a new friend."

His second serve went into the net. "Love fifteen. Well, good luck to her. I always thought Peggy could be another Mrs. Robinson. She's so foxy."

Whatever I had been looking for, this was not it. Thankfully Steve did not press me but began to talk about the lunatic parent who wanted him to teach creationism. When he fell silent, I changed the subject. What was his opinion of the middle school Marcus was due to attend?

"Pretty good," he said. "Some dedicated teachers, decent labs. They could do with more money and equipment, but who couldn't? The head teacher is a dynamo. She knows what's going on in every corner of that place."

I filed away his comments, ammunition for the next round.

At 2–2 we called it a draw. I walked home through the twilight. At the corner of our street I stopped to stroke the neighbor's elderly chow. As I patted the dog's thick coat, I caught sight of the yellow house with its blackened walls. Since the night of the fire I must have seen it scores of times, but that evening I was struck by the realization that someone had come home, just as I was doing, planning to make supper, or repair a lawn mower, or read a book, and found the life in which those things were possible utterly gone.

My own house looked reassuringly, misleadingly, the same. In the living room Marcus and Trina were sitting on the floor, playing Monopoly with Drew, the babysitter. "Viv said she'd be home by five," he said, shooting me an accusing glance from beneath his long eyelashes. "Neither of you answered your phones."

Drew was an unusually good-tempered teenager, and I was at first more worried about placating him than about Viv's whereabouts. When I apologized—I hadn't heard my phone on the court—he relented; he'd only been going to study for a physics test.

"He took all our money," said Trina. "I've been in jail for three rounds."

"And I'm going to give him even more." I paid him, adding an extra twenty.

After Drew let himself out, I turned on the oven and called first Viv and then Claudia. As I stood in the study, listening to the phone ring, I stared at a photograph I had taken that summer of Viv and the children on the beach at Wellfleet, all three smiling.

"Donald," said Claudia. "I've been meaning to call you about Viv's birthday party. You know how down she's been."

Down? I thought, bewildered, eyeing the smiling woman in the photo, but there was no time to go into that now. I explained why I was calling. Claudia said she'd left Viv at the stables.

"What time was that?" I asked. "Do you think she's had an accident?"

Her laugh was brief and gloomy. "Not the kind you mean."

"What do you mean, 'not the kind'?"

"You're thinking thunderstorms and car crashes. She's had another kind of accident. She's fallen in love with Mercury."

We agreed to discuss the party tomorrow and hung up. I held the photograph under the light. Marcus and Trina, it was true, were smiling, their hands full of shells. But Viv's eyes were hidden by sunglasses, and her mouth was raised at the corners in a smile more like mine than hers. I turned off the oven, bundled the children into the car, and headed for Windy Hill. But as we reached the main road, a familiar car turned in our direction.

5

My father used to claim we were distantly related to Robert Louis Stevenson, and as a teenager, I had a phase of reading his work. Safe in my bedroom in Cambridge, Massachusetts, I delighted in his tales of adventure and wickedness, particularly *The Strange Case of Dr. Jekyll and Mr. Hyde*. So I can report that Dr. Stevenson did not that evening meet Mr. Hyde at the crossroads, but he did glimpse some dark part of himself. Even as I followed Viv down Green Street, across Herbert and onto Milton, I was turning away from the street of honesty, and heading down the avenue of duplicity.

Inside the house Trina ran to find her mother. From the kitchen I heard her voice, then Viv's, then the sound of the shower. I turned on the oven again. By the time Viv came downstairs, Marcus had laid the table, the pizza was hot, and I had put together a salad.

"I'm so sorry," she said, hurrying into the room, her damp hair falling almost to her waist. "I only just got your message, and poor Drew's. Thanks for making dinner. What can I do?"

"Nothing."

She studied me for several seconds and then, although we don't usually drink during the week, went to open a bottle of wine. As we helped ourselves to pizza, she asked her nightly question: "What did everyone learn today?"

Marcus announced that he'd learned he was entitled to life, liberty, and the pursuit of happiness. "So you ought to let me stay up late," he said.

Before Viv or I could explain the true meaning of the phrase, Trina said that today was elephant appreciation day. "There used to be millions of elephants in Africa," she said. "Now there are only thousands. I want to dress up as one for Halloween."

Marcus sniggered. "You're not even five feet tall."

"So I'll be an Indian elephant," she said resolutely. "They're smaller. They can eat three hundred pounds of grass a day."

I said that when I was her age, I had dressed up as a walrus for Halloween and collected money for Guy Fawkes. Then I had to explain who Guy Fawkes was and how in 1605 he, and his fellow Catholic conspirators, had plotted to blow up the Houses of Parliament in London.

"He was an early terrorist," said Viv.

Even as I wanted to contradict her, Marcus and Trina were nodding—they were familiar with terrorists—and I realized she was right. If the Catholic monarchy had been restored, then Fawkes would have been a freedom fighter, but it wasn't, and he wasn't. His story had all the modern ingredients: dreams of radical change, betrayal by anonymous letter, torture, confession.

After the children were in bed, Viv refilled our glasses and told me what had happened at the stables. Claudia had had to leave early, but they were both worried about Mercury; he'd been pacing his paddock all afternoon. They thought he might kick down the gate if he didn't get some exercise. And then, once she was riding, she had lost track of the time.

"He's just a horse," I said. I was used to her enthusiasms.

"Not just," she said. "Imagine if you were suddenly given the keys to a Porsche. I barely touch the reins, and he knows what I want. And he remembers things. The first time around, he clipped the tallest jump. The next time he adjusted his stride and took off a foot closer."

Only afterwards, as she was rubbing him down, had she remembered that it was Thursday, that she was due home. "I'm sorry," she said. "I was bewitched."

She went to load the dishwasher, leaving me to ponder the discrepancy between Claudia's account and hers. Claudia hadn't mentioned being worried about Mercury. It was Viv, I was sure, who had adjusted the truth. At the time it seemed a small subterfuge, the kind of white lie anyone might tell. The main thing, I told myself, was that Mercury had cheered her up.

The next day I phoned Claudia to plan Viv's birthday party. I was writing "potato salad" when she suggested we invite Hilary and Diane.

"We're not asking Merrie," I said.

"But this is Viv's party."

Talking about his first wife, Steve once said, "She began every sentence with 'but.'" Even as she urged the invitation, I understood that Claudia shared my reservations about Mercury and his owner. If only I had stood firm, my story would end here.

6

MUCH OF WHAT I learned at school has vanished from my brain, but I do recall reading a tale of Chekhov's in which a man exclaims about his neighbor, "If only I knew what the old stick did in bed." I have never felt that way. I am, however, deeply interested in what I myself do in bed. The first time Viv and I slept together, it was clear that we pleased each other, and until recently the bedroom was a happy priority. Jack told me that long before the decline of the Roman Empire was apparent, the percentage of base metal in the gold and silver coins had begun to rise. Months before I admitted what was happening with Viv, the pattern of our lovemaking changed. After a frenzied period prior to my father's death and a long blankness following it, in September our normal pattern of two or three times a week had resumed. Then suddenly—was it before or after she cut her hair?—Viv was often too tired, even at weekends.

We did, I remember, make love the Sunday before we went whale watching with our neighbor Anne and her daughters. The expedition was Trina's idea, and she brought her sketch-pad, a book about whales, and huge excitement to the occasion. As we drove to Boston Harbor, she recited various facts about whales, including that they see the world in shades of gray. It was late in the season, the boat only half full, and as soon as we left the harbor, Trina and Viv went to talk to the naturalist who was guiding the trip. In the lounge Anne leaned across the table and began to praise Greenfield School.

"It's not just about education," she said. "It's about the whole child." Glancing at the next table, where Marcus and her daughters were playing hangman, she added that Ivy hadn't gotten into a single fight this year.

"Excellent," I was saying as Viv and Trina reappeared, Trina waving the naturalist's sample of baleen. We all admired the dusty black fringe and listened to her explanation of plankton. When she darted off to return it, Viv sat down and Anne resumed her attack.

"Don't you want your children to grow up believing they can do anything?" she said.

"No," I said, "because that's patently false." I offered Viv's equation. X—our taxes fund public schools + Y—everyone deserves a good education = Z—we should send our children to the schools and work to improve them. Beside me, Viv gave no sign of encouragement.

"Of course we should campaign for better schools," said Anne, "but Marcus needs skilled help now to fulfill his potential."

Outside the windows of the lounge the sea was growing choppy. "Who knows what his potential is?" I said. "Maybe he'll be a trade union leader, or a dairy farmer, or a swimming coach. Right now he's an ordinary ten-year-old who's mad about swimming. I'm happy for him to be an ordinary eleven-year-old, an ordinary twelve-year-old."

But the ordinary had no place in Anne's vision; she was an unabashed elitist. Her daughters could grow up to be Nancy Pelosi or Serena Williams or Zaha Hadid. She was describing the mentoring program at Greenfield when someone shouted, "Whales!"

Over the years I must have seen hundreds of images of these large beings, but the reality took my breath away. The naturalist announced that we were meeting the four-month-old Millie and her mother, Ruby. Millie rolled back and forth, a few yards away, waving her flippers as if in greeting. As for Ruby, she lazed alongside the boat companionably. Her skin was the deepest navy blue. Leaning over the rail, I stared down into her small, dark eye, willing her to look back, and just for a moment she did. Then she dipped her head and blew a spout of water. A few drops, fishy and exhilarating, spattered my jacket.

PERHAPS THAT EXHILARATION WAS partly responsible for what happened the next day. From her questionnaire I knew that Bonnie Dawson was twenty-nine, married with two children; she worked in a middle school cafeteria. Of the five people in the waiting room that morning, three were women around thirty. Bonnie, I guessed, was the one in the corner, a little heavyset, listening to her iPod. But at the sound of my voice a woman in the middle of the room lowered her magazine. She wore a cream sweater with a cowl neck, jeans and black boots, clothes Viv might have worn but that were, I somehow knew, of cheaper quality.

"Thank you for seeing me," she said, offering her hand.

Not many patients shake hands, and her clasp was warm and firm. Her eyes were that color we call hazel. I made some comment about the weather, nice for late October, and then we were in my inner sanctum. "So tell me why you're here," I said.

She took off her ugly tortoiseshell glasses and rubbed her eyes, two-fisted, like a child, as she told me that her husband had said she was imagining things. "But I don't do imagination. There's this shadow inside my head. A few months ago it was skinny as a knife. Now it's like a door I'm trying to see around, but how can you see around a door in your head?"

"Look at the wall. Can you show me where the shadow is?"

She covered one eye and slowly raised her other arm. "Just below that certificate. If it gets much bigger, I won't be able to see what I'm putting on the kids' plates."

I asked if she'd had problems with her eyesight before, and she said as a baby she'd had a lazy eye. "You can see me in pictures, looking two ways. I wore a patch like a pirate."

I turned out the lights. As I told her to blink, look up, look down, I noticed something moving in the gloom. Bonnie's head was perfectly still, but her hands were writhing. When I said I needed to dilate her eyes, she said she was already late for work; she'd make another appointment. Before I could protest, she was out of the chair, out of the room. Two minutes later I was discussing the weather with my next patient, but for the rest of the day I found myself thinking about Bonnie. I had watched the marriages of several friends blow apart, but this, I told myself, was only a slight breeze. My mother might be on the move; I was not.

LIKE MANY OF THE events in this narrative, I recall Viv's birthday party in two ways: as I experienced it, and as I later came to understand the role it played in our story. At the time the party was notable for one thing: Viv's new haircut. For as long as I had known her, her hair had hung almost to her waist. She arrived at the party with it shorter than Marcus's.

"I felt like a change," she said, running her hand through the feathery tufts. "New age, new look. Don't you think it suits me?"

I was so dismayed I could barely speak. The children, with no such scruples, protested vehemently. "You look like someone else," Trina said. Marcus announced that hair grows at the rate of half an inch a month. It would take two years for her to look like her old self.

"But I don't want to be my old self," said Viv.

Besides my mother, Claudia, and her great-aunt Helen, the guests included friends, neighbors, and Hilary and Diane. Claudia had organized everyone to bring contributions, and Steve ran the barbeque in the backyard. It was a lovely October day, the sun shining, the leaves resplendent. We sang "Happy Birthday," and Viv closed her eyes to blow out the candles.

"Did you wish for your hair back?" Trina asked.

Claudia hushed her. I assumed Viv had wished what I always wished on such occasions: good fortune for our little family. Months later, when she told me she had wished for success with Mercury, I slammed the microwave door so hard the hinges broke.

But that was still to come. As we ate the cake, I found myself next to Hilary. Diane was doing so much better, she said. She was speaking up in class, making friends.

"Excellent," I said. "Viv told me you help people sell houses."

"Yes, I do this weird thing called staging. I help owners present their houses in the best possible way. Who's the guy with the camera?"

"Claudia's friend, Rick. In real life he's an accountant."

"Oh, that's Rick. And what about the guy who looks as if he's hiding from the camera?"

Following her gaze, I saw a handsome man wearing sunglasses, a black shirt, and black jeans, playing cat's cradle with Trina. When he first came to see me, Jack had described how for years he'd denied his poor eyesight, going to the movies, rollerblading, cycling, running for buses. Even now, when he often used a cane, he was adamant that his blindness did not define him. I'm not your blind friend, he insisted. So I was only following his orders when I failed to mention that his dark glasses too were a kind of staging.

"That's Jack Brennan," I said. "He teaches Latin and Greek at the university. Don't you worry that you're deceiving people?"

"No more than a woman wearing makeup, or a man in a suit." She smiled easily. "There's nothing wrong with trying to look one's best."

"But a house is the most expensive thing most people ever buy," I persisted. "Shouldn't they be making a rational decision?" Near the barbeque, Viv was talking to her friend Lucy. Why, oh why, had she done something so irrational, without even asking me?

"People make decisions in lots of different ways." Hilary slid her fork into the cake. "Only a few of them rational."

"Hear, hear," said Steve, who had joined us. "My wife believes people think more clearly if they frown. She marched around open houses with a scowl. I knew we'd found our new home when she looked furious."

"So Donald probably makes excellent decisions," Hilary said.

I served them more cake and went to ply the other guests. The next time I looked, she was talking to Jack. Head on one side, he was listening to her light, pleasant voice. How could any of us have known what would come of their conversation on that warm October afternoon?

7

THE WEDNESDAY AFTER HALLOWEEN, I attended the funeral of a patient. Mr. Lombardo had died in his sleep the night before he was due to have his first cataract operation. I was sitting in a pew near the back of St. Catherine's, gazing at a stained glass window showing the saint on her wheel, when the buzz of conversation ceased. The only sound as the priest entered was a piteous sobbing. My patient, I learned, buried his fig trees every winter and made excellent wine. He had gone out in the middle of the night to help a young family whose boiler had sprung a leak. The day before he died, he had played bocce with friends.

Afterwards I waited in line to shake the hand of Mr. Lombardo's oldest son. When I introduced myself, his face darkened. "You're the one who made him get surgery," he said, dropping my hand.

I nodded dumbly and hurried away, guilty as charged.

That evening on the sofa I told Viv about the exchange. "It was as if he blamed me for his father's heart attack."

"That makes a kind of sense," she said. "His dad was fine. Then you announce he has cataracts, and the next thing he's dead. Everyone knows there's a connection between stress and heart attacks. Maybe you didn't pull the trigger, but you loaded the gun."

If there was a gun, I argued—at the time it was only a metaphor—then it was loaded by genes and habits. The autopsy had found three of his four arteries almost entirely blocked.

Viv shook her head. "Sometimes, Don, for all your lenses, you can't see what's right in front of your face. Think how you felt about Edward's death. And you had years to prepare yourself."

Before I could argue further, she said her day too had been difficult. That morning the police had appeared at Windy Hill. During the night someone had broken into the nearby farm stand, destroyed a greenhouse, and set fire to two sheds. "They wanted to know if we'd seen anything," she said. "Which we hadn't."

"They're bound to have insurance," I said.

"But imagine if someone broke into the stables."

She looked so dismayed that, for the moment, I forgot the Lombardos and did my best to be reassuring. The stables were set back from the main road, I said; lightning didn't strike twice.

OSTRICH-LIKE, I HAD BEEN hoping that Viv had forgotten Greenfield, but the next morning she reminded me of our plan to meet at the open house that afternoon. Despite myself, I was impressed by the airy classrooms, the language lab, the library and Thoreau room (for contemplation and religious practice), and especially by the polite, articulate students. Trina was thrilled by the art room and asked voluble questions; Marcus throughout was monosyllabic. Viv wisely didn't press him and afterwards suggested his favorite restaurant: China Garden. Not until the next morning, when I was walking him and Trina to school, did I ask what he thought of Greenfield.

"The kids are stuck up," he said, "and the diving team sucks."

"They're meant to have great labs," I pressed. "Challenging teachers."

"Who wants to be challenged? It's school, not a duel to the death."

Sensible boy, I thought. Before I could praise his answer, his friend Luis joined us. The two began to argue about whether their new history teacher wore a toupee. Trina asked if I'd noticed that Nabokov was losing his feathers.

"I saw some on the bottom of his cage last night," I said. "Has he been losing them for long?"

"Since before Mom's birthday. He pulls them out."

"Why didn't you say anything?"

"I didn't think it mattered. You and Mom have been so busy."

Walking beside her, I couldn't see her face, but I knew from her tone that she felt blamed. "No busier than usual," I said. "And it probably doesn't matter. At certain times of year birds lose their old feathers to make room for new ones. It's called molting."

"Isn't that in the spring?" She stooped to pick up an acorn. "Busier in your heads. There's a kind of buzzing around you, like the fridge."

"I'm sorry," I said. "Sometimes you just need to shake me. Will you do that?"

She reached for the sleeve of my jacket. "Like this?"

I can date our conversation to November 5, the four hundred and fifth anniversary of Guy Fawkes's botched attempt on Parliament and the first anniversary of the killing and wounding of more than two dozen people on a Texas army base. Merrie had brought me the news of Fort Hood between patients. We'd both remarked how lucky we were to live in Massachusetts where guns were harder to come by.

That evening, after Viv left for her Pilates class, I went to the computer and opened the folder labeled "Finances." For several years she and I had kept our money separate, writing checks back and forth, but after we bought our house we had opened a joint account. Only our credit cards remained separate and private. I was the one who paid our bills, mostly online, yet still I felt oddly stealthy as I clicked from account to account. I had insisted, on principle, that we couldn't afford $30,000 a year. Now I found abundant evidence that this was true. Among our non-negotiable expenses were the mortgage, property taxes, insurance, groceries, utilities, the children's various lessons, summer camp, college funds, and retirement savings. And there were always surprises. Last year the roof had leaked. This spring my car needed a new catalytic converter. When Marcus broke his leg, we had paid for tutors and extra physiotherapy.

As I studied the figures, I could hear my father quoting Mr. Micawber: "'Annual income twenty pounds, annual expenditure nineteen nineteen six, result happiness. Annual income twenty pounds, annual expenditure twenty pounds ought and six, result misery.'" I shut down the computer and telephoned my mother. Since my father's death we had met less often; now she seemed pleased by my suggestion of lunch. After checking her diary, she said she could manage Monday. I hung up with the sense that my problems were already solved.

The glorious weather that day seemed to confirm my optimism. In the autumnal sunlight even our shabby main street had a kind of splendor. When I stepped into the windowless bar, I stood blinking for several seconds, waiting for my eyes to adjust to the merry underworld of bottles and TV screens. My mother was already seated at a corner table, with a glass of wine.

I bent to kiss her cheek. "Sorry I can't join you," I said. "My patients might rebel."

"Is one clearer? Or two? Or don't you give a toss?"

She began to talk about her new account with a chain of bowling alleys. I bided my time, waiting to bring up Greenfield. But when our sandwiches arrived, she said, "I want to tell you something, and ask you something."

The eye is the fastest-moving part of the body, beyond the control of the brain. Who knows how many saccades my pupils made as they tried to avoid my mother's next sentence?

"I'm seeing someone."

Of course: the waiter, our fellow customers, the football players, me.

"I never thought it would happen," she went on. "I was devoted to Edward. But Lawrence—Larry—is a lovely man."

I was as shocked as if she'd thrown her drink in my face. Despite my glimpse of her in the restaurant and my subsequent comment to Steve on the tennis court, I had banished any thought of her replacing my father. "Are you trying to tell me," I said, "that you're getting married?"

"No." She laughed. "But I'd like to ask him to Thanksgiving."

I studied a crack in the table and said she was welcome to bring him. My mother, still Scottish after thirty years in the States, did not comment on my frosty manner. "Another man to keep you and Marcus company," she said. "He's looking forward to seeing you again."

For a moment I thought he had spotted me in the street. Then she explained she had known Larry for years; his wife had Parkinson's. "The four of us used to play bridge. You met them one evening when you were dropping off groceries. Larry had to put Jean in the home last year. He keeps saying he wished they lived in Oregon, where he could honor her wishes."

"And get into your bed."

"He's already in my bed," said my mother, not so Scottish

after all. "Fran says I'm going to set my grandchildren a terrible example and live in sin."

That she had told my sister first only deepened my vexation. I took a too-large bite of my sandwich and was still chewing when she asked what I wanted to talk about. I swallowed, drank some water, and described Viv's sudden infatuation with private schools: how I didn't think we should separate Marcus from his friends, how I was anxious about the fees.

"Edward and I had the same argument," my mother said. "He worried we were shortchanging you and Fran, sending you to public schools."

"I didn't know that."

She raised her shoulders to suggest there was much that I didn't know. "We weren't really arguing about schools," she said thoughtfully. "Edward, after being very keen to stay here, suddenly got cold feet, but he didn't want to say so. And I had this great job, so I didn't say anything either. We struggled through the year, arguing about everything except the thing we were really arguing about. Then, suddenly, he was happy again. Maybe you and Viv are fighting about something else?"

If she had pressed me about the "something else," what would I have said? My wife is in love with a horse? I can't live without my father? But she didn't. I got out my credit card.

I knew that not one person in fifty would share my disapproval of Larry, and not one person in a hundred, including me, would understand it. When Viv had remarked that if Peggy were a man, women would be lining up round the block, I had staunchly agreed. I prided myself on being a man who opposed the double standard, who valued character in women over youthful beauty. Yet now my disapproval was a dish I kept eating even as it grew cold and stale.

That afternoon Viv was scarcely through the door before she started exclaiming: how wonderful, Larry sounded great. "Peggy said you were grumpy," she added.

"No." I was at the stove, stirring spaghetti sauce. Some onions had stuck to the bottom, and the spoon kept snagging.

"Now is the winter of our discount tents," said Nabokov, stepping smartly back and forth on his perch. It had been one of my father's favorite jokes.

Still holding her jacket, Viv approached the stove. "But you're not pleased," she said. "You're not glad that your fabulous mother, who took care of your father for a decade, has someone else."

Her dark green sweater was dotted with white marks, which I had assumed were toothpaste. Now that she was closer, I saw that moths were to blame; her shirt was showing through the holes. "You should darn your sweater," I said.

"No one darns nowadays. Perhaps"—her head was cocked at the same angle as Nabokov's—"you're finally coming to terms with your father's death. Someone's stepping into his shoes, so he really must be gone."

"I know he's dead," I said shortly. "Larry's wife isn't."

"And he takes excellent care of her, according to Peggy. But she's no longer his wife in anything but name."

"My mother stuck with my father through thick and thin." I kept stirring and stirring. A spot of sauce landed on Viv's sweater, between two moth holes, but she didn't seem to notice.

"She was amazing," she said. "And I'm thrilled for her."

She paused as if about to say something more. Would she finally acknowledge how abandoned I felt? How absent she'd grown? But she said nothing. In the face of my unfaltering stirring, she stole a slice of pepper and offered it to Nabokov.

8

ONCE ON A PLANE I read a quiz in a woman's magazine: "How well do you know your partner?" Brief scenarios were described, and the respondent asked to pick among possible answers. After a lovely dinner the waitress forgets to put the second round of cocktails on the bill. Does your partner (1) Pay and sneak away? (2) Point out the error? (3) Point out the error and ask for free desserts? Until a year ago I could confidently have answered such questions about Viv. She was impetuous, ambitious, staunch in her left-wing beliefs, and devoted to animals. Here is my evidence, four examples so specific that, despite everything, they still stand firm.

1. The June after we met, Viv and I were walking to a restaurant near the seaport in Boston when we spotted the ferry to Provincetown. Before I could protest, she was pulling me up the gangway. Everything will work out, she insisted. And it did. We found a hotel, bought underwear and toiletries, and had a sunlit day and starry night.

2. When Marcus was only three months old, she had gone back to work and taken on an extra project to secure promotion. The following year, to maintain her

visibility, she attended conferences in Scottsdale, Cincinnati, San Diego, and Montreal.

3. In 2008 she spent every Sunday in New Hampshire campaigning for Obama, and several nights a week telephoning reluctant voters.

4. Once, when we were having a drink on the porch of the apartment she shared with Claudia, a mouse had appeared and started running in slow, tipsy circles.

    "It's sick," Viv exclaimed. "Can't you help it?"

    "With what?" I held up my empty hands. "Besides, I don't know about mice."

    While I sat down again, she bent over the tiny creature, murmuring, "There, there. You'll be all right." She called Claudia for advice and insisted on watching over the mouse's last hour with an old towel and a saucer of water.

So in answer to the question: An animal is in pain. Would your partner (1) Drop everything to help? (2) Say I'm not a vet and drive on? (3) Urge someone else to help? I would have chosen 1, unhesitatingly. But since Mercury's advent, my sense of knowing Viv was under siege. A battlement fell here—Hilary. A turret there—Greenfield. A major stretch of wall fell when, not long after lunch with my mother, Viv asked me to go to the stables to help Claudia with Nimble; they were sending him to the vet's to be euthanized. She had a doctor's appointment, and the Brazilian men who worked at Windy Hill had a family birthday. "You don't need to do anything," she assured me. "Just offer moral support." I rearranged my appointments and drove out to the stables. A trailer hitched to a faded black truck was standing near the indoor arena. As I got out of my car, Claudia appeared in the doorway of the barn, leading a gray pony.

She thanked me for coming. Nimble nudged me, searching my pockets. Poor beast, I thought, showing him my empty hands. It was almost cold enough for snow.

"Come on, Nimble," said Claudia, leading him towards the trailer. It was surely no different from many others he had entered during his long life, but twenty feet away he came to a halt. Neither tugging nor coaxing would budge him. When Claudia changed direction, heading for the water trough, he limped along obligingly, but as soon as she turned back to the trailer, he stopped. I could see the whites of his eyes.

"What's the problem?" said Claudia, offering a carrot. Nimble ate the carrot but did not move. I felt the first drops of rain.

A man wearing a shiny blue jacket got out of the truck. "Step up," he said, and slapped Nimble's rump. The pony gave a feeble kick. While Claudia went to fetch some oats, the man tugged at the halter and swore. Nimble—I was by now entirely on his side—put his ears back and stood firm. At the sight of Claudia and the bucket of oats, he nickered, but he knew better than to take a single step. Still swearing, the driver returned to the cab.

I stepped over to stroke Nimble's neck. "Can't he stay?" I said to Claudia. "He's not doing any harm. I'll pay for his hay. Doesn't he deserve a good retirement?"

"Donald," she said, "his kidneys are failing. Really, this is the kindest way."

"How can this be kind? He's terrified. Let's phone Viv. I'm sure she'd want him to stay."

Claudia put her hand on my arm. "The shot will calm him," she said.

Even as she spoke, the driver reappeared. With no preparation, he rammed a needle into Nimble's shoulder. Nimble
reared halfheartedly. Claudia hung on to the halter until he was
again standing quietly. While she and the driver argued about
vets, his head sank lower. I stood watching out of a sense of
duty. At last Claudia declared him ready. Nimble lurched up the
ramp, paused on the threshold, and stumbled into the trailer.

All of this was harrowing, but worse, much worse, was Viv's
reaction when I described the gruesome scene. "He didn't know
what was happening," she said.

"He absolutely did. He knew that horse trailer was his death
sentence. I felt like an accomplice to murder."

I would have bet ten thousand dollars, a month of my life,
that my kind, animal-loving wife would agree with me, but
like Claudia, she was adamant. Nimble was old, he was ill, he
was fit only for dog food and glue. At some point the woman
who watched over a dying mouse had disappeared. I had missed
her departure.

And I had missed something else, something even more crucial. I have never believed I was exceptional, but Viv secretly,
passionately, believed that she was destined for greatness. When
her attempts to compete on Dow Jones failed, when she found
herself thirty-seven years old with two beautiful children, a devoted (if grieving) husband, a pleasant home, dear friends, and
a job she loved, she felt as if her life was over. Everything tasted
of ashes until Mercury arrived.

9

I MISSED MY FATHER ALL the time, but the major holidays, those days when I had reliably been in his company, were particularly hard. For the last few years we had celebrated Thanksgiving at Claudia and her great-aunt Helen's house. Now, as I helped Viv make stuffing and cranberry sauce, I kept picturing him standing in their living room, reciting the Scots grace, using his walker as a prop in charades. How could we celebrate without him? How could my mother have already replaced him? But as soon as Larry came into the room, I could see that he was, as she had said, a lovely man. He went round greeting everyone. He endeared himself to Viv and Claudia by asking about the stables, to Helen by praising the house, to Marcus by talking about diving, and to Trina by describing the time he'd ridden an elephant.

"I doubt you'll remember," he said to me. "We met years ago." His lower teeth were endearingly crowded.

"Of course," I said, although I still had no recollection of our meeting. What had my mother told him about me? A wonderful doctor. Gave up surgery to care for his father. Devoted to his children. Or a less flattering description?

But Larry was asking after Nabokov. He too had an African grey. "I remember your father telling me that Henry VIII owned one. We joked about what it might say. 'Wife number three. Watch your head.' "

My mother, once the introductions were past, behaved as usual, helping Claudia with the turkey, but something about her was different. In private she must often have bemoaned my father's illness, but in public she always behaved as if she were glad to be married to this man who towards the end, could not button his own shirt nor finish a sentence. Watching her now, I remembered a long-ago afternoon, bicycling on Cape Cod. I had gotten ahead of the others, and when I turned around to wait, I saw her pedaling towards me, her face bright with happiness.

Needless to say, Larry was good at charades and his baked squash was delicious. As I sat looking down the candlelit table, everyone talking and laughing, it was as if my father had never existed. Just then my mother tapped her glass.

"Ladies and gentlemen." Her gaze settled on me. "May I propose a toast? To absent friends."

It was the toast my father had made year after year. We raised our glasses.

But the most significant event of the holiday was still to come. Viv and I drove home, put the children to bed, and went to bed ourselves. An hour later we were woken by the phone. I answered on the second ring, half expecting to hear my mother's voice. A man asked for Viv Turner.

I hovered, uselessly, while she said, "Yes," "Yes," and "I'll be there as soon as I can."

The alarm had gone off at Windy Hill. The police needed her to check that no damage had been done and reset it.

"Probably just a raccoon," she said, as she pulled on her clothes.

"This is Massachusetts," I reassured her. "People don't steal horses."

But we were both thinking about the break-in at the farm stand. She turned out the light, and I heard the familiar sequence: her feet on the stairs, the back door, the car door, the engine.

When Marcus was four, he had gone through a phase of dreading sleep, sure that if he closed his eyes, some dragon or demon would pounce. As I lay there, alone in the dark, clicking back and forth on the abacus of my nocturnal accounts, I had new sympathy for his fears. My father was dead; my patients were dying (only one); my mother was changing (she had found happiness); my wife was obsessed with private school and a horse (she was an enthusiast); we were close to bankruptcy (not really). At last I pulled on my bathrobe and went downstairs. I still have the British belief that almost any situation can be improved by a cup of tea.

The water had just come to the boil when I heard a car turn into our driveway. But as I heated the pot, measured, and poured, I heard nothing more. Thinking I had been mistaken, I opened the back door. There was Viv's car in the usual place, and there was Viv, still sitting behind the wheel. Something terrible must have happened.

At the sight of me hurrying down the steps, she jumped out of the car. "Don," she said, "you'll freeze."

In the kitchen she opted for Scotch instead of tea, which suddenly seemed like a very good idea. We sat down at the table. Two policemen, she told me, had been waiting at Windy Hill. They had walked around the barn and the smaller building, looking for signs of entry. Inside the barn, the younger policeman had checked the windows again while she and the older one went round the horses.

Our kitchen overlooks the garden, and we seldom close the curtains. As she described how, outside Mercury's stall, they had found a man's glove lying on the floor, I watched the pale gleam of her face reflected in the dark window. "People drop gloves all the time," I said.

She shook her head. "I fed him just before I locked up. I couldn't have missed it. Someone broke in and visited his stall." She set down her glass and reached for my hand. "I need you to promise something. Don't tell anyone about this. I don't want Hilary to move him."

"Maybe she should," I said. "He requires all this special care, and now some burglar is interested in him."

"No!"

The single syllable was so piercing that I was again sure something terrible had happened. Had she cut her hand on her glass? Developed appendicitis? But before I could speak, she was pointing to the ceiling. We listened for the children. When no sound came from above, she went on, her voice steely. "There's no need for her to move Mercury. We'll make the stables safe. Promise me, Don."

I promised, and she kissed me, but in bed she turned away.

THE PHRASE "DON'T TELL anyone" nearly always has a silent exception. In this case, I assumed it was Claudia. She and Viv were best friends; she owned the stables. Whether Viv had already decided not to tell her about the break-in, or whether circumstances conspired to make that choice, she herself scarcely knew. The police paid a follow-up visit the next morning and were gone by the time Claudia arrived. They recommended a new alarm, security lights, and grills at the windows, all of which Viv justified by reminding Claudia about the break-in at the farm stand. By the end of the following week the measures were in place. The bill was paid, again I learned only later, with Viv's credit card—which is to say, by our joint account.

What I knew at the time was that our household was not running smoothly. Viv no longer walked the children to school but left first thing to ride Mercury; most afternoons she stayed late at the stables. At home she spent hours online, looking up things about horses: tack, nutrition, training, competitions. Trina missed a violin lesson, and we had to pay for it. Marcus missed a crucial swimming practice and wouldn't speak to us for two days. I was irked by these errors, but I held my tongue. In the weeks following my father's death Viv had carried the household uncomplainingly. My silence was rewarded when one night in early December she arrived home to find Marcus and his friend Luis making tacos.

"How are the horses?" Luis asked. "Marcus said maybe some-day you'll let me ride." He smiled at her over the cheese grater.

"I didn't know you liked horses," said Viv.

"Yes, you did, Mom," said Marcus. "Luis went to a ranch last summer. His whole family learned to ride."

That night, when she joined me on the sofa, Viv said what a nice boy Luis was. I said he was, all credit to his mother, who worked two jobs and still helped with homework every night.

"So how can they afford to go to a ranch?" she asked.

In the last few months she had often accused me of not pay-ing attention. Now I refrained from retaliating as I explained that Luis's uncle managed a ranch in Wyoming. He had hired the mother to cook for his summer guests. I was turning back to my book when Viv spoke again.

"I've been thinking," she said, "you're right about Green-field. There are all these good things—smaller classes, terrific teachers—but Marcus's friends are important. We can volunteer at the middle school. Get him extra tutoring."

"It is what he wants," I said, trying not to sound too eager. Luis, I thought, with his tacos and his interest in horses, had changed her mind.

10

PAINFULLY, ON PAGE AFTER page, I record my myopia. My wife was choosing a horse over our family, and what was I doing to lure her back? But I had my own distractions, some I was aware of, some not. On the anniversary of Pearl Harbor, Diane came to my office. The vision in her left eye was a little blurred. I checked the prescription and said that the eye had improved in the last couple of months. It sometimes happened when you first started wearing glasses.

"Will it keep improving?" she said.

"Maybe—eyes are unpredictable—but any further changes will probably be very small. You like science, don't you?"

She nodded. "What's the problem with Jack's eyes? He wasn't always blind, was he?"

"Jack?" I said.

"Mom's friend, your friend."

The week before, Jack had remarked that since he started carrying a cane, people often told him their secrets, but he found it hard to reciprocate. "All I can picture," he said, "is me pouring out my heart, my listener yawning." At the time I'd assumed he was rehearsing a new section of his book: how people treat the blind differently. Now I understood he'd been telling me that he too had his secrets. I hid my hurt from Diane behind a stuffy speech about patient confidentiality.

"Ask Jack," I said. "I'm sure he'd be happy to explain his condition."

"He tried, but it was hard to follow. He can't draw a diagram."

Something about her seriousness made me reach for my model eye. "This is the iris," I said. "And the pupil." I was pointing out the optic nerve when Merrie knocked at the door: my last appointment of the day was here. I thanked her and finished my explanation. "So we think we see with our eyes," I said, "but really we see with our brains."

Fifteen minutes later I emerged from the last appointment to find Merrie sitting on the edge of her desk. "If you want to give a biology lesson," she said, "use the waiting room, or my office."

"I didn't realize Mr. Kearney was waiting."

"Mr. Kearney's not the point. You shouldn't see children alone in your office, with the door closed, beyond the necessary appointment."

How fast does sight travel? Diane had asked. As fast as Merrie's meaning reached me. "Did Diane say something?"

"Only that it's cool that the eye has a lens like her contact lens."

"But something happened? Come on, Merrie, what are you really saying?"

Still frowning, she said that a teacher at her daughters' school was in trouble. "Ginny's taught there for ten years. Now she's been accused of 'inappropriate behavior.' She was helping a girl with extra homework, and the two of them were alone in the classroom. There's no way she can prove her innocence."

"It sounds like that famous case in Edinburgh," I said. "You seem very sure the girl is lying."

"Lots of famous cases." The girl had briefly been friends with her oldest daughter. Several times Merrie had caught her in a blatant lie. "She's a little cat, but she made me realize you do have to be careful. Men are even more vulnerable than women."

When I moved back to Boston, colleagues had warned me about the dangers of lawsuits. Be careful about apologizing, the head of surgery admonished. But I had not considered other kinds of danger. All day long I saw women alone, with no nurse or assistant. Now I promised to heed Merrie's advice. We locked up, and I watched her stride away into the darkness. Then I phoned Drew to ask if he could babysit for an extra hour and Jack to ask if he'd like a drink. Both said yes.

The door of Jack's apartment was ajar, and when I stepped inside, the air had a spicy fragrance. He was at the stove, stirring a saucepan of mulled wine; his building was having a party that evening.

"Diane came to my office," I said.

He added a pinch of cinnamon to the wine. "She's a smart cookie. Let's give this a shot."

He filled two mugs and led the way to the living room. "So what's up? The air is vibrating. Are you mad that I'm going out with Hilary?"

"She just doesn't seem your type."

"The type to have a blind toy boy? Did you notice my new decor?" He waved his arm.

I had grown accustomed to the bare functionality of Jack's apartment. Now I took in the pictures on the walls, the three new lamps. A wicker basket of papers sat on one table, a large bowl on another. As if following my gaze, he said, "She hasn't just prettied up the place for my sighted friends. She's made my life easier."

"Brilliant."

"Brilliant," he mimicked. "What's the matter, Donald? You're worried about my morals? You think I don't deserve Hilary?"

"If anything, she doesn't deserve you. I just feel stupid that I never thought you might want a girlfriend."

Jack smiled. "You, and everyone else," he said. "Lo, the blind are not celibate. It's nice to break a long dry spell, and nice to be with someone who treats me like a normal person. What do you think of the wine? Hilary says you don't like her."

I was startled to learn that they had discussed me, and startled that the feelings I thought so carefully concealed were apparent. I said I hardly knew her. "We didn't get off on the best foot, but you like her, and so does Viv. Clearly I need to get on a different foot. The wine is good."

"Maybe a splash more brandy. Why did you get off on the wrong foot?"

No point in saying that Hilary had struck me as shallow and flirtatious. Instead I said she seemed to disapprove of her daughter liking biology.

"Oh, that's just Hil, wanting Diane to have more friends. And now"—he set down his mug—"you may ask the obvious question."

"Why is she going out with a blind man?"

He clapped mockingly. "I'll tell you my guilty secret. She didn't know I was blind until after we'd slept together."

"How could that be?" Even as I asked, I guessed the answer: his vivid eyes had misled her.

"When she introduced herself at Viv's party, I assumed she

knew. 'My blind friend Jack'—isn't that what everyone calls me? I gave her my card, and she phoned a couple of days later. I invited her over for a drink. With disgraceful speed, one thing led to another. Only afterward, when she asked if I needed help hanging pictures, did it dawn on me that she hadn't a clue."

"So what happened when you told her?"

"She said 'Wow, my first blind guy.' Then we went through chapter and verse. When did I lose my sight? Can I see anything? Is sex more or less intense? I answered as best I could and said she was welcome to get the hell out. I hadn't meant to deceive her. She said she didn't feel deceived, but she was hungry. We went out for Thai food. She told me stories about her job, and growing up in Ontario. I told her about my students and growing up in Gloucester. She walked me home, said she'd be in touch—maybe I could buy some condoms?—and drove away."

I imagined Hilary's light voice saying "condoms."

Gleefully Jack described the pharmacist's surprise. She too, apparently, had never realized that the blind have sex lives. But then he was home with his little purchases, waiting. After sixty-seven hours Hilary phoned to say she liked him but she didn't know what she was up for. She hadn't been with anyone since Diane's father, and she didn't want to be a person who wasn't kind to cripples. He said he liked her too. Whatever happened, he wouldn't play the cripple card. On that unsteady basis they were stumbling forward.

"Brilliant," I said again.

"Come on, Donald. At first there was nothing to tell: I saw someone last night, and I may or may not see her again. It's not as if Hilary is a friend of yours."

"But"—I studied the wicker basket—"you are." Three words I would never have said to a sighted person.

Jack seemed to understand what they cost me. "I am," he said, "and I'm sorry I kept you in the dark. Believe me, I know what that's like."

Suddenly my resistance, my anger, whatever it was, disappeared. "Christ," I said, "I'm being a dickhead."

"Hurrah, he swore in American." He clapped his hands again.

As I got ready to leave, I asked whether Viv knew about him and Hilary.

"Wouldn't she have said something?"

"The way things are nowadays, who knows?"

I saw him register what I was telling him, but for once he did not press me. Instead he told me about Mercury, the Roman god, with his winged hat and winged shoes. Like the Greek god Hermes, he carried messages and guided souls down into the underworld, but he had many other duties.

"He's a busy fellow," Jack said. "He's the god of eloquence, of commerce, and of travel, but he's also the god of thieves and trickery. People used to paint his image on their doors, thinking that he would protect them from lesser thieves. And he carries a staff, a caduceus, with two serpents that people often confuse with your doctor's staff."

"Asclepius's rod," I said. "We only have one snake." The idea of sharing anything with Mercury made me prickle.

I thanked him for the wine and left him to his party. Outside, the first snow of the winter had begun to fall. Tiny crystals glinted in my headlights as I drove home. In the kitchen Drew was teaching Trina, Marcus, and Nabokov to sing "Good King Wenceslas."

11

THANKSGIVING HAD BEEN HARD, but it was only one day, an American day. Christmas had always been our family's holiday. Every year had found us together, first in Scotland, then in the States, playing games, eating goose, hoping for peace on earth. Over the years Viv and I have invented our own modest traditions. On Christmas Eve we go to a carol service at Merrie's church, she and her daughters sing in the choir, and after supper we read an abridged version of *A Christmas Carol*. On Christmas Day, unless the weather is appalling, we go for a walk before making dinner and playing games. At some point during the holidays we drive into Boston to skate on the Frog Pond, and my mother treats us to tea at a fancy hotel. I assumed we would continue these traditions, sadly marking my father's absence. But then my sister announced she was staying in Nashville with a new beau. My mother, deep in her own romantic entanglements, was going to Philadelphia to meet Larry's children. As we bent over Marcus and Trina's advent calendars, exclaiming at each new picture, I could feel what Viv called my astronaut's suit growing thicker by the day. She had first used the phrase in August, the evening we got back from the Cape. When I asked what she meant, she said, "You're like a man in a space suit. Everything has to make its way through layers and layers to reach you." I had nodded, startled that she understood me so well. But later, as I put the groceries away, it occurred to me that her image was only half right: my astronaut's suit kept me aloof but it did not keep me safe: no oxygen, no water, no warmth.

On the solstice Steve thrashed me at tennis, and when I got home, Viv asked if we could invite Hilary and Diane for supper on Christmas Eve.

"We scarcely know them," I said.

"You scarcely know them. Hilary's become a good friend. It's not like we exchange presents or anything." She was, I recall, cleaning her riding boots.

"What about *A Christmas Carol*? The kids always complain, but they'd miss it."

"She thought it sounded fun. And I'm sure Jack will enjoy it."

She had, I realized, already issued the invitation. "When did she tell you about Jack?" I said.

"I don't think there's much to tell." She rubbed a muddy heel. "She likes him, but she's wary." She dabbed some polish. "Who can blame her?"

She did not seem surprised that I knew about their relationship and had said nothing, so why should I be that she had done the same?

On Christmas Eve I woke to the silvery light of new snow, Viv's side of the bed empty as usual. In a few months I would be forty, and this was the first Christmas, save for one as a student in Edinburgh, when I had not been in my parents' company. Dear Robert, I thought, do you remember the year we had lots of snow at Christmas, and went sledging in the local park? Happily Marcus and Trina burst into the room, rescuing me. We spent the day in seasonal activities: baking Christmas cookies, making a snowman and a snow-woman, decorating the house. Viv, when she came home, was in a wonderful mood, teasing the children and taking even their most fanciful suggestions for decorating the tree seriously. Marcus made a boy diver for the top, and Trina made an elephant family, a baby, mother, and three aunts linked trunk to tail, which we hung in the lower branches. At the carol service I could hear our voices, separate and distinct, blending with the others.

Back at the house we had a fire going and dinner ready by the time Hilary, Diane, and Jack arrived. Hilary and Viv embraced warmly, and I did my best to follow suit. When everyone was seated at the table and the lasagna had been served and praised, Hilary said she'd met a woman who trained miniature horses to guide the blind.

"Wouldn't that be cute, Jack?" she said. "You could go everywhere with a little horse."

"How little?" said Trina. "Could it sit at the table?"

"I bet they make great guides," said Viv. "They live a long time."

"I'm sorry," said Jack. "My housekeeping skills are already challenged. What if I had a horse to clean up after too? You know who I think would make a good guide? Nabokov. He could say things like, 'Boring colleague to the left.' His feathers are sticking up in a weird way."

Trina said that he'd been pulling them out. I repeated my molting theory.

"But birds don't molt in winter," said Diane. "That's when they need their feathers."

"Maybe it's a cry for help," said Jack. "He must be lonely without Edward."

Suddenly everyone at the table was looking at me reproachfully. I promised to take Nabokov to the vet as soon as possible, and offered seconds.

In the living room we settled ourselves around the fire with *A Christmas Carol*. I read, as my father had always done, Dickens's epigraph—"I have endeavoured in this Ghostly little book to raise the Ghost of an idea"—and we were off. Jack, with his braille version, was Scrooge, Diane and Trina enjoyed being pathetic orphans, I was the narrator, and Marcus and Viv shared the other parts. Hilary had volunteered to be the audience, and when we reached the last lines, she jumped to her feet, clapping and shouting, "Bravo. Encore."

The children disappeared to play Ping-Pong in the basement, I poured more wine, and Viv asked Jack and Hilary one of her questions: How had they celebrated Christmas as children? "If you celebrated," she added, in cautious American fashion.

"We did," Jack said. His whole family—aunts and uncles, cousins, grandparents—had gone to the midnight service on Christmas Eve. "It's the closest I've come to a religious experience without drugs: the church lit by candles, everyone wishing each other merry Christmas. Afterwards, walking home, I'd be so sleepy I could hardly put one foot in front of the other, and so happy, knowing that when I woke up there'd be presents and no one getting mad at me for an entire day."

But that world, he went on, was utterly gone. His father was dead. His mother didn't know Christmas from Easter. His older sister lived in Baltimore and had no money to travel. His younger sister, a Christian Scientist, lived in Malden and didn't want her kids to meet him.

"Horrible people," said Hilary, reaching for his hand. "What I remember is Michael, my brother, carrying me out to the barn to wish our horses Merry Christmas."

Viv had mentioned Mercury's previous owner. Now I learned that Michael was nine years older than Hilary and believed there were five elements: earth, air, fire, water, and horses.

"He died very young," I said.

"He did," Hilary said. We were all silent as she blinked back tears. "He was riding alone, late in the day, and he fell at a jump. Mercury made his way back to the stables. They said it was an accident, but I still find it hard to believe. Michael didn't have accidents involving horses."

Listening to her, I was struck by how we crave precision around death. We want to know the exact minute of passing; we note where we were and how we heard; we ponder that strange interval of afterlife during which we assumed the other person to be still alive and how that interval vanishes when we learn the news. I was with my father at the nursing home when he died. I had been sitting by his bed for an hour, holding his hand and talking to him, when I wandered over to the window. In the parking lot a woman was clearing the snow off her car. As she swept the hood, I noticed that the room had fallen silent. It was eleven minutes past four.

Hilary had been working on a house, hanging a mirror, when her phone rang. "As soon as Mom said hello," she said, "my reflection turned white." She had flown to Ontario for the funeral and brought his ashes back to the States—her parents couldn't bear to keep them. She still hadn't decided what to do with them.

"You'll figure it out," said Viv. "He'd be glad you're taking such good care of Mercury."

It was then that Jack asked what I'd wondered on several occasions: How much was the horse worth? Hilary looked over at Viv. "Five thousand dollars?" she said. "Ten?"

"More," said Viv. "A good jumper, his age, athletic, well trained"—she spread her hands—"you might be surprised what he'll bring. When he starts to win competitions, people will see what he's worth."

"But who's going to ride him in competitions?" said Hilary. "Besides I'll never sell him. He's all I have left of Michael."

Her voice shrilled with dismay. Jack put his arm around her and leaned over to whisper something. Neither of them heard Viv's answer to her question.

"I will," she said. "I will."

ON TUESDAY THE VETERINARIAN confirmed Jack's diagnosis. Nabokov was pulling out his feathers because he missed my father.

"So should we get him another parrot for company?" Viv asked that evening when the four of us gathered around his cage.

"The vet thought that might be tricky," I said. "Parrots mate for life, and we couldn't be sure we were choosing a bird that would suit Nabokov. What he needs is human company."

"We have to talk to him more," said Trina. "Hello, Nab. What did you learn today?"

We each came up with ideas for spending more time with Nabokov, but still he would be mostly alone. "Could you take him to the office?" said Viv. "I bet he'd enjoy the waiting room."

"You mean drive him back and forth every day? What if he catches cold? Or swears at a patient?" My mind was crowded with possible disasters. Was it even legal to have a bird in a waiting room?

"Please, Dad," said Trina. "It would be so sad if he made himself bald."

Once again everyone was looking at me, even Nabokov, his pupils growing larger by the second. I promised to talk to Merrie and see what could be done. The idea of my father's last companion being lonely was more than I could bear.

ON ONE OF OUR early dates Viv had told me about Clever Hans, a horse famous for being able to add 4 and 2, or 3 and 5. Only after many trials did investigators discover that Hans was not doing arithmetic but picking up on the cues given, unconsciously, by his audience. If no one present knew the answer, neither did Hans. "The scientists felt vindicated," Viv said, "but actually he was doing something much more complicated than counting." All autumn she had been praising Mercury's intelligence. Her superlatives reached new heights when she came home from riding him with the saddle I had given her for Christmas.

"There was this barrier between us that I didn't even know was there."

"Excellent," I said. After nearly a month of consultations with the saddle fitter, I was glad she was finally pleased.

Our annual expedition to the Frog Pond was usually a high point of the holidays, but this year my mother was missing, the ice was rough, the wind vicious. A superstitious person might have said the omens were bad. After less than an hour we headed across the snowy Common to the hotel where we always had tea. In the lounge, with its beautifully decorated tree, we grew almost giddy, drinking hot chocolate and eating little sandwiches. It was dark by the time we got home. While Viv and the children took off their outdoor clothes, I moved through the house, turning on lights, drawing curtains. When I saw the blink of the answering machine in the study, I pressed play, thinking Merrie had phoned. She and her daughters were due for supper, another tradition, in a little over an hour.

"Why the hell didn't you tell me about the break-in at Thanksgiving?" Anger rendered Claudia's voice almost unrecognizable. "Have you forgotten I own the stables? All that crap about getting a new alarm because of the farm stand. How could you treat me this way?" And so on until the machine cut her off.

Back in the kitchen I took refuge in unloading the dishwasher. When Viv came in, I said Claudia had called. "Oh, good," she said, and went to listen. I heard again the furious crescendo, muffled by the wall. In the silence that followed, I began to put away the cutlery. Viv appeared in the doorway. She walked slowly to the table and sat down with her head in her hands. I kept putting knives in the drawer.

"Viv," I said, "why didn't you tell her?"

"Because of Mercury." She spoke as if the answer were utterly obvious.

"What do you mean, 'because of Mercury'?"

Still she kept her face hidden. "Claudia already thinks he takes too much of my time. I didn't want to give her an excuse to ask Hilary to move him." Then she told me that we, not the stables, had footed the bill for the new alarm and grills. She let her hands fall, and I saw her face, flushed with cold or emotion, or both. "It was only seven thousand dollars," she said.

As I stood watching her, half a dozen forks in one hand, a dishtowel in the other, it came to me that her change of heart about Greenfield was due not to the importance of Marcus's friends but to the many expenses around Mercury. Even our son came second to her horse. For a moment anger robbed me of speech.

"Why," I said at last, "why would you spend all this money on someone else's horse?"

"We've been very lax about security. The changes were long overdue."

"If that's true, then why go behind Claudia's back, and spend my money secretly?"

"So now it's 'my money'? What about for richer, for poorer?"

Useless to point out that, in our abbreviated ceremony at city hall, we had never made such a promise. She stood up and headed towards the coatrack.

"Where are you going?" I stepped forward to block her path. "Merrie and her daughters will be here any minute."

"They'll understand," she said. "It's an emergency."

"No, Viv. It's not an emergency. Claudia said nothing about needing you at the stables."

I put my hand on her arm, meaning only to remind her that her place was here, at home, but when she started to pull free, my grip tightened. Suddenly we were struggling, both using all our strength, Viv glaring as if I were her enemy. She was almost free when Trina appeared.

"I'm hungry," she said. "Is something wrong?"

Somehow we got through the evening. We both drank too much; Viv told stupid jokes and insisted we play serial Ping-Pong. No one else, I thought, noticed her frantic edge. At last Merrie and her daughters left; the children went to bed. I stood in the kitchen doorway, watching Viv scrub a saucepan, wondering if she was about to drive to Windy Hill.

"I'll be up in ten minutes," she said, not raising her eyes from the sink.

Dutifully I climbed the stairs and prepared for bed. I was sure she regretted her earlier outburst and everything else: keeping the break-in secret, paying for the alarm without consulting me. It never crossed my mind that I too was in the wrong. She had tried to tell me about Mercury; she had given me my chance; I had failed her. When she came upstairs, I closed my book, still hoping for an apology, but she only reached for me.

12

ILLNESS SAVED US FROM further argument. Viv awoke the next morning complaining that her skull was too tight. Her temperature rose to 103. For two days she lay in bed. We celebrated New Year's Eve at home, watching DVDs, and were asleep by eleven. Not until January 2, when Marcus needed a lift to a friend's house, did I have a chance to visit Windy Hill. As I got out of the car, Charlie and another girl were pushing wheelbarrows of hay towards the little barn. We exchanged Happy New Years.

Claudia was in the tack room, standing at the table, sorting bridles and halters. "Donald," she said.

I knew at once that she was not pleased to see me. Despite everything, there was never any question who she would save from a burning house. "Happy New Year," I said. "I heard your message. I'm sorry about all this stuff with Viv."

Her gloved hand tightened around the bridle she was holding. "I was so mad I didn't realize I'd called your home phone. By 'stuff,' I take it you mean not telling me about the first burglary, and not telling me why we were suddenly going overboard on security, and not allowing me to tell Hilary what's going on, and probably a few other things that I'll find out about months from now."

This time the burglars had borrowed the ladder they used to replace lightbulbs in the arena and come in through the hayloft.

"But why break in and not take anything?" I said. "It's a lot of trouble for nothing."

"That's what the police said." She held up a bridle, testing the strap. "They think it must be someone who knows the stables, but we have so many people coming and going."

Nearby I heard Charlie's hearty laugh. I dropped my voice to ask about Hilary.

"You mean, have I told her?" Claudia gave me a quick glance. "The answer is, not yet. I mean to every day, but I haven't seen her since before Christmas, and I know Viv will kill me."

"You could," I spoke hesitantly, "insist she move Mercury."

Her face grew still. "I'd love nothing more than to see the back of him, but it wouldn't do any good. Viv would just hate me and follow him to a new stable. He's the horse she's been waiting for."

Two walls of the small room were lined with saddles, including presumably the one I had just given Viv. "Have you ever seen her like this before?" I said. "So obsessed?"

Claudia set down the halter she was holding and sat on the edge of the table. "I was asking myself that yesterday, and the answer is yes. As long as I've known her, Viv's been ambitious. She ruined her favorite horse, overtraining him. Then she was determined to be a CEO by the time she was thirty. When she decided not to have an abortion, I knew she was in love with you."

One of my most cherished memories was of the night Viv told me she was pregnant. Now, in response to my broken question, Claudia described how the two of them, over margaritas, had listed the pros and cons: abortion versus baby. Viv had phoned Planned Parenthood the next day. "But the night before the appointment"—Claudia was smiling—"she had a dream. She and the baby were having a picnic by a river, paddling. He was so happy, Viv said."

My first reaction was neither sorrow nor anger but a kind of astonishment that my past life, which I had thought safely stowed away, could change so radically. All the milestones on the journey to my present self—a father, a husband—were suddenly up for negotiation. "I didn't know any of this," I said. At the time I did not stop to wonder why Claudia was, at last, telling me this long-ago story. Later I would understand.

She stood up and turned her smile on me. "Viv loves you, Donald," she said. "I've never seen her happier than with you and the kids, but Mercury has started something in her. Or maybe he's reminded her of something that never entirely went away. In Ann Arbor we used to daydream about a horse that could jump anything, like in *National Velvet*. Most people grow out of those dreams. Not Viv."

She went to check on the stable girls, and I made my way to the rows of stalls. Samson came over to the bars and lost interest as soon as he saw I was empty-handed. Mercury was standing at the back of his stall, wearing a red blanket, swishing his tail. I said his name softly and he looked at me, ears pricked.

"You're causing a hell of a lot of trouble," I said.

My family was founded on a dream, a dream of a baby paddling in a river. As Mercury whinnied, it came to me: we should buy Viv her own horse, a good horse she could ride in local shows. Ever since her failure with Dow Jones, she had been complaining about the horses at Windy Hill—how hard it was to train them above a certain level—but I hadn't taken her seriously. Now, I told myself, she wanted more. But the more didn't have to be Mercury, with his huge talents and demands.

13

So this was how we started 2011. My father's African grey sad. Claudia and Viv at odds. Viv training Mercury every minute she could, convinced he was her last great chance. Marcus's swimming team enjoying a winning streak. Trina, her mother's daughter, obsessed with drawing and elephants. Hilary and Jack making their way unsteadily from day to day. My mother, as she liked to joke, happy as Larry. And me, still deep in grief, worried about our finances and how seldom Viv turned to me in bed, or talked to me on the sofa.

On the first Monday of the year I drove Marcus and Trina to school and returned to the house. Leaving the engine running, I covered Nabokov's cage and whisked him into the car. When he was safely strapped in the seat beside me, I removed the blanket.

"We're going to work," I told him.

"Hey ho, hey ho," he chanted.

For the next fifteen minutes he kept up a cheerful commentary, including a recital of a railway timetable—the eleven o'clock for Inverness will depart at eleven oh six—that perfectly captured my father's intonation. At the office Merrie had set up a table in a brightly lit corner with a large cage and two ficus plants. As I arranged his perch, a fresh maple branch, she appeared, coffeepot in hand.

"Welcome, Nabokov. Do you remember me? I'm Merrie. You must be sure to tell me what I can do to make you a happier bird. Does he peck?"

"No, he's mostly very affectionate. He likes conversation and sunflower seeds."

I showed her how to approach him from the side, not the front, and the place behind his head where he liked to be scratched. When I returned from hanging up my coat, Leah had joined the conversation. Then Jo showed up. How this would have tickled my father, I thought: three intelligent women giving Nabokov their complete attention.

On his third day at the office, Bonnie Dawson, the patient with a door in her head, finally returned. She had made a follow-up appointment, canceled it, rescheduled: kids, she said, work. But the shadow was still there, still growing. "It's scary," she said. I put in drops to dilate her eyes and sent her out to the waiting room. Three patients later, when I called her back to the chair, she said, "Your parrot kept saying 'Shall I compare thee to a summer's day?'"

"He belonged to my father, who taught him poetry. Put your chin here."

Looking into the eye is like looking into a room where, ideally, all the furniture is in the same place. In Bonnie's left eye the furniture had moved. A tear in the retina had allowed fluid to accumulate; now the retina was becoming detached. I turned on the lights and broke the news: she needed surgery. In the meantime she had to be as careful as possible—no lifting, no bending or stretching, no running after children.

"It looks," I added, "as if you had surgery as a child, perhaps more than once."

"Are you sure? Wouldn't I remember?"

The idea of a past operation seemed to alarm her almost as much as the prospect of one. I said not to worry. The main thing was, she needed surgery now.

"But I'm not in pain. What about wearing a patch again? Or new glasses?"

"Bonnie, you said yourself the shadow is getting bigger. New glasses can't stop that. If it gets too big, you won't have any vision to improve."

She stood up and took a step towards me, her eyes fixed on my face. "And if I let someone mess around in my eyeball with a knife, what then?"

"We don't use knives. If all goes well, your vision should stabilize. You should be able to continue with your normal life."

"'Should'? What does 'should' mean? Will I be okay?"

She was looking at me so fiercely I had to turn away. "'Should' means there's every reason to think the surgery will be successful, but no one can give you a hundred-percent guarantee."

"I'm out of here." She seized her bag and headed for the door.

"You ought not to drive. You might hurt someone—your daughters, a friend of your daughters."

My last remark stopped her. "Shit," she said. She sat down on the edge of my desk, glaring as if this too were my fault. I was reaching to touch her shoulder when I recalled Merrie's warning. I let my hand fall and suggested she phone her husband.

Greg arrived twenty minutes later, straight from his job unloading trucks at a supermarket. He had the build of a linebacker, tall, short necked, and thick thighed. His bulky presence made my office seem instantly smaller, but as soon as he spoke, his fundamental niceness was apparent. I again explained the need for immediate surgery and how careful Bonnie must be.

"Treat her like a princess," he said. "Got it."

I escorted them to Merrie's desk, and was almost back at my office when I heard footsteps.

"Doctor," Greg said. "Are you saying Bonnie could go blind? You can tell me straight."

He was standing a few yards away, his uniform stretched tight across his chest, his muscular arms flexed, ready to pick up whatever burden I handed him. Remembering Jack's mockery of my circumlocutions, I said, "That is the very, very worst case scenario."

"Thank you. That's what I needed to know. Bonnie's stubborn. We'll get home, and she'll start charging around, but I'll tie her to the bed sooner than let her do one bad thing."

Before I could respond, he was hurrying back to Bonnie. I gazed after him with a feeling that, at the time, I did not understand. Now I suspect it was envy.

EITHER THAT WEEK OR the next, Viv began to drive up to New Hampshire to observe the master classes at a riding school. At the time I paid this new activity no heed; it was just more of her endless busyness around horses. Only later, in what I have come to think of as my afterlife, did I understand that on these trips she crossed much more than a state line. The new university term had begun and the day after Bonnie's appointment, Jack asked if I could pick him up at his office. I left work early, took Nabokov home, and drove to the campus. As I approached his second-floor office, a student was leaving.

"Thank you so much, Professor Brennan," she said.

As soon as her footsteps faded, he turned to me. "Is she attractive?" he said.

What I'd noticed was the young woman's gratitude, not her appearance. "Moderately. She was beaming as she thanked you."

"Makeup?"

"Not much. Maybe some mascara. How did you picture her?"

"Nice looking, but not in a slutty way." He reached for his backpack and began to gather his possessions. "It's one of the things I've always despised about myself: I care so much how women look. In grad school I shared an office with this woman Sandra. She was smart, funny, kind, and I knew she liked me. But I couldn't imagine going out with her because she was so homely. Sometimes I think I deserved to go blind."

"If everyone who misused their eyesight lost it, we'd all have white canes," I said. "Hilary is attractive, in case you're wondering."

"I can tell from the way waiters speak to her." He picked up a stack of CDs. "God, I'm such a pig. Even now, when I ought to be grateful that any woman will give me the time of day, I still want to have a pretty girlfriend. It's the opposite of every value I hold dear, yet I can't fucking change."

I thought of Bonnie's hazel eyes; of the shadow only she could see. "So what happened to the brilliant, homely Sandra?"

"She married a millionaire who worships the ground she walks on—I wish." He smiled and zipped up his pack. "She's a single parent, teaching high school in Syracuse. Friends report she works too hard and is happy."

On the short drive to his apartment he made me describe the journey. It was Hilary's idea; if he learned that the bad pothole was by the post office, the long traffic light was at School Street, then, even in a car, he would always know where he was. When we were settled in his living room, he told me she had taken him to meet Mercury.

"Beforehand I was thinking all horses are the same to a blind man. But then I held out my hand, and he gave a big, warm snort. His breath smelled of grass, and summer."

"You could ride," I said. "Helen Keller did."

"Are you suggesting I climb onto a tall animal, over which I have zero control, and allow it to carry me around? No thanks. So what's this about a security issue at Windy Hill?"

Hilary had noticed the new alarm, and Claudia, in response to her question, had used this vague phrase. Which is worse: breaking a promise or telling a lie? As ten-year-olds, Robert and I had debated this choice and voted for the former. A few months before, when I asked Marcus and Trina, they had said the same. Now, in response to Jack's question, I followed Claudia's example, lying to keep my promise. I mentioned the break-ins at the nearby businesses, how the police had advised updating the alarms.

"Hilary would go ballistic," he said, "if anything happened to Mercury."

"But she never rides him nowadays." I was not sure if I was asking, or telling him.

"And there's the rub." Gradually he had begun to understand that behind her grief about Michael lay a more complicated narrative. For nearly a decade brother and sister had scarcely seen each other. He disapproved of her husband; she disapproved of his feckless lifestyle, his living like a stable rat in his forties.

The room was growing dark when I said, "I had this patient yesterday. She made me feel I owe you an apology. You were so calm about losing your sight, I never said how sorry I was. I must have seemed like an unsympathetic oaf."

"Actually you seemed like a Hippocratic oaf." He gave the glint of a smile. "Your stoicism was easier to deal with than the hysteria of friends. You helped me understand that nothing—

shouting, praying, smashing every glass in the house—was going to change things. I take it she's attractive?"

"She has beautiful eyes, and she works in the cafeteria at the middle school."

I would have said then, and I still say now, that I was not in love with Bonnie, but some emotional gear had shifted. Otherwise I would not have copied her number into my phone, and I would not have dialed it the following morning. Fortunately I called her landline, where no missed call would register. Fortunately she did not answer.

14

I BLAME THE SNOW FOR what happened next. It fell and fell. Our cars were buried, the stables were buried, our lives were buried. The horses had to be kept indoors and exercised in the arena, which meant vastly more work for Viv and Claudia. Jack organized a roster of students to guide him back and forth to his office. My mother worked at home. Marcus and Trina had frequent snow days, and we scrambled to make child-care arrangements, trading with Anne and other parents. I know Viv talked to Claudia and that some kind of peace was brokered, but I did not dare to ask the particulars. Nor did I dare to ask about the dream that had stopped her from getting an abortion. It was long ago, I told myself. What mattered was our family, our shared life, that we had been happy for more than a decade.

I was still waiting for the right moment to suggest that Viv buy a horse of her own, but she was even more distant, a distance only emphasized by meals. While the rest of us ate winter food, pasta and baked potatoes, she ate fish and quinoa. When Marcus and Trina asked why, she said, "I need to be stronger to ride Mercury."

"But it's not kind to eat animals," said Trina. "We ought to eat less of them."

"Fewer," said Viv. "What did everyone learn today?"

Marcus said he'd learned that the Sami have nearly a thousand words to do with reindeer. Trina said she'd learned that her friend Rachel's mother was whitening her teeth.

"Is that good?" I asked.

"No, it's weird. Like there's a light on in her mouth."

I glanced at Viv, hoping to share the pleasure of our daughter's wit, but she was slicing her tuna.

DURING THOSE SNOWY WEEKS first Steve, then my mother, asked if something was wrong, leaving the "something" vague. Ask Viv, I told them. Steve, my docile friend, obediently changed the subject, but my mother was more persistent. "What do you mean, 'Ask Viv'?" she said.

I was at her house, helping to rearrange the ground-floor room. It was here that I had often joined my father in the late afternoons to drink tea and talk about whatever caught his attention: the best way to boil an egg, the skunks that attacked his garden, Basho's travels. On one of these afternoons, sitting by the window, he had described the Simurg, a bird in Persian mythology, large enough to lift an elephant. It was very old, and very benevolent. "I picture it having beautiful brown feathers," he said. "Like an owl. Sometimes, when I'm having a bad day, I wish the Simurg would carry me away."

Now I was more sorry than I could admit to see my mother reclaim the room. "Just what I say," I told her. "Viv's off on Planet Mercury. I'm the last to know what she's doing." I set the cardboard box containing a new bookcase on end and began to cut it open.

"She loves that horse, doesn't she?" My mother was kneeling on the other side of the room, surrounded by books. "It'll be exciting when they start competing."

"It'll be a nightmare when they start competing. She's already gone all the time. It's as if she forgets she even has children." The sound of the blade, pushing through the cardboard, seemed to both echo and amplify my anger.

"Would you say that if she were a man?" Still on her knees, my mother was watching me. "With your father, and your work, and the kids, Viv has come last for years. Then, finally, Edward died. Mercury is an amazing horse, an amazing opportunity. Marcus and Trina won't feel neglected if you help them understand that."

" 'Finally'?"

"Finally," she repeated. "Did you ever wonder what it would be like if your life had revolved around taking care of Viv's father?"

"But Dad—" I started to say. But Dad was part of me. But Dad's illness brought me back to Boston. "No," I said. "I didn't."

"Nor did I," she confessed, "until I started seeing Larry." While they were in Philadelphia, his wife had fallen and broken her hip. He was convinced it wouldn't have happened if he had been nearby. "We won't be leaving town again any time soon."

"I'm sorry," I said. "I know you'd love to travel."

"And I will." She smiled. "Just not with Larry, not now. It's frustrating, but I admire his loyalty to Jean." She stood up and came over to inspect the bookcase. "I hope you and Viv can work things out so you both get a part of what you want."

"I hope so too," I said. But what would a part be? A fetlock for her? A scalpel for me?

THE DAY AFTER THE conversation with my mother, as we yet again dug out our cars, I asked Viv if she was glad Edward was dead.

"Not glad," she said, angling her shovel into a drift. "But these last few years, everything was hard. And it was all for nothing. He wasn't going to get well. He wasn't happy. I hated to see him struggling day after day." Her blue eyes regarded me across the snow. "Didn't you feel that way, at least sometimes?"

"I don't think so." But even as I spoke, I remembered standing in his room, on another snowy day, holding a pillow while he slept, wondering if I had the courage to use it, knowing I didn't. I had never spoken of that moment, tried never to think of it, but standing knee deep in snow, I silently acknowledged that I had thought of killing my father.

"You've had a lot to put up with," I said, "being married to me."

I know the date because in my appointment book there is a note: "Call Bonnie D. re op." Later that same morning, when I went to the mall to get supplies for Nabokov, I sat in my car outside the pet shop and dialed her number. She answered so swiftly she must have been holding the phone.

"I just want to make sure you're all set for tomorrow," I said. Her operation had been postponed because of a cold.

"Thanks for calling, Dr. Stevenson. I'm okay. Greg's taken the day off work. He won't even let me put on my own shoes."

The snow was falling in tidy flakes that melted the instant they touched the windshield. I turned off the engine to hear her voice more clearly. "And what about your daughters? Are they old enough to help?"

"Alice waits on me hand and foot, and she keeps Suzie in line. What's that noise?"

"A van reversing. I'm at the mall, picking up supplies for the parrot."

Bonnie did not comment on the oddity of this. "Oh, the

parrot," she exclaimed. "He was so cute, spouting poetry. I was telling Greg we ought to get a bird. It would be someone for me to talk to when I'm here alone all day."

The windows were misting up, cutting me off from the quotidian world. Idly I drew a bird on the glass—the Simurg—and watched its wings blur. Bonnie was still talking. She'd never had a pet, but when she was a kid, her neighbors had a Pekingese. "Rollo had these huge brown eyes, and his owners were at work all day. I used to sneak into their yard to play with him. Somehow they found out. They came and shouted at my parents. Rollo was worth thousands of dollars. If I didn't stay away, they'd call the police. I never got to play with him again."

Her own eyes, I realized, had a little of that exophthalmic quality so marked in those of Pekingeses. "Well," I said, "I just wanted to make sure you're all right. Don't eat or drink anything after midnight."

"Thank you, Dr. Stevenson. I appreciate your calling, especially after I stomped out of your office. I know you were doing your best."

As I bought Nabokov's bird food, I thought how there was no art to detect inappropriate behavior. I always called patients before surgery—by some standards, in not calling Bonnie, I would have been remiss—and yet our conversation had crossed a line. When I got back to the office, Nabokov and Merrie greeted me warmly, and my patients for the rest of the afternoon were punctual and grateful. Later, when I drove to the stables to collect Marcus and Trina, the sky in the west was still light. A van was parked in my usual spot by the trailers. As I maneuvered between two cars, a light went on in the car in front. Two heads came together. Then a door opened, and Charlie loped towards the barn.

15

PERHAPS ONLY THOSE WHO are, or were, married will understand how Viv and I saw each other every day, slept together every night, and yet seldom found time to talk. At last on a Saturday, when both the children had play dates, we decided to tackle the long-postponed task of painting the basement. As I stirred the sky-blue paint and Viv lined the doors and windows with masking tape, I said I'd been thinking about returning to surgery.

"Why not?" She unfurled more tape. "You used to enjoy it."

She spoke as if we were discussing returning my library books. Later, when she claimed I had been oblivious for months, I would say the same about her. As I started rolling paint onto the walls, I explained I would have to study to requalify. For a while I would earn less.

"How much less?"

At once she registered her misstep. Since our conversation about the alarm system, money had been a dangerous topic. Switching to the ultrareasonable voice she used to urge the children to tidy their rooms, she said we should discuss the pros and cons. Maybe when Marcus was settled in middle school? She kept talking, but the phrase "pros and cons" had carried me back to my conversation with Claudia in the tack room. Had the dream baby looked anything like our son? Now, writing this, I wonder what would have happened if I had asked Viv that question—if one of us had adjusted our orbit to cross paths with the other. But when she paused, I said I'd also been thinking she should buy a horse of her own.

"Buy a horse?" She was painting around the door, her hand deft and steady. "Why would I do that? Claudia and I were just saying we've finally got the right ratio of horses to students to boarders. We're not going to replace Nimble."

"I meant a horse just for you, to train for competitions."

"I have Mercury." She hurled the sentence across the room.

"But you don't own him," I said. "You don't have a legal arrangement with Hilary." What I wanted to say was that he was too good for her, that he made her want too much.

"Don, I used to be in business. We have an understanding. She pays his board, the veterinarian's fees. I take care of him and pay the expenses of competing. She doesn't want to sell him but if she did, she would sell him to me."

Years ago, when Marcus was still a baby, someone had asked Viv if we were married. No, she said, we have an understanding. As she spoke, she smiled at me, and I heard the word with new meaning; we were standing on the same ground. "And is this understanding written down?" I asked now. Paint oozed beneath the roller. "Witnessed?"

I can name only some of the muscles involved in the hard stare she gave me. "I thought you Scots believed a woman's word is her bond."

For several minutes the radio filled the silence until, by way of a peace offering, Viv brought up Burns Night. Every year we joined with my parents to celebrate the Scottish poet; my father, as long as he was able, had acted as master of ceremonies.

Now Viv reported that my mother was making the vegetarian haggis. I said Steve would offer the "Address to the Lassies." We finished painting the basement, and the following evening I found myself presiding over a table full of friends and neighbors. When we joined hands to sing Burns's most famous song, "Auld Lang Syne," I felt we were honoring both my father and the poet.

Later I would learn that the next day Viv drove to New Hampshire and spent six hundred dollars on a handgun, ammunition, and a bribe to the man who made the purchase.

16

By early February Nabokov was uncrowned king of the office. Merrie rationed his treats, her daughters provided him with fresh tree branches, and Jo had taught him to say, "Better? Or worse?" His feathers were growing in, smooth and thick, and in the morning he often urged me to hurry. One day, when I was collecting the children from the stables, he started calling from the front seat: "Hurry up. Hurry up."

"He sounds like us now," Trina said.

At once I realized she was right. Only when he quoted poetry or recited the railway timetable did Nabokov still sound like my father. In my dismay I failed to ask the children if they had everything. After supper Marcus discovered he'd left a crucial schoolbook on the office table.

"You'll just have to explain to your teacher," I said.

"But there's a test tomorrow. Ms. Fisher hates to give makeup tests. Please can we get it?"

Viv and Trina were watching a show about a game reserve. Lions were roaring. "I want to see this," Viv said. "Can you go, Don? I'll explain the alarm."

"I'm paying the bills. Marcus needs to take responsibility when he forgets things."

"He does, but all the shuttling around is hard on the

kids." She smiled up at me. "Everyone gets to make a few mistakes."

All the shuttling around is because of you, I thought, but I wrote down the instructions for the alarm and told Marcus to start studying while I fetched his book.

The night was cold and starless. Outside town I passed only a few other cars, and when I turned up the road to Windy Hill, my headlights shone on the empty paddocks. As I walked towards the barn, I was grateful for the brightness of the new security lights I had unwittingly paid for. I pressed the buttons of the alarm once, then again. Nothing seemed to happen, but the door opened silently. Inside I heard a faint rustling. Only a mouse, I hoped. I hurried along the dimly lit corridor and retrieved Marcus's book from the office. Back at the door, I reset the alarm. I was turning towards my car when I noticed the windows of the arena glowing. Someone had forgotten to turn out the lights.

The arena, I know from the Windy Hill website, is seventy-five feet by two hundred. As I stepped through the side door, I saw an almost white horse cantering at the far end, a dark figure on his back. Charlie was riding Mercury. In the middle of the arena stood a young man who seemed to be alternately checking his phone and taking pictures. Even at this distance I could smell his cigarette. Now I understood why the alarm had behaved oddly; it was already off. Neither of them noticed me. For several minutes I remained standing in the doorway, spellbound by the drama of the solitary horse and rider. As Mercury approached, cantering up the nearest wall, I could see his breath streaming in the cold air. Charlie, beneath her helmet, was radiant.

By the time they approached for the second time, I had come to my senses. I stepped forward, arms raised. "Charlie," I called. "Stop. Stop."

Both horse and rider startled. Then Charlie was lying on the ground, and Mercury was again heading to the far end of the arena. I bent over Charlie, asking if she was all right.

She was already scrambling to her feet. "Dr. Stevenson— Donald—you scared the shit out of me. Don't you know not to shout at a horse?"

"What are you doing here, riding Mercury? How did you get in?"

The young man was running towards us, shouting, "Are you okay? Who the fuck is this?"

"Viv loaned me the keys last month when she had to leave early. Ben and I were driving by—and I so wanted to see Mercury."

"Who the fuck is this?" Ben repeated. Despite his swearing, he was not a threatening figure. He was wearing far too few clothes for the cold night—a hoodie, tight jeans, and sneakers— and his face, even scowling, had a good-natured look.

"This is Viv's husband." As she spoke, Mercury cantered by, showing no signs of slowing. If anything, he was going faster, stretching into a full gallop, stirrups flying. We all three turned to watch him.

"Mercury," called Ben. "How are we going to catch him?"

"Food." Charlie stepped out of the side door and returned with an armful of hay, which she dropped in Mercury's path. He slowed to a trot. A moment later he was greedily nudging the hay. Charlie captured his bridle, and order was restored.

Only then did she turn to me. "Please, please, please," she said, "don't tell Viv. I promise we won't ever do it again."

Until she asked, it had not occurred to me that I had a choice. I imagined Viv seizing the phone, firing Charlie. But of course

I must tell her. Not to do so would be a terrible betrayal. I became aware that my face and hands were freezing.

She sensed my hesitation. "Riding is my favorite thing in the whole world," she said. "I know it was wrong to come here like this, but I was desperate to see Mercury." Her eyes were brimming.

I remembered Bonnie's story about losing her beloved Pekingese—"I never got to play with him again." What would my silence cost me? Nothing, other than the pain of lying to Viv. She had often said Charlie was their best worker.

"Put him back in his stall," I said. "Bring the keys to my office tomorrow."

"And you won't tell Viv?"

Her eyes were very wide and her lips very red, but that was not what made me decide, between one moment and the next, to keep her secret. At the time I thought it was because of Bonnie. Now I suspect that I also wanted to punish Viv, for her almost abortion, her obsession with Mercury, her betrayal of Claudia, her falling asleep, night after night, without turning to me.

"I won't," I said, "but you must never do this again. If Mercury got hurt, there'd be hell to pay."

She promised fervently—cross my heart and hope to die—and led him towards the door. Ben followed. I heard the ring of hooves on the icy snow. I was turning to leave when something lying in the middle of the arena caught my eye: a black scarf. I hung it on a railing, like any other piece of lost property, and turned out the lights.

At home the safari show had ended. Trina reported that the baby hippopotamus had learned to swim.

"Here," I said to Viv, handing her the keys. "Did its mother teach it?"

"Not really. She just led it into the water. The father was off somewhere."

"Fetching missing schoolbooks," I said.

And so in a couple of sentences, in less than a minute, I did to Viv what she had done to Claudia; I let the opportunity to tell the truth pass. I lied. I was helping Trina choose her pajamas when it came to me that the glove of the first break-in was not some sinister message, but the result of Ben's inability to hang on to even his few items of clothing.

The next day when I returned from my lunchtime walk, an envelope lay on my desk with the words "Thank you!" written in black marker. I put it at the back of my desk drawer and noted the code for the alarm in my appointment book. Like those householders who hung a picture of Mercury on their doors, I was committing a small crime, I told myself, to prevent a large one.

17

As the anniversary of my father's death approached, each day was both itself and the day it had been a year ago. I woke with the same feeling of terror that he might have died in the night, carried the same burden of dread through my appointments and duties. If only I was stronger, or cleverer, or richer, or more eloquent, if only I was a better person, I could save him. The actual anniversary was an abyss. I could not imagine how I would get from the day before to the day after. Then my mother phoned and suggested we go to Gloucester to mark the occasion.

"I thought about Walden," she said, "but Edward loved the beach, and we'll be closer to Scotland."

"It's a Tuesday," I said, as if this were an insuperable objection.

"I already told my assistant I won't be in. Can't Leah take over your appointments?" She had it all planned. The five of us would drive to Gloucester, remember my father on the beach, and have lunch in a local restaurant. I put down the phone, my dread deeper than ever. Later that day in the bathroom mirror, I noticed how the lines on my forehead had begun to mimic my father's.

My mother must have phoned Viv separately. That evening

at supper she announced she'd arranged for the children to have the day off from school. "What shall we do?" she said. "We could bring some of Edward's favorite poems to read? Or put a message in a bottle and throw it out to sea? Or tell stories about him?"

Trina said she would draw a picture of Edward to go in the bottle. Marcus said he'd write something and attach it to a kite. He had heard about some country—Japan? Korea?—where people used kites to send messages to the dead.

I spent several evenings going through family albums, searching for a photograph to put in the bottle. My father's illness, which in life I had often managed to ignore, was in pictures clearly visible. He was always holding on to something—a tree, a wall—or someone—my mother, me. There were even several photos of him at Windy Hill, holding on to a horse. I chose one of him walking in the Adirondacks and slipped it into a bottle along with one of Nabokov's tail feathers.

Tuesday was overcast, miraculously still and a little above freezing. My mother arrived at our house soon after ten. Viv had offered to drive, but as we approached her car, she suddenly exclaimed: she'd forgotten to get gas. Could we take mine? Later I realized she had already begun to keep the gun in the trunk of her car.

We were nearing Gloucester when Trina asked if Edward would be able to hear us.

"I don't think so," said my mother, "but no one knows for sure. We're honoring his memory."

"Like Greyfriars Bobby?" Marcus said.

My father had told the children the story of the little dog who, for years, went every day to sit by his master's grave. Viv and I had visited the churchyard when we were in Edinburgh.

Even on the beach there was almost no wind. The sea was a dark green and the sky was like a painting, the gray streaked with yellows and pinks and oranges. It was a perfect day except for Marcus and his kite. We'll take a walk, Viv promised, on the next windy day. We lined up, my mother and I, the children, and then Viv, looking across the ocean to Scotland.

"We're here," my mother said, "to remember Edward John Stevenson, our beloved Edward, who died a year ago today." She described how they'd met at university in Edinburgh. How they'd walked around the city, talking about politics. At one point he'd thought of trying to run for Parliament. Then he got a job working for British Rail and fell in love with trains. Life wasn't fair, he used to say, but everyone deserved a good train service. She read a poem he had known by heart: "The Night Train."

Next Trina read a list of the things she liked about Edward: that he did double knots in his shoelaces, that he called jimmies hundreds and thousands, that he gave her a guinea pig for her fourth birthday, that he talked to Nabokov and tried to answer her knock-knock jokes. Marcus explained about his kite and how it had a private message for Edward. He liked that Edward could imitate all kinds of machines and always came to watch him swim.

Viv described her first meeting with Edward—he had shown her his asparagus beds—and how much he'd enjoyed visiting the stables. While the waves came and went, she read several haiku, some by Basho, some by my father.

"Dad," said Trina. She tugged my sleeve, and I understood it was my turn to speak.

"Edward—"

I cleared my throat and tried again. "Dad, I don't know what to say. I remember coming home from school. It was June and you'd been cutting the lawn and everything smelled of grass. Mum was away, and we had supper in the garden. You said we could stay up as long as the swallows were flying. You taught me to be kind and truthful and not to judge other people. You're the person I feel standing behind me—"

I stared at the waves and blinked and stared. Then I raised the book I had brought and read Shakespeare's sonnet: "From you I have been absent in the spring." Line by line, I thought, I can't continue. Line by line, I did. Line by line, my father drew closer until, by the final couplet, I sensed him standing beside us on the wet sand.

> *Yet seem'd it winter still, and, you away,*
> *As with your shadow I with these did play.*

My mother had brought a bunch of white roses. She gave each of us some flowers to throw into the waves. I waded out as far as I could in my rubber boots and threw the bottle containing the photograph, the feather, and the message towards Scotland.

18

I KNOW NOW THAT DURING those snowy weeks, when Viv claimed to be so busy at the stables, she was also visiting a shooting range. She used her weekly trips to the riding school in New Hampshire to cover her tracks and to justify the sudden increase in take-out meals, which delighted the children. At the range she found herself in the company of people who regarded a gun as no different from a screwdriver. Live free or die. Scotland was united with England in 1603 and, despite the efforts of Bonnie Prince Charlie (and others), has remained part of that more populous, more prosperous country for four centuries. Perhaps that is why honesty and integrity have always mattered more to me than freedom. Of course there are degrees, but who, after all, is ever free? As a son, a brother, a doctor, a father, a husband, an employee, and an employer, my life has been governed by rules, and mostly for the better. I am glad that someone paves the roads, makes me send my children to school, regulates my business, checks the ingredients in my food, stops my neighbor from burning down my house, sends the fire brigade when they do.

But I am getting ahead of myself. A few days after our visit to Gloucester, Jack phoned to ask if Marcus had swimming practice that afternoon. "I've got cabin fever," he said. "Can I come and watch?" I was about to refuse—my day was already complicated—but something in his voice stopped me. Leah took over my last appointment. I whisked Nabokov home, collected the children, and was at Jack's apartment a few minutes early. While he got ready, Marcus and Trina played with his computer, talking nonsense into the microphone and giggling when it appeared on the screen.

"There's a picture of Mercury," Trina said.

She was pointing to a photograph, one I hadn't seen before, on the wall over Jack's desk. A white horse stood in a field; a man was holding its bridle. "Actually," Jack said, "that's his mother, Moonshine, with Michael." Hilary had hung it there, not wanting to see it every day.

So this, I thought, stepping closer, was the architect of all my troubles: a slight man of medium height, wearing a white shirt and jeans. Save for the intensity with which he gazed at the horse, he looked entirely unremarkable.

We dropped Trina off for her violin lesson and drove to the pool. While Marcus headed to the changing rooms, I led the way to the bank of seats, where half a dozen parents were already checking their phones. When we were seated in the front row, Jack said, "Swimming pools are so intense. Shut your eyes."

I did. Breathing in the warm, muggy chlorinated air, listening to the splashing and the echoing voices, I felt calmer than in days. "Tell me what they're doing," Jack said. I opened my eyes and described Marcus, his teammates, and their coach, a woman with hair even shorter than Viv's and the endearing habit of clapping her hands and exclaiming, "Good work." Then I asked if he and Hilary were still going swimming. He had told me they'd started going to the Y together.

"We're not doing anything," he said. "Hil phoned saying she

wasn't feeling well and then left a message saying she had the flu. Since then I've heard nothing for three days and seven hours."

"So call her."

"I have." He slammed his hand down on the bench. "I called asking how she was feeling. I called asking if there was anything I could do. I called asking if I should get tickets for a concert. In the old days I'd have gone over to her house. When my girl-friend Marie-Claire dumped me, I tore a sink out of the wall."

I said that flu was very debilitating. "Viv was completely flat-tened at New Year. I could take you to her house."

"So could a taxi. If she doesn't want to see me, there's no point. My charging around never did really work. Now I'd just be some blind guy, tripping over chairs."

His words were so bitter, his expression so bleak, that I turned back to the pool and said they were practicing flip turns. Marcus's was a bit splashy. Jack said he used to do great turns.

"You still could," I said, "if someone counted down the dis-tance. Did the two of you have a row?"

"The good old British row. Not that I'm aware of. The last time I saw her, we went to the movies and ate Mexican food. I don't think I got salsa on my face. But a dozen things could have happened to make her realize having a blind lover is crazy. That's the trouble with silence. It can mean so many things. An atom bomb might be about to fall. A dog might be taking a crap."

Beside him I shifted uneasily. "Sorry," he said. "Rampant self-pity is a drag. People have ditched me before, but I always had anger to fall back on."

"So why not get angry now?" From the pool came the sound of clapping, followed by "Good work."

Jack spread his hands. "It was only ever a way to hide from the pain. Now I can't do that shit anymore. I just have to sit with the pain, and let me tell you, it's torture to feel so fucking helpless."

I remembered Bonnie in my office, swearing. As if I'd spoken aloud, Jack said, "How's the school dinner lady?" He might have given up on anger, but he had not lost his edge. I said her surgeon had reported that, as I'd suspected, she had had several operations as a child. There was significant scarring, which might compromise the success of her recent operation.

"'Compromise,'" Jack mimicked. "Is that another word for blindness? Do you plan to tell her?"

I pictured Bonnie, like one of Linnaeus's swallows, blindfolded, wintering beneath the ice. "Should I?" I said.

He asked if there was anything she could do that would make a difference. I said no. Her only hope, like his, lay in research.

"Then I'd say leave her in ignorance. Does she know you have the hots for her?"

"I'm her doctor," I said stiffly. "We're both married."

"And I'm a jerk." He began to describe his latest research. He'd discovered this remarkable and obvious thing: people who are blind from birth have no images in their dreams. "They just have sounds and smells," he said. "And touch. Whereas people like me keep dreaming in images for a long time. And another interesting fact: the blind dream about transportation four times more often than the sighted."

Before I could ask if this was true of him, his phone buzzed. His voice rose hopefully as he excused himself, and sank into ordinary politeness: only a student.

On our way home, after we had dropped him off, Trina said, "Jack's sad."

"Yes, he is," I said. Marcus was in the backseat, engrossed in his phone.

"Why?" She eyed me gravely.

"It's hard being blind, and sometimes it's harder than others."

She was silent for a few seconds. Then she announced, "He's like Nabokov. He's lonely."

During the busyness of homework and supper, I kept thinking about her simple insight: Jack was lonely. Doubly so, in his blindness and his estrangement from Hilary. When the children were in bed, I asked Viv if she'd spoken to Hilary. She said they hadn't talked in nearly a week.

"Maybe you should go by her house," I said. "She told Jack she wasn't feeling well."

Viv said she would go tomorrow, and I went to bed, thinking I had done my best to help my friend.

DAY BY DAY I had been teaching myself to usher Bonnie out of my brain whenever she appeared there. Now Jack's questions had undone my lessons. Once again, on the pretext of doctorly interest, I dialed her number. Once again she answered promptly.

"Dr. Stevenson!" She had been about to ring my office. The bandages had been removed and the shadow was gone, but her surgeon said it would be six months before they knew how much vision she would recover. Was there anything to be done about her glasses? she asked. I said we had an opening at three that day. If she took a taxi to the office, I could give her a lift home on my way to pick up Marcus and Trina.

Which was worse, I wonder now: my posing as a Good Samaritan, or my using my children to do so? My offer did not harm them, it did not harm Bonnie, but something I couldn't name was harmed. At the time I gave these subtleties no thought. I went to tell Merrie about the appointment and, wanting to distract her from the unusual fact of my dealing directly with a patient, asked about her friend, the teacher.

"Oh, it's been a nightmare," she said. The girl had contradicted herself several times but still clung to her story. "I don't know if Ginny will ever recover."

I echoed her outrage. All that morning I was especially diligent, and there as my reward, when I came into the waiting room at ten minutes past three, was Bonnie. She was standing beside Nabokov's cage, talking to Merrie.

"What's Nab telling you now?" I said.

Merrie smiled. "He's urging us to lie still and think of England, which, if you don't have a dirty mind, is pretty good advice."

"I'm not sure I've ever thought of England," said Bonnie.

She was still wearing her ugly tortoiseshell glasses, but her hair was pulled back in a way that framed her face; her slender gold earrings moved as she spoke. Once she was sitting in the chair with the lights off, she announced that there was something she wanted to ask me. The machine was between us, hiding her expression; only her hands, fluttering above the armrests, were visible. Just for an instant I imagined her saying, Dr. Stevenson, you're all I've ever wanted.

"This is stupid," she said. "Greg says it's stupid, but I keep worrying about Alice and Suzie. What if they've inherited my problem? Alice is crazy about basketball. I worry all the jumping up and down will ruin her eyes."

My ventricles resumed their normal activity. I said that wasn't stupid. I didn't know the answer, but I would consult a colleague. In the meantime she should have her daughters' eyes checked, just to be safe. "Put your chin here," I said.

By the time we emerged, Merrie had Nabokov ready to

travel. I went to warm up the car and came back to get him and Bonnie. As I pulled out of the parking lot, I felt a rush of exhilaration. At this busy time of day the journey to her house might take as long as twenty minutes. In the confines of the car I could smell some fragrance: her shampoo, or hand cream. From the backseat, Nabokov began to recite a railway timetable.

I told Bonnie that my father had worked for the MBTA, and she said she'd wanted to drive a train when she was little. "I always wave to women drivers on the subway. Did you get to drive one as a kid?"

"No. My best friend and I wanted to be pilots. Then I had a brilliant biology teacher." We were behind a bus; I made no effort to pass.

"Lucky you," said Bonnie. "I was planning to go to college, but my dad died and there was no money."

"Your girls are growing up," I said. "You can still go."

"I hope so—I want to be a good example for them—but sometimes things happen."

Before I could ask what things, she told me to turn left and pointed out the supermarket where Greg worked. His cooking had improved while she'd been out of action. Soon she was directing me to stop in front of a small green house. A neatly shoveled path led to the front door.

"Doctor—," she began.

"Please call me Donald."

"Donald, this has been an ordeal, but you've made things easier. When I'm up to speed, I'll bake you and Merrie my famous chocolate cake."

I was saying there was no need when she leaned over and kissed my cheek.

. . .

I HAD SEEN BONNIE only three times, spoken to her on the phone only twice, and yet for several hours she had displaced any thought of my old friend, alone in his private darkness. But Viv was already acting on her promise. After another failed phone call, she drove to Hilary's house and found the sidewalk piled with snow. She knocked, she rang the doorbell, she shouted and got no answer. She decided to walk around the house, banging on the windows and calling Hilary's name. "The snow was so deep," she told me later. "It was like swimming." She was at the back of the house when she heard a faint answering cry.

Hilary had been in bed for almost a week, with only Diane, who was at school all day, to take care of her. Viv set to work. She made soup and tea; she changed the sheets; she did laundry, loaded the dishwasher, emptied the trash and the cat's litter box, went through the fridge, ordered groceries. From Hilary's house she drove directly to the stables, and from the stables to her book club. Not until she was getting ready for bed did she tell me what had transpired. The next morning at the office a patient was waiting. It was almost 11:00 a.m., thirty-six hours after our conversation at the pool, when I at last phoned Jack with what I hoped was good news.

He didn't answer, and it was only later that I heard how, with the help of his regular driver, Carlos, he had already embarked on his odyssey. He stopped at a florist's, a liquor store, a jeweler's, and finally at Hilary's, where Carlos led him to the back door and wished him luck. If Jack didn't reappear in ten minutes, he would assume the best and drive away.

"After you took me to the pool," Jack told me, "I thought and thought and what it came down to was, I could give up on Hilary, or I could go for broke. Both were terrifying. Then in the middle of the night I woke up and I heard a voice saying, 'Ask her to marry you, you numbskull.' I couldn't walk away from the best person I'd met in years without even trying."

He knocked. Hilary, wearing her clean nightgown, opened the door. He drew a discreet veil over what happened next. Did he ask her immediately? Did they go to bed first? Did she say you're all I've ever wanted? Whatever the route, by the time Diane came home from school, they were standing on the same ground.

19

As a schoolboy in Edinburgh I learned the rhyme, "For want of a nail the shoe was lost, for want of a shoe . . ." The logic of the poem, the idea that a small thing I did in our house, on our street, might make a large difference in some distant place, fascinated me. Even now I cannot list all the factors that contributed to the events of that night in early March when, as swiftly as if someone had severed my optic nerve, my life changed. The snow, Viv, Mercury, Charlie, Jack, Hilary, my well-meaning mother, me—we all played our parts. And there were others—Claudia, her boyfriend, her great-aunt—of whose role I learned only later.

My mother, as our discussion over her new bookcase made clear, was worried about my marriage. In an effort to give Viv and me what she thought we needed—time alone together—she invited Trina and Marcus to go bowling on Saturday. They would stay the night, and on Sunday she and Larry would take them to the Museum of Science in Boston. I did not want to spend another evening listening to Viv talk about Mercury, but I dutifully made a reservation at a nice restaurant. Perhaps, later, she would turn to me. I had just got home from taking the children to my mother's when Viv phoned. Samson had colic: she was going to walk him for another hour and see how he progressed.

"Why don't you use the reservation with Jack," she urged. "I don't know when I'll be home."

My first impulse, if only I had acted upon it, was to get some take-out barbeque, open a bottle of beer, and watch bad television with Nabokov, but that seemed too pathetic. I rang Jack.

"Let me ask Hil," he said. "Diane's with her dad."

I had forgotten that Jack now came with Hilary. Our private conversations of the last few years were going to be hard to come by. On the drive to Il Giardino I lectured myself about trying harder with her. Perhaps she had made the same resolution. From the moment she kissed my cheek and thanked me for suggesting this, I could tell we were in for a jolly evening.

We ordered several appetizers, and Jack posed as the blind food critic with the amazing taste buds. "This baby octopus comes from the cold waters of Labrador. Note how it embraces the marinade. Though actually," he added, "research shows that we blind have no better sense of taste or smell than you sighted. We just pay more attention."

"So what do you think the shrimp is spiced with?" Hilary asked.

"Coriander. Perhaps a touch of fennel?"

"Donald and I need to close our eyes too."

We did and made silly guesses. Jack joked about the challenge of fancy restaurants: finding your portion on the plate. They described the film they had watched the night before. Hilary said that if Jack knew the setup, he could follow most of what was happening. In fact he often figured out the plot before she did; he wasn't distracted by trivial details like clothes and hair.

We were on our second bottle of wine when a text came from Viv: *Samson OK Going to bed xo V.* I passed on the news and we raised our glasses to Samson. "The ultimate advertisement for the importance of hair," Hilary joked.

Not until we were having dessert did she bring up Mercury. One afternoon while she was sick, she had dreamed about him. "You know how some dreams are so real," she said. "They seem like they've just happened? Or are just about to? I was back in Ontario with Michael. Mercury had escaped, and we were searching for him along the railway line that led into town."

Slowly, as if she were again walking along the tracks, she described the scene. "Michael was very calm. He had a stick he was clicking against the rails; I suppose that was Jack's cane? But I kept feeling that Mercury was in danger, that he needed our help. Then I heard the rumbling of a train, and suddenly we were both running, stumbling over the sleepers, trying to reach him. I woke up feeling wretched. I haven't been to see him in weeks."

I said Viv was taking good care of him.

"I'm sure she is, but I wish we could go there now. Michael believed that at night we can hear what animals are thinking, and vice versa."

"We can," I said. "We can go there now. I have a key."

Somehow, as we drank the last of the wine, the three of us agreed that this was the best possible plan. We finished our crème brûlée and chocolate bread pudding. I insisted on paying the bill. A month later my credit card statement showed we had spent $270. I drove us to my office, and while Hilary and Jack waited, I collected the keys from the back of the drawer and checked the code in my appointment book.

When I returned to the car, Hilary had put on one of the CDs Fran had sent me for Christmas. She and Jack were in the back, sitting as close as the seat belts permitted. "This is so nice of you, Donald," she said.

"I feel as if I'm going on a mission with my friends," Jack said. "When I was a kid, almost all our bad behavior started with a car at night."

"My bad behavior occurred on foot," said Hilary. "We just passed Diane's school."

Outside of town the sky was filled with high white clouds. I said that they made me think of Russia.

"Or Ontario," Hilary said. "Somewhere with large skies and low temperatures. We're on the main road to the stables. Michael was always high. That was part of what went wrong in Kentucky. I used to lend him money, 'lend' in quotes, until I realized he was spending it on speed."

"Michael took drugs?" I too, I realized, had put Mercury's owner on a pedestal.

"I think it's quite common in the horse world," said Jack. "Certainly among jockeys."

I was still grappling with this revelation as we turned off the main road. "We're passing the paddocks," Hilary said. "No horses and lots of snow."

Out of habit I parked in my usual place behind the trailers. Another lost nail. If I had parked outside the barn, my car in plain view, there would be no need to write this story. As we approached the door, the security lights came on. I remembered the code; the key worked; we were inside. I turned on the lights, and the two rows of stalls stretched out before us, the main one by the bank of lockers, and the other, farther from the door, with the stalls on either side. I led the way towards the latter, where I had found Mercury at New Year's. Jack commented on the smell, and Hilary said, "In five minutes we won't notice it."

Mercury was in a different stall, near the middle of the row. He was standing at the back, wearing two coats, one slung over the other.

"Do you think he's asleep?" whispered Hilary.

Neither Jack nor I answered.

"Mercury," she said, and then again, louder, "Mercury."

At the sound of his name he looked up, his dark eyes gleaming. Two ropes, a red and a black one, were looped around the door and the bars of the stall. Hilary hung them on the saddle post and slid open the door. She stepped inside. Jack put his hand on my arm. We followed, and I slid the door closed. Hilary reached out to stroke Mercury's neck.

"Are you awake? Good boy. Were you dreaming of nice pastures and sunny days? We're here to see you. Jack and I need your blessing."

Mercury shifted from hoof to hoof. She continued to talk, and I led Jack over to stand beside her. We were all slightly drunk, Hilary and Jack perhaps more than slightly, yet the occasion had a solemn feeling. None of us mentioned Michael, but it was clear that Hilary was trying to lay her regrets about him to rest. Mercury gave a half snort, half sigh. Hilary took Jack's hand and placed it on the horse's neck.

"Talk to him," she said.

"Mercury," said Jack, "you fucking amazing horse, you emperor of quadrupeds, you king of equines. You represent what's noblest in us. No, that's not right. You embody what's noblest in us. If you're thinking tonight, think noble thoughts. If you're dreaming, dream noble dreams."

Mercury snorted again, more vigorously, and Jack stepped back. "I've asked Hilary for her hand in marriage," he went on, raising his own hand. "I hope you give permission. We'll get married in a field so you can—"

There was a loud, precise, frightening noise.

Mercury reared in a mad scramble of hooves.

Hilary screamed.

Jack stumbled against the wall of the stall and fell to the ground.

In the confusion neither Hilary nor I stopped to think about the dangers that lay outside the stall. Our only thought was to get away from Mercury, to get Jack away. Somehow we dragged him into the corridor. On all sides the other horses were whinnying, kicking, screaming. Viv had told me that horses scream in anger, or pain; now I heard the sound for the first time.

As soon as the stall door was closed, I dropped to my knees. I knew little about gunshot wounds, but I had to make sure Jack didn't bleed to death. "Where are you hurt?" I said. "Can you tell me?"

"My arm," he whispered. "Or my shoulder."

Beside me Hilary, also on her knees, was crying. "What happened? My God, did someone shoot us? We've got to get him to the hospital."

"I need to make sure he's not bleeding."

Mercifully Jack fainted as I tried to get his arm out of his jacket. In the dim light I saw that the wound was bleeding steadily but not furiously. I stood up with the thought that I could use a wheelbarrow to get him to the car. And then, at the end of the row of stalls, in the gloom, something moved. Viv was standing by the last stall, holding a black object in both hands. In less than a heartbeat, less than a saccade, I understood that Viv, the woman I loved, my wife of almost a decade, was holding a gun, and that she was pointing it in my direction.

Our eyes met for a brief, appalling moment. Then she lowered the gun and stepped back into the shadows.

Hilary noticed nothing; all her attention was on Jack. With her help, I hoisted him into a wheelbarrow. We hurried along the corridor, she steadying him, me pushing, Jack groaning. At the door I ran to get the car. Between us we lifted him into the backseat. Then we were spinning away over the snow. The CD Hilary had put on was still playing. *"Give me bread and give me honey. Fill my wallet and fill my boot."* I did not think to turn it off. Jack kept groaning.

"You'll feel better soon," Hilary said. "We'll be at the hospital soon. I love you."

I drove as fast as I could, using the horn ruthlessly when we reached traffic. The alcohol I'd consumed made everything vivid and ferocious. I could have lifted a car off a baby, climbed a burning building. All three of our lives, not to mention those of my wife and children, were at stake.

PART TWO

VIV

1

I HAVE ONLY ONE CHANCE to plead my case, and only one person to plead it to.

When I was eleven, I presented my mother with a list of reasons why I absolutely had to have riding lessons. I remember four of them:

> *I love horses.*
> *I want to win rosettes.*
> *I was a horse in my last life.*
> *My best friend rides.*

Mom countered with her own list: the cost, the inconvenience of chauffeuring me to the stables, the importance of school. I said I'd contribute my dog-walking money, and Claudia's mother could drive me. I promised to study hard. Finally she agreed to three months of lessons. She hoped I'd forget when I went to camp, but that summer every girl in my cabin was in love with Misty of Chincoteague. Back home, I didn't risk asking for permission again. I took my riding clothes to school and got a lift to the stables with Claudia. Soon the teacher said I was the best rider in our group, and I believed her. It was as if I had a sixth sense about what the horse wanted, how to make it do what I wanted.

By the time I entered high school I mostly rode Nutmeg, a chestnut gelding with four neat white socks. The first day I led him in from the paddock, a cat spooked him. I hung on to his halter and broke my little finger. I didn't tell my mother—she might have stopped me riding—and by the time she noticed, the bone had set crooked. The accident gave me a special bond with Nutmeg. We started to enter shows. Soon the frame of my bedroom mirror was filled with rosettes—some firsts, lots of seconds and thirds. I wanted to go to bigger competitions, farther away, but this time my mother stood firm.

The week after I got into Yale, my parents announced, almost as if they too had filled out applications and written personal essays, that they were getting a divorce. My father was joining a dental practice in San Diego. I was shocked, but Claudia wasn't. "Your parents always looked like they were going different places," she said. Hers had been divorced since we were in middle school, and she moved back and forth between their households like an airline pilot, a suitcase permanently packed.

My parents kept saying the divorce didn't change anything. I knew what they meant, but it wasn't true. I had to make two phone calls instead of one. I had to accept that they were people who wanted things. Dad offered to come back from San Diego for Thanksgiving, but I said I'd visit him at Christmas. California in December made sense. Mom joked she'd come too, and he said we were both very welcome. Their good humor made my last months at home easy, but I found it weirdly upsetting. Didn't the breakup of our family merit some passion? Some bad behavior? Claudia's parents had fought for months. "But yours are older," she said. "Money isn't a problem."

Do you remember, when we first met, I quoted Margaret Fuller? "Let them be sea captains," she wrote, "them" being women. At seventeen I didn't think of myself as a woman. That word belonged to my mother and her friends. But with their fulltime jobs, their hobbies, and their houses, they were more like hard-working first mates than captains. They would never shine as brightly as Fuller, nor end up like her. On her way back to America from Italy, she was shipwrecked off Fire Island. Our English teacher described her huddling on the deck with her husband and baby, waiting to be rescued. Then the tide turned, and they were drowned. Could you be a woman and a captain, I wondered, and not end up on the rocks?

The worst part of going to Yale was leaving Nutmeg. The day before my flight I rode him along the trail by the river. "Don't forget me," I said. "I'll be back in three months." Even as he shied at a willow tree, I realized that wasn't true. By Thanksgiving I would be a different person. Wasn't that why I was going to college?

I met a hundred people the first week, another hundred the second. At high school I'd been the best at math and computer science and debating. Now the bar was raised; everyone was used to being the best. I joined various clubs and agreed to do far too many things. I didn't have the time, or the money, to ride.

My roommate, Tamar, came from Manhattan and seemed to know instinctively how things worked. So when she suggested we go to a Big Sisters meeting, I agreed. As we walked across the Green, she told me she too was an only child; she had always wanted a sister. Of course I said I felt the same, but the truth was, I already had Claudia; we'd sworn an oath of undying friendship when we were nine. The Big Sisters' organizer gave a predictable speech about making a difference one person at a time, and I started meeting Jade every Thursday. She lived with her grandmother and three half brothers. With her grubby pink leggings and dirty hair, she was the opposite of cute. I took her to the library: boring. I took her to the playground: dumb. When I asked her the question my parents asked every night—What did you learn today?—she said "Zilch" or "Crap."

Tamar was struggling too. "I hate my little sister," she burst out one night. Then she listed so many nasty things about her that suddenly Jade didn't seem so bad. The next day I phoned the organizer and told her we were overcommitted; we couldn't be Big Sisters. Our mutual failure sealed my friendship with Tamar. We studied together and joined the fencing club. But Claudia was the only one who knew how, after my first year at Yale, I had given up on riding; how I was waiting to discover something else I loved, to hear a professor say, "Ms. Turner, you have a gift for this." Much too soon my parents began to ask about plans. Mom suggested law school; Dad said dentistry was a great career for a woman. My friends talked about Silicon Valley and Wall Street. By senior year, I was panicking. Once again Tamar intervened. She signed us up for recruitment meetings, and we each got three job offers. I started reading business magazines, picturing myself as a CEO.

My job was demanding, which I'd expected, and a struggle, which I hadn't. I was good with numbers, a quick learner, interested in politics and business, but I didn't have the sixth sense I had with horses. I was seldom at the office less than ten hours a day, often twelve. Then I went out with friends or back to the apartment I shared with Tamar and her boyfriend on the Upper West Side; it belonged to her father. My room was very peaceful, with a single tall window.

That first spring my mother visited the city for a conference on hospital administration. On her free Saturday we went to the Frick. Of all the paintings I remember only one: *The Polish Rider.* Last September you and I looked it up on the computer. You commented on the young man's intense expression, but that afternoon at the museum my attention was on the badly painted horse, with his thick neck and odd proportions. The only horses I saw in New York were the ones in Central Park, and the occasional police horse.

I told myself my life was amazing, but sometimes, catching the subway to work, or in the line at the Starbucks near the office, or in the lobby waiting for the elevator, I had a kind of vertigo. Where was the sky? Who were all these people? If someone had told me 50 percent of them were robots, I would have believed it.

My second year in New York, our building had a blood drive. You know how scared I am of needles, but I lined up dutifully. So long as I kept my eyes closed, it didn't hurt too much. That afternoon, though, my computer screen, and everything around it, seemed a little fuzzy. At seven I went downstairs to catch the subway; I was meeting a friend in Williamsburg. Waiting for the second train, I fainted.

I came to lying on the platform, with two men bending over me. "What happened?" I said. "Where's my shoe?"

One of the men—he had a sharp widow's peak—helped me to sit up and pointed to my black pump, lying beside the rails. A moment before I'd been lying there too. I must have asked again about the shoe. The other man—he wore a purple tracksuit— said, "Oh, Christ." Before I understood what he was going to do, he jumped down, grabbed it, hauled himself back up, and handed it to me. The train came, and the men were gone.

The police took me home. In the empty apartment I got into bed and phoned Claudia. She was almost as slow to grasp what had happened as I had been. When she did, she was furious. How could I be so stupid, after giving blood for the first time? "Eat something," she said, "and go to sleep."

The next day I stood far back on the subway platform. I still hadn't seen Tamar, and I didn't want to turn my narrow escape into another New York story. I went through that day with my secret, and the next. Soon it became a story I would never tell. Occasionally, on crowded trains, I thought I saw one of the men, but already their faces were growing vague. At Yale a friend had told me how his father celebrated two birthdays: the actual day, and the frigid November day in 1956 when he'd been shot and left for dead on the banks of the Danube. Now I had a second birthday, and I wanted to do better by my second life. I was sure I'd been saved for something special.

But what that was, I didn't know. Once I'd thought it was winning shows, being a champion. Now I thought it was to rise up the ranks of a company. Walking home at night beneath the ginkgoes, I would gaze up at the penthouse windows and worry I'd been left behind. Several friends had already been promoted.

At last, my third spring in the city, my boss summoned me. On the way to her office, I fantasized: The China team? Securities? "I think you'll be a good fit for our Boston branch," she said. Was this a step up or a step down? I didn't know, but I did know refusal would mark me as difficult. I made my eyes bright, asked interested questions. That night, in a bar at Columbus and Eighty-eighth, I ordered a margarita and toasted Boston. Surely this was the door to my second life.

New York, now that I was leaving, displayed its best self. Two transactions that had been stalled for months went through; the weather was warm but not humid; several men I liked asked me out. Departure made me sexier, safer. Walking along the south

side of Central Park after one of these dates, I came across a
small crowd. A carriage horse was lying on the ground, taking
big, racking breaths. Her owner had got her out of the harness
and driving lines and was leaning against the carriage. I went
over and said I thought his horse had colic. She needed to walk.

"How's she going to walk?" He squinted up at me from beneath his baseball hat. "She can't even stand."

"People will help," I insisted.

He squinted at me for a few seconds longer, then turned to
the crowd and announced we were going to try to get Rosie
back on her feet. Half a dozen women stepped forward, and
some men, ashamed not to. The man tugged at Rosie's bridle and said, "Come on, girl. Ups-a-daisy." Two women and
I heaved at her rump, but she kept slipping out of our hands.
After a couple of minutes we stepped back. The owner gave a
little shrug and returned to his carriage. I stayed with Rosie,
talking to her, until the men came.

A week later I took the train to Boston and moved in with
Claudia. Every morning she put on a T-shirt and jeans and
walked to the vet's office; I put on my business clothes and
caught the subway downtown. On Saturdays, when we were
both free, we drove out to Windy Hill. Helen was in her late
sixties then, tall and upright, her hair already gleaming white.
She ran the stables with the help of Stu, who sounded like he'd
left Donegal last week, and two men from Brazil. I remember
one day watching her ride a stallion called Hotspur. He was
eighteen hands, stubborn and distracted, but Helen didn't give
an inch. She rode him around and around until he was obey-
ing the slightest twitch of the reins. It was a beautiful sight:
the elegant, white-haired woman in control of the powerful
animal.

When I first started riding again, I was dismayed. I'd grown so stiff, so clumsy. Slowly, as I helped with lessons and exercised the horses, my skills began to return. Then there'd be a deadline at the office; I'd miss a couple of weeks and slip back. When I complained to Claudia, she told me Helen had ridden almost every day for sixty years and never competed outside New England.

"You have to be a fanatic," she said, "to get to the top."

"What about to be good?" I said. "To be really good?"

Claudia smiled. She knew what I was asking. "You need to ride six times a week, five to ten horses a day, and push yourself all the time. Which is hard with a job like yours."

She was right. I didn't want to give up anything for anything. I wanted to be a star rider, and I wanted to make killer deals. It turned out I was a good fit for the Boston office. After six months I was promoted, and I liked my colleagues. Sometimes on Fridays we went out for drinks. Sometimes, after drinks, I went home with Robert, who worked in accounting and played jazz cello.

The day of my second birthday, I was coming home on the subway when I noticed a man. He was reading the *New Yorker* as if he were alone on the train. He had beautiful hands, and his upper lip was a perfect M. I sat down beside him, got out my own copy of the magazine, and took a deep breath. Let him notice me, I thought. And you did.

You wrote down my number, you called me, and on our first date you told me you'd recently broken up with your Scottish girlfriend. I couldn't believe my luck. On our third date, you used the ominous phrase, "There's something I need to tell you," but the "something" was that your father had Parkinson's.

A few weeks after we met, I went out for Friday drinks. When

Robert nodded toward the door, I hesitated. Then I picked up my bag and followed him. You hadn't mentioned monogamy, but I knew you took it for granted. Would you have been able to understand that Robert helped me to be casual with you? I'd ruined several relationships with premature intensity.

That Sunday when we were eating breakfast in your kitchen—I wonder if you remember?—you said I'd murmured the name Robert in my sleep. You weren't suspicious, just curious.

"The only Robert I know is at work," I said, reaching for the strawberries. "He has no business in my dreams." Between one breath and the next I vowed not to sleep with him again, not to risk the sweetness I had with you.

You told me then about your Robert, how you still felt bad about not answering his letters. "I didn't want to tell him I wasn't coming back," you said.

"Because he'd be mad at you? Or because it would have made it real?"

Behind your elegant glasses your eyes grew thoughtful. "Because I'd have lied," you said, "and promised to see him soon."

"Isn't it better to lie than to hurt someone?"

"I suppose, but I hate that messy middle ground." You lined up the strawberries on your plate, largest to smallest, and said something I've thought of often since Edward died. "When I see trouble coming, I tend to hide. I hope I never hide from you, Viv."

A month later you announced you were going to be tested for HIV; there was no way I couldn't do the same. As the phlebotomist released the tourniquet, the room began to spin. Remembering my shoe in the subway, I insisted on taking a taxi home. I spent the rest of the day in bed, fingering the little bandage on my arm. One of two possible futures was already running through my veins, but I could only picture the worst. I couldn't tell you about my fears, and I didn't tell you what happened when I phoned for the results. A young man's voice, cool and cocky, said, "Cambridge morgue. You kill 'em, we chill 'em." I was not the first person to have misdialed.

After I stopped shaking, I called the correct number. A woman answered. She said the lovely word "negative," a word that led to your not using a condom and to my getting pregnant.

At that time I had only one close friend with a baby. Lucy was already living in Duxbury. When I visited, I enjoyed playing with Leo, but really what I wanted was to talk to her. At Yale we had stayed up late, arguing about William James's theory of the scapegoat and the Iran-Contra affair. Now, even after he was in bed, Leo was her main topic. Had all our studying been in order to discuss why he didn't like his sippy cup?

I hadn't faced a choice while I waited for the HIV results. This time I did. My life could continue with work, riding, you, friends. Or it could change radically. I knew you'd be pleased. You'd already suggested we live together, and when we visited Lucy, you devoted yourself to Leo. But did I want to be colonized by a small, helpless being? Was this my second life? After a long evening in a bar with Claudia, I called Planned Parenthood.

The Monday before my appointment I arrived at the office to find Gabe and Nathan deep in conversation. They changed the subject, but not before I understood that a deal I'd worked on, fruitlessly, months before, was going through. Nathan was in the next cubicle, and Gabe and I often shared meals. I had thought they were my friends, not each other's. Why had they cut me out? Had I drunk too many margaritas one Friday? Or revealed a shocking ignorance of South American politics?

That evening I walked over to the vet's office. Claudia lent me a white coat, and I helped her feed the cats and dogs and two tremulous angora rabbits. As we ladled out pellets, refilled water containers, I told her what had happened.

"But Viv," she said, "there must be dozens of times when you've made people feel left out."

She was watching me, but I kept my gaze on the beagle we were feeding. "It's not about popularity," I said, stroking his silky ears. "It's about not being the best."

"Of course you're the best. Look how much they pay you."

I tried to explain—good enough to head a team, run a company—but she didn't understand. My world was too different from hers. And I was too different. She didn't believe she was destined for greatness; she didn't have the hunger, the ambition.

That night I dreamed I was sitting by a river, the river where I'd ridden Nutmeg, and a little boy, dark haired, blue eyed, with a rosebud mouth, was sitting beside me. He took my hand, and we played in the warm, shallow water. The next morning I told Claudia I'd changed my mind. "Can I be godmother?" she said. My lingering doubts were banished by your delight. And you were still delighted when I persuaded you we didn't need to get married. Being a mother was already overwhelming; I didn't want to be a wife as well.

But even Margaret Fuller finally succumbed. When I got pregnant for the second time, something shifted, and I was ready. Once again we got blood tests and went to city hall. Beforehand I told myself it was just a formality—I already loved you and Marcus—but when the justice of the peace asked us to stand, my heart leaped. In bed on our wedding night, I remember holding up my hand with my new gold ring. "I'll never take it off," I said.

"Nor will I," you said. Then you said some very un-Scottish things.

FROM OUR THIRD DATE it was clear that your parents would play a large part in our lives, and mine a small one. It wasn't that I disapproved of Dad's bubbly new Californian wife, or Mom's violinist boyfriend, but, seeing them only once a year—New Year in San Diego, Memorial Day in Ann Arbor—I scarcely knew them. Whereas your parents invited us to meals and movies, took an interest in my work, and babysat often. Edward in those early years was so gentle and witty, it was easy to forget he was ill. Then, soon after Trina was born, he grew worse.

I knew you were stretched thin, but I didn't know how thin until that afternoon we went for a walk in the park. As we passed the playground, you told me that on Friday you'd had to cancel two patients. Then you got home late and made Marcus cry.

At the top of the park we sat down on the bench overlooking the track. A man and a girl were jogging. The man's tracksuit was the same purple as that of my savior in the subway. While they circled the track, you laid out your argument: we should move closer to your parents, and you should start your own business so that you could help them and still be a good father. "And husband," you added.

I came last, but I still thought I had a choice. Hadn't we promised each other never to live in the suburbs, where Republicans and ax murderers roamed the streets? You listened quietly to my arguments. When you spoke again, your words came from far away. A few days before, operating on a young man, you'd almost made a fatal mistake. "I'm not sure I believe in nervous breakdowns," you said, "but I may be having one anyway."

The next Sunday, Scott whisked us through six houses and then, turning to me, said, "Tell me why all of those are wrong?"

"They're wrong because I don't want to live in the suburbs," I said.

"So we must find a place that doesn't feel like the suburbs. Make a list of the things that will make you happy to move here."

He went to get coffee, and we both began to laugh. "He should be a therapist," I said. "Or a politician," you said. But I started on my list.

In one of those odd coincidences—what Edward used to call serendipity—Claudia phoned a few days later, her voice brimming with excitement, and begged me to meet her for a drink. At the bar near our old apartment, she had two margaritas waiting. Helen had asked her to manage the stables.

"It's the best thing that's ever happened to me," she said, "but I hate that there'll be no more last-minute dinners, no more babysitting."

The floor of the bar was sticky with beer. I pulled my feet free, first one then the other, and told her our news. "Maybe you won't be farther away," I said.

It helped that Scott found a house we liked, and it helped that Marcus and Trina, after a shaky first week, begged to go to day care each morning. It helped that your business flourished and that Edward responded to treatment. But I had become someone I'd hoped never to be: a commuter. Despite the World Trade Center, despite Iraq, new markets were opening up. Nathan, Gabe, almost everyone who'd been at the office when I arrived, had moved on. I wanted to follow them, but a new job would have meant even longer hours.

Most of the mothers on our street didn't work, or worked part-time. They helped out when you had another crisis with

Edward, but I was the one who paid back the favors. "You're so busy," they said, and I caught the criticism beneath their smiles. When Marcus threw a tantrum, when Trina kept re-arranging her books, I worried my work was warping my children. Meanwhile my colleagues complained that I missed late meetings and was slow to respond to e-mail. Those weekend mornings I spent at the stables were the only times I felt like myself. Do you remember how I cried over the film *Seabiscuit*? Those were tears of rage because I only got to ride once a week.

But as Jack used to say, we don't step in the same river twice. Suddenly Edward's balance was worse again. Marcus went through that phase of bad dreams and bedwetting. I started going to work even earlier so I could be home earlier. There was no end in sight. Or to be exact, the only end was the one you dreaded. Then Helen needed her first hip replacement, and Stu quit to move back to Donegal.

The first year at Windy Hill was exhilarating. I overhauled the business side. We had a dozen new students, and I bought three more barn horses. Every stall and paddock was filled. I was still busy but much more flexible. When Trina was sent home from school with suspected chickenpox, I was there in twenty minutes. But sometimes as I drove to and from the stables or helped a girl saddle a horse, I was plagued by the feeling I'd had in New York: Was this really my second life?

One day, after watching me ride Dow Jones, Helen told me I was holding the reins too wide. She started giving me lessons, and I started entering competitions. But it was hard to train a horse that other people were riding badly. We kept coming third or fourth. When we failed to place in a small local show, I gave up competing.

Then one fall afternoon I came home to find Anne looking after the children. You had taken Edward to the emergency room, again. "Shouldn't he be in a home?" she asked.

That night I asked you the same question. Your beautiful mouth tightened. "I hate to think of him being a patient, not a person," you said.

"But he's been both for years. Think how stressful it is for him. He knows he might fall at any moment, and that Peggy can't lift him."

You stared at your book and insisted that they were still fig uring out the dosage of a new drug. When they got it right, his balance would be fine.

Finally I drove into Boston and took Peggy to lunch. I had barely uttered a sentence when she interrupted. "For years," she said, "people have been telling me to put Edward in a home, and I've said over my dead body. But he and I have talked about it; the time has come." For the rest of the meal we discussed solar panels.

Gradually we got used to visiting Edward in his small room overlooking a grove of birch trees and the parking lot. Or at least the children, Peggy, and I did. I'm not sure you ever did. When he died, I guessed the size of your distress from what you didn't do: you didn't phone me right away, you didn't take time off from work, you didn't want to deliver the eulogy. You listened stony-faced as your sister spoke about how Edward had negotiated with his illness rather than fought it, and how he had never stopped being interested in other people.

In bed that night, when I asked how you felt, you said, "Like an orphan, which is ridiculous for a man of my age."

"Especially for a man whose incredible mother is very much a part of his life."

As I fell asleep, I could feel you lying awake beside me, and when I woke, you were in exactly the same position. "I want the Simurg to carry me away," you said. Then you told me about the Persian flying creature, very kind and so large that it could carry an elephant.

I knew I had to let you grieve in your own way. I tried to make sure you never missed a tennis game with Steve. I tried to make sure you did things with the children. But most of the time it was as if you were walking around in a large protective suit, your astronaut's suit. Was it protecting you from us, or us from you? When I told you my fears about Marcus, the information vanished between one layer and the next.

A few weeks after Marcus broke his leg, I ran into another mother at the school gates. She asked how he was doing. I said he was great. His crutches were like a new toy.

"They heal so quickly at that age," she said. "Nick says the other boy was mostly to blame."

"To blame for what?" Marcus had been vague about the accident. One minute he was fine; the next he had a broken leg.

"Charging around," she said. "Chasing the little kids."

Before she could say more, her son appeared.

"Everyone charges around in the playground," you said when I described the exchange. "Especially ten-year-old boys."

But I was worried that our son was becoming a bully. The following week, when Ivy and Lynn came over, I noticed how they avoided being alone with him. I began to listen to Anne's arguments about Greenfield: the fantastic teachers, the structure, the individual attention.

As for our new student at the stables, I didn't even try to tell you about her. Tiffany was thirteen, horse crazy, desperate to improve. One day she had her lesson on one of our trickier horses. Mrs. Hardy kept nipping at the other mares. Afterward Tiffany's mother complained, and Claudia said how about half off for today.

"You shouldn't have done that," I said when she told me. "It sets a terrible precedent."

"I know, but she works in a 7-Eleven, and she was wearing that godawful sparkly sweater."

We agreed I'd take Tiffany's next lesson and suggest she go on our budget plan. I had seen her ride before, but I was impressed by her seat, by how easily she posted. I explained about the plan: twelve lessons for the price of ten. Her mother said great. She'd bring a check next week.

After the next lesson, I again praised Tiffany and asked for payment. Her mother reminded me they were on the plan, and I reminded her about the check. Next week, she promised.

But the next time Tiffany came with a friend, and the lesson after that, her father brought her and knew nothing about any check. For the fifth lesson she once again came with a friend. When I said we couldn't keep teaching her on account, tears spilled down her cheeks. I handed her a Kleenex and relented. It was a quiet, hot afternoon, and by the end of the lesson she was riding Sir Pericles in graceful circles. Her friend had already left, and I gave her a lift home. As I pulled up outside the ramshackle triple-decker, I offered to talk to her parents. She was out of the car before I finished. "See you next week," I called. But I didn't.

"Good riddance," said Claudia. "We can't do battle for every payment."

"But she's really talented," I said. "It doesn't matter if we don't get paid once in a while."

"Viv, she got five free lessons. You see our cash flow."

She was right—everything about the stables cost money—but I couldn't get Tiffany out of my head. She was my younger self. I had failed her, and somehow that failure connected with all my other failures. At my job. With Nutmeg and Dow Jones. With various men. Even with my Little Sister Jade. I had failed my second life. You were in the grip of your grief, and I was in the grip of mine. When we went to Wellfleet, we hardly spoke to each other, but you didn't seem to notice.

Back at Windy Hill I found we had a new contender for our worst rider award. Week after week Diane slouched around on Samson. So when her mother asked if she could board a horse, our expectations were low. I was walking back from the paddocks when the trailer pulled up outside the barn. From it emerged the most amazing horse I'd ever seen: a dapple-gray Thoroughbred, almost seventeen hands, five years old. Mercury backed out of the trailer, tail clamped, legs ready to kick, ears pinned, nostrils wide. Given half a chance, he would have galloped back to Ontario. The driver held out the forms for Hilary to sign, but she simply stood there, frozen. I stepped forward to take delivery.

Hilary didn't come by the next day, or the next. Between giving lessons, I brought Mercury up to the stalls and brushed him using the softest rubber curry. Claudia appeared while I was picking burrs out of his tail.

"I thought you were checking the supplies," she said. "It's not our job to groom him."

"I'll get to them. I don't think anyone's been near him in months."

This brief conversation set the pattern for our exchanges about Mercury: my enthusiasm, her disapproval. The next day, when Claudia had to go to Boston, I phoned the one person who I knew would appreciate him as much as I did. Helen said she would love to see him.

I went to fetch her at lunchtime. When we pulled up beside the paddock, he was grazing in the far corner. "Help me out," she said. I hovered, worrying she'd lose her footing as she moved her walker over the rough ground. Mercury had caught sight of us and was trotting toward the gate.

"Good shoulders," Helen pronounced. "Good pasterns. Good suspension. The last time I saw a horse like this was when my first husband took me to the regionals."

At the gate Mercury fixed his large dark eyes on me and nickered softly. Then he scraped the ground, twice, with his right front hoof, choosing me.

2

Suddenly I was full of hope. Think about the best thing that ever happened to you, not counting Marcus and Trina. That was how I felt during the days following Mercury's arrival. Even simple things—cutting the crusts off Trina's sandwiches, putting gas in the car—were filled with meaning. But he was Hilary's horse. Without her permission I could do little other than feed and groom him. She came to ride him once when I was supervising the stable girls. Then nothing. Eight days passed before she phoned to ask if she could visit Mercury after work. She hadn't boarded a horse before and didn't know the rules. That afternoon, the minute Claudia left, I went to get Mercury from the paddock. Walking up the road, he pulled like a yearling. When, instead of fetching his saddle, I cross-tied him outside a stall, he snorted.

"I can't," I told him. "Your mistress is coming."

As soon as I saw Hilary heading our way, wearing a flowery skirt, carrying a bag of carrots, I knew she wasn't planning to ride, but I gave no sign. "Mercury's waiting by the stalls," I said. "Do you need help finding his saddle?"

"Oh, I'm not riding him again." She was startled but quite definite. "I'm too out of practice, and he's too strong. I'm just here to pet him."

"He really needs to be exercised," I said.

"Why can't he just run around in a field?"

I explained that he was a Thoroughbred; besides, we didn't have a large enough field. "I'd be happy to ride him," I said, "as part of your boarding him here." I could hear my voice cracking with casualness.

She started to smile—you know how Hilary nearly always looks as if she's about to smile—and asked if we could discuss the arrangements over dinner. Diane was away. Now she was the one trying to sound casual. I phoned you, and you said, "Fine." My absence made no difference.

At the sight of me, Mercury stamped the ground and tossed his head. Where had I been? He danced from hoof to hoof as I saddled him. Normally, riding a horse I didn't know, I would have walked him around the arena, letting him get used to me and his new surroundings, but as soon as I mounted Mercury, I could feel the energy coursing through him. He was ready, eager, unafraid. I decided to break my own rules and take him out to the large field. As we stepped onto the grass, his ears came forward. We walked two sides of the fence. Then I let out the reins, and that was that. All I had to do was push my hands into the crest of his mane, and his body unfolded beneath me. He had been cooped up for much too long. And so had I. Do you remember the picture you showed me of the Roman god with his winged shoes? Riding Mercury, it was easy to believe his hooves had wings.

Afterward, as I followed Hilary's rear lights down the road and back to town, even my car seemed different, the steering more sensitive, the accelerator more powerful. How many horsepower was it? A hundred and fifty? Two hundred? I imagined a cavalcade of horses, like Mercury, galloping before me.

In the restaurant we took turns telling our life stories. Hilary had met her husband in Toronto, buying Gouda at Kensington Market. Franklin was a computer programmer who loved to cook. They'd married after three months and moved to Providence, where they bought a ramshackle Victorian. For nearly a decade they'd been absorbed in wainscoting and moldings. But after the house was finished, Franklin just wanted to get stoned and play guitar. Or so she thought.

Then some elderly neighbors asked Hilary to stage their house. It sold in a weekend. The next day she quit her job, technical writing for software manuals. "Once I started earning decent money," she said, "I was even less patient with Franklin. He wasn't interested in my houses, didn't like my new friends. One day he forgot Diane's school play. I said maybe we should try living apart. I thought he'd argue, promise to change, but he said not a bad idea."

Two days after she moved out, her friend Beth had moved in. She couldn't stand it. Beth enjoying the window seat she'd built in the kitchen, Beth getting Franklin to do the things he'd never do for her. Hilary hadn't planned to leave Providence, but one weekend she'd been visiting a cousin in Lincoln and driving around, she'd seen a cute house for sale in our town. Diane still hadn't forgiven her.

I nodded, asked questions, waiting to ask about what really interested me: Where did she find the amazing Mercury? When I did, a shadow fell across her face. "He belonged to my brother," she said. "I'll tell you another time, when I'm not going home to an empty house."

To our left, a couple was holding hands; to our right a couple was studying the menu. I remembered all the empty rooms I'd gone back to, before you, and apologized for prying.

"You're not prying. I just hate Diane being away. You understand I can't pay you for riding Mercury? I can only manage the
boarding fees because Michael had life insurance."

She was very firm about this point. I said she was providing
me with a mount, which meant there was one more horse we
could use for lessons. My jumbled logic seemed to satisfy her.
We each had an agenda. Then I gave the quick version of my
life story. When I mentioned you, she exclaimed that she'd seen
you at the stables and assumed you were just another parent.
You'd been great with Diane. I said I was glad you were doing
a good job with your patients. At home, since your dad died,
you'd been MIA.

Hilary shook her head. "I'm not sure grief has a timetable,"
she said. "Just when I think I've come to terms with Michael's
death, I find myself spiraling down again, braking at a green
light, wearing odd socks."

We split the bill and promised we'd do this again soon. Driving home, I thought how long it was since I'd made a new
friend, not as a parent, not as a wife, but as myself. I'd forgotten
the pleasure of revisiting my past with another person. It wasn't
only Mercury that filled me with hope, but Hilary too. When
I told her how I used to work in mutual funds, she said, "Viv,
you're a Renaissance woman."

The next day, as we brought the horses up from the paddocks, I told Claudia about the arrangement. She was leading
Sorrel and Dow Jones. I had Mrs. Hardy and Nimble.

"Lucky Hilary," she said, "finding a free groom. What time
is the hay arriving?"

"You were the one who said we needed more boarders," I
persisted. Three owners had taken their horses to North Caro-
lina last winter and never returned, and we'd had a run of bad

luck with our own horses: a mare with colic had to be put down, a gelding was lamed by a split hoof, another gelding kicked in the face, his tear ducts damaged. Five of our twenty-four stalls were empty. And Matheus and Felipe had asked for a raise.

"Not boarders like Mercury," said Claudia. "He doesn't belong in our cozy, second-rate stables."

As she spoke, Sorrel and Dow Jones crowded forward, objecting to her description. I did too. "We don't have to be second-rate," I said. "He can help us attract better horses, better riders."

"I'm not saying we have to be." She tugged at the reins. "But I like the stables the way they are. I like that anyone can come here and ride. Of course, I'd love to have prize-winning horses, stellar riders, but I'm satisfied with what we do have."

And Mercury, I tried to explain, was a way for me to be more satisfied. "He's been so well trained. I'm hoping to take him out to a few shows."

Claudia gave me a quick, sideways glance, but all she said was, "Okay, I'll stop being a Grinch. I just want you to be happy."

I would have said the same. We were both nearly thirty-eight, but Claudia was childless, living with her great-aunt, dating a married man. In her twenties she'd gone out with a series of willowy, Frisbee-playing boys. I'd thought their youth mere coincidence until one night I made a joke about cradle snatching, and she said, "But you know I like younger guys."

She was my closest friend, and I had had no idea. When I asked why, she said, "They're cute, and they don't think I'm a failure."

"You're not a failure," I protested.

She laughed. "Come on, Viv. I love my job, but there's no ladder to climb, no glass ceiling. I can't afford to do the things you and your fancy friends do."

Suddenly I recalled all the times she'd claimed she wasn't interested in a play, didn't feel like going out for tapas, and I'd taken her at her word. I felt dumb as a post. A few months later Helen asked her to run the stables. Then she met Rick; he was taking photographs at a horse show. The good news was, she'd overcome her ageism. The bad news was, he had a wife and three sons, the youngest still in college. His wife used to teach nursery school. Now she raised money for her church and had migraines. It wasn't a question of if they got divorced, Rick said. Only when.

Claudia was incandescent, but as the months passed, his divorce seemed permanently on hold. One son was depressed, another got sick, the dog had cancer, his accounting firm was restructuring. Rick was doing his best, she told me, seeing a therapist, but there was always a good reason why it was a bad time to leave.

The afternoon he came to photograph Mercury for our website, Claudia had a dentist's appointment. I spent an hour grooming Mercury—washing him with whitening shampoo, oiling his hooves. I had just finished combing his tail when Rick arrived.

First he photographed Mercury grazing with Sorrel and Sir Pericles, then on a lunge line. At last I rode him. For the final shots Rick suggested a couple of jumps. We hadn't jumped before, and as we approached the first pole, I felt him hesitate. Then he gathered himself, and we were flying. By the third jump I knew what Mercury was born and trained to do.

Back in the barn, while I rubbed him down, Rick set up his tripod. "It's so quiet," he said. "Don't you ever get frightened, being here alone?"

"It's safer than walking around downtown at night," I said.

"That's what Claudia says. I told her she should get a gun."

Had I heard him correctly? I turned to look, and there he was, frowning slightly, gold-rimmed glasses glinting as he adjusted the camera. "I have a pistol at my cabin in New Hampshire," he went on. "I take it out once a year to oil it, but just knowing it's there makes me feel safer."

"You own a gun?"

"I know, it surprises me too, but in Franconia no one gives it a second thought. It doesn't mean I've turned into a redneck."

Suddenly I couldn't stop myself from asking, "Are you ever going to leave your wife?"

It was his turn to be surprised. "The answer is yes. Believe me, I don't like having to lie. I don't like Claudia having less than she deserves. I don't like Nan having less than she deserves."

"So what's stopping you? Thousands of people get divorced every year." I moved to Mercury's off side.

"I don't know," he said, and I could hear that he didn't. "Three months after I met Claudia, I was all set to leave. I'd had a good day at work, and as I drove home I was sure I could find the right words. Our marriage had run its course. We'd both be happier apart. Nan would have the house, money, etcetera. But when I stepped into the kitchen, she was waiting with a bottle of champagne. Her church had gotten planning permission for their extension."

"I can see that was a setback," I said, "but there can't have been good news every day."

He clicked his fingers along the bars of the nearest stall. "All I can say is that looking after Nan has been my job for nearly thirty years. If I die tomorrow, that'll be my epitaph: 'He was a good husband.' Everyone will hate me for leaving her."

I asked what his therapist thought, his sons.

"My sons are devoted to the status quo. My therapist thinks I should shit or get off the pot, but being a polite woman, she says we should try couples counseling."

Nearby a horse whinnied. "Claudia loves you," I said. "She deserves a chance to have what you have: a partner, children. If something doesn't change"—I was amazed at my boldness— "I'm declaring war."

Rick stepped over and placed his right hand on Mercury's neck. He was swearing an oath on what he knew I held sacred. "I am trying," he said. "If I can't, then I promise I'll break up with Claudia."

"Soon," I said. "Not years from now. Months from now."

Mercury, with a fine sense of timing, let fall a stream of droppings. As I fetched a shovel, Rick asked if I'd tell Claudia about our chat. "Will you?" I said, trying to sound as if I didn't care.

He wasn't fooled for a second. "What good would it do? She'd just be mad at you, and she wouldn't break up with me."

When I began to apologize, he started to laugh. "You're a scary woman, Viv. I'll send you the photographs by the end of Sunday." Then he looked up from folding his tripod and said what I'd been hoping Claudia would say ever since Mercury emerged from the trailer: "That's a horse in a thousand."

3

I CAME HOME AND TOLD you I'd just heard something as-
tounding: Rick, the liberal, artistic accountant, owned a gun.
You were in the garden, picking tomatoes, the last of the season.

"Maybe he's like you," you said. "He learned to shoot at
camp?"

"But that was a game. Shooting clay pigeons. Rick owns a
real gun. If someone broke into his house, he could kill them."

You removed a few faded leaves and held out an almost ripe
tomato. "Hopefully that won't happen," you said. "But you never
know about people and guns. Remember Melanie's father?"

I did, and I remembered, longingly, your response. It was you
who noticed that Trina had come home from Melanie's with a
picture of a girl holding something small and black. You who
gently questioned her and learned that the small black object
was a gun. Melanie's dad had one. He kept it in a box.

"Sure," Mr. Nichols had said when you phoned. "What's the
problem? I have a permit."

"Excuse me," you said. "No one has a permit to show a gun
to six-year-olds." After you hung up, you had phoned all the
parents in Trina's class.

Now the news about Rick's firearm barely reached you.
Could I start the water for pasta? you asked.

. . .

AT THE TIME THAT I studied Margaret Fuller I had intense ideas about sharing everything with my affinities. And I still feel that way. I want to be truthful, and until last fall, barring my colleague Robert, I mostly was. Then you and Claudia, the two people I was closest to, disapproved of Mercury, and in the face of that disapproval, I began to follow your example: I began to hide things. I hid the amount of time I was spending with him; I hid the scope of my ambitions. You asked only practical questions—who was taking Trina to her violin lesson? Should we have the furnace serviced?—but Claudia was more perceptive. Why did the vet see Mercury every time she came? Why did he have special food and the largest paddock? So when Rick's photographs appeared in my in-box, it was Hilary I phoned. We arranged to meet at a café near her office.

I arrived to find her already seated at a corner table with two coffees. "I hope you like lattes," she said as I opened my laptop. The photographs began to slide across the screen, Mercury growing ever more lustrous as the sun set.

"He *is* beautiful," Hilary said wistfully. She asked who had taken the photographs, and when I said Claudia's boyfriend, she said, "Oh, I'm glad she has someone."

"She does, and she doesn't." I described the situation and, lured on by her attentive smile, confided my attack on Rick.

Her phone buzzed, but she didn't even glance at it. "You're such a good friend," she said. "What would happen if Claudia delivered her own ultimatum?"

I explained Claudia's theory that Rick had never recovered from being sent away to boarding school. He was twelve years old, two thousand miles from his home in Nebraska, and allowed one phone call a week. "She says he has to decide for himself," I said.

We both paused to watch Mercury approach a jump in one photograph, soar over it in the next. The neat way he folded his hind legs gave him several inches advantage over a sloppier horse.

"Perhaps," Hilary suggested, "Rick's a Good Man." Then—at first it seemed like a digression—she told me about her abortion. When she got pregnant, soon after she moved to Providence, her mother had phoned with the news that she'd once had a sister. Jessie had been born with Down's syndrome when Michael was three, and had died soon after her second birthday. "I'm telling you now," her mother had said, "so you can make sure there aren't any problems." But there were.

On what was already one of the worst days of her life, Hilary had arrived at the clinic to find a group of middle-aged men holding up bloody pictures, shouting "Murderer!" "Whore!"

"I kept thinking," she said, gazing at me intently, "that these men went to church on Sunday, and for the rest of the week they looked at porn and hit their wives and molested their kids' friends. Or their kids. All that mattered was that everyone thought they were good. I hate Good Men."

Rick's not like that, I wanted to say, but I recalled his anxious frown, his fear that everyone would hate him. Before I could speak, Hilary's phone rang again. She was needed at the office.

"Thank you for showing me the photos," she said. "I wish Michael could see them."

I was nearly back at the car when I caught sight of Jack across the street. Two minutes earlier, and Hilary would have met him, tapping along with his white cane. I went over to say hello, and he asked after you. You'd been so distant since Edward died. I'd been glad when Hilary said you were doing well by your patients. Now I was glad Jack had noticed your astronaut's suit. I told him about our whale-watching expedition, and how it had seemed to cheer you up.

"So maybe Donald just needs to be in the presence of large mammals," he said.

"Do you think there's anything we can do to help?"

He tapped his cane thoughtfully. "Besides keeping him company, and waiting for him to come back? No. He's on his own journey. Someday soon he'll realize how lucky he is to have you and the kids."

I offered him a lift, but he shook his head. "It's my civic duty to remind my fellow citizens that, however bad things are, they still have their eyesight."

"You'll only serve as a reminder," I said, "when you're less handsome."

THE PHOTOS OF MERCURY were my version of porn. When I was alone, I looked at them all the time. I pinned up half a dozen on the bulletin board. Matheus pronounced him superb; Charlie and the other stable girls were wild about him; Claudia said nothing. At my birthday party she led the singing and teased me about my hair, but the next week we had another quarrel. She tracked me down in the stalls, where I was getting a horse ready for a lesson, to tell me Hilary had phoned to complain about the bills from the vet and the farrier. "She said there's even a charge for silicone pads."

"Mercury was a little off," I said. "I needed the vet to do a full lameness exam. And he was due for new shoes. The farrier suggested the pads." With another horse I would have waited a day or two to see if he recovered before paying for a vet's visit; as for the pads, they helped to absorb the shock of jumping. Of course Claudia knew all this. What she didn't know was how much I was riding him. Already he recognized my car. When I arrived in the morning, he was waiting at the paddock gate.

"But why didn't you consult Hilary?" she said. "At least let her know about the shoes? And Matheus says you're giving him special food."

"Just vitamins and alfalfa hay. I buy them myself."

The mare I was saddling tried to nip me. She sensed my anger, and so did Claudia. "Viv, it's not the food or the farrier that's the problem. It's you. You're acting as if Mercury is the only horse at Windy Hill. He's not, and he's not your horse."

Twice in elementary school I was sent home for hitting other children. Maybe that's why I was so worried about Marcus. For a few seconds I could have thrown my helmet at Claudia, or shoved her to the ground. Then my vision cleared. I was tightening a girth, talking to my oldest friend. I said I was sorry; I didn't want to lame an expensive horse; I'd let the farrier's zeal carry me away.

She nodded doubtfully. "You're so different." She sighed. "It worries me."

"I'm not different," I said. "I'm myself again. Now I know why I didn't die in the subway."

I smiled, hoping to win her over, and she returned my gaze, not smiling. She'd been there when Nutmeg broke my finger, when the *Challenger* disintegrated and we stood in the school playground, staring up at the sky, when I won first place in the Medway show, when my parents separated, when I met you: all those hours of riding and daydreaming and planning to change our lives.

"Okay," she said at last. "But be careful. Remember what happened with Nutmeg."

"I was twenty then. Just a kid."

That afternoon, as I taught my lessons, what I kept thinking about was not Claudia's warning but Hilary's betrayal. She and I talked or texted several times a week, and at my party she had joined in like an old friend. Now she had gone behind my back to Claudia.

After supper I went to the study and dialed her number.

"Viv, I was just wondering which to do first: sew on a button, or go over Diane's homework?"

"The button. Listen, Claudia spoke to me about the bills. I'm sorry I didn't ask you first." I explained that Mercury would need to see the farrier every five weeks but, barring emergencies, there wouldn't be any more major expenses. The vet had given him a clean bill of health. As I spoke, I drew the outline of a large M on the notepad you kept on the desk.

"Did I screw things up, phoning Claudia?" Hilary said. "I think of her as the money person, and you as the one who knows horses."

I felt a rush of gratitude; she had seen past my apology. "Actually," I said, "I'm the money person."

"Oh, Viv, I did screw things up. Of course after a decade in business you'd deal with the bills. I'm sorry. You're my friend, and I didn't want to bug you, so I went to Claudia. I'll know better in future. Listen, I wanted to ask you about Jack Brennan."

"Jack Brennan?"

"Yes. We've been hanging out since your party. He seems really nice."

I could hear her smiling. I said he was great, one of your closest friends, and got off the phone. Hilary and Jack? Jack and Hilary? Alone in the study, I felt my cheeks grow warm. The thought of them together seemed to break some unwritten rule. I told myself it wouldn't last. There was no reason to tell you.

4

ONE DAY SOON AFTER we moved here, Marcus rode his tricycle straight into Main Street. In the instant that he shot out into the lanes of cars, I was running after him, shouting, "Stop! Stop!" My love for him was like a skyscraper, dwarfing the danger. All that mattered was his safety. I had the same single, towering emotion when the police called at Thanksgiving to say the alarm had gone off at Windy Hill. You know what happened that night at the stables. What you don't know is how it made me feel. When the police escorted me to the corner of Milton Street, I saw our house, dark except for the kitchen lights.

Who lives here? I thought. For a moment I was sure I'd step into rooms I'd never seen before.

Do you remember when we visited Edinburgh, we went to a pub called Deacon Brodie's? You told me that Brodie had inspired Robert Louis Stevenson's *Dr. Jekyll and Mr. Hyde.* By day he was a respectable cabinetmaker; by night he became a burglar, robbing the people who bought his cabinets. "Surely everyone feels like that sometimes," you said. "Like inside us are two people who want completely different things."

I was still sitting in the parked car, still trying to remind myself I was Marcus and Trina's mother, when you appeared in your bathrobe. At the kitchen table I gradually returned to myself. I told you about the police, the glove. Suddenly it occurred to me that you might mention the break-in to Jack; he might tell Hilary; she might worry about Mercury. I could see you were bewildered when I swore you to secrecy.

What happened the next day was nothing I planned. The police came back early to finish their report and were gone by the time Claudia arrived. At lunchtime she and I were in the office, eating our turkey sandwiches. The clock above the filing cabinet sounded like a man with a little hammer. "Tell her, tell her," he was saying.

Instead I praised last night's pecan pie: not too sweet. Then I mentioned that the police had come by that morning. "There've been a couple of break-ins in the neighborhood," I said. "They want us to update our security. I thought I'd make some calls."

"That would be great," she said. "The other day Helen was telling me about the summer two horses were stolen and a third poisoned. They never did find the culprit."

So you were wrong, I thought. They did steal horses in Massachusetts. And Mercury was so well trained he would be easy to steal. I arranged for the workmen to come when Claudia was busy, minimizing work and cost. When she queried the latter, I invented a windfall. Some bonus stocks had finally matured. My Christmas present to the stables.

"Viv," she said, "that's so generous of you."

I tried not to think about my credit card bill. That afternoon, when I rode Mercury, I raised all the jumps.

WHEN I WAS TRINA'S age, I loved stories about the great hunters who could track a bear to its cave, find the buffalo by the way the grass bent. Later, in my office near the Prudential Center, I sometimes thought of myself as a modern hunter, tracking the market. So I noticed that Claudia was drinking more mint tea, that she asked me to lift a bale of hay, but I didn't follow the signs to their conclusion. When I came into the office the day after the security lights were installed, and saw her sitting at the table, clasping her head, my first thought was that she'd discovered the break-in.

"Do you have a headache?" I said.

Silently she pointed at a chair. I stared out the window, longing for a bird to fly by, or a plane, anything to fill the empty sky.

"Viv," she said. "I'm pregnant."

I was so happy I nearly knocked her to the floor. When we stopped laughing and embracing, she told me she was nearly nine weeks. Around the time I lectured Rick, one of his sperm, more intrepid than its owner, had reached its goal. "Have you told him?" I asked.

"Not yet." She was smiling and frowning at the same time. "But already everything's different. For nearly three years I convinced myself that his going home to Nan every night was proof he loved me. He tells me the truth, not Nan! He hurts me, not Nan!" She shook her head in amazement. "Now I'm scared. If his first reaction to the baby is fear, or anger, then my love will sink without trace. Whatever happens, I want this baby."

"Oh, Claudia," I said helplessly. A flock of black birds flew by the window.

"I was worried about you too," she said. "That you'd think I was crazy to keep it."

I said again I was thrilled; this was the best possible news. When did she plan to tell Rick? After the holidays, she said. With his sons coming home for Christmas, and Nan's father visiting, he couldn't cope with one more thing. Then she swore me to secrecy, even from you.

As I helped the next rider to adjust her stirrups, I thought this was the best possible news for me too. Now Claudia wouldn't care how long and hard I trained Mercury.

I came home to find Marcus and his friend Luis making tacos. After dinner, when they were playing in the basement and you were in your usual position, reading a book, the TV on mute, I seized the opportunity to tell you I'd changed my mind about Greenfield.

5

WITH YOU UNAVAILABLE IN one way and Claudia in another, I turned increasingly to Hilary. We each had something the other wanted. She knew about Mercury's past. I knew about Jack's. In the weeks since she'd confided their relationship, I had begun to get used to the idea. The week before Christmas, we met at the reservoir to go for a walk. It was a cold, clear afternoon, a half moon already rising over the straggly oaks. We talked about holiday plans. She had decided not to go to Ontario, flights were so expensive, and would spend Christmas here with Jack. Then I brought the conversation around to Mercury. Did she know how Michael had come to own him?

"Only bits and pieces," she said as a golden retriever loped past. "He was working at a stable in Kentucky when he won a mare in a bet. He started breeding her. Mercury was the second foal. By the time he was a year old, Michael was obsessed with him. This was the horse he would ride to victory. Then something bad happened—I don't know what—and he moved back to Ontario."

She stepped squarely on a frozen puddle. "For a while it seemed like a good move. He worked hard; his boss appreciated him. But last winter he became convinced that Mercury was in danger."

"Why would he think that?" I pictured the black glove lying on the ground.

She made an exasperated sound. "Why would Michael think anything? He got it into his head that someone was riding Mercury secretly. He started spending all his time at the stables, sleeping in Mercury's stall. He even went so far as to make a will and take out life insurance, two things I never would have expected of my brother. My parents were beside themselves. All he could talk about was Mercury and the Spruce Meadows derby, this big show in Alberta. They gave up on him, but I never did. I hate that he's dead, and I hate that nothing came of his dreams."

His dreams aren't over, I wanted to say; I can take Mercury to Spruce Meadows. But she was pointing at the sky. Four mallards were flying across the half moon. "Would you like to come to dinner on Christmas Eve?" I asked.

SOMEHOW, DESPITE YOUR MOTHER'S absence, we got through Christmas. Then we came home from the Frog Pond, and you told me Claudia had left a message. At first all I heard was her anger. Only when I pressed repeat did I grasp that there'd been a second break-in. I walked back to the kitchen, counting my steps. When we'd had our fight and you'd blamed me for the things you'd promised never to blame me for, I headed for the door. I needed to see Mercury. You stepped forward, your face furious, blocking my path. Finally I had reached you.

How cheerful you were that evening with Merrie and her daughters. Meanwhile I looked at my watch twenty times an hour, wishing them gone. I had given you your chance; I had tried to tell you about Mercury. Now what I wanted was for you to go back to being oblivious. I did the dishes, hoping you'd fall asleep. But upstairs you were still awake. We made angry love, and afterward my dreams were full of violence. A stranger wrapped his hands around my neck. Ice cracked beneath my feet. Flames leaped from doors and windows. The next morning, even before I opened my eyes, I knew I was sick.

Hours passed like a clap of the hands. It was eleven; it was four; it was dark, and the air smelled of fried onions. By the next day, as you and Trina came and went, offering drinks and magazines, my head had cleared. I kept thinking about Michael: his fear that someone else was riding Mercury, his falling at a jump, an accident that was perhaps not an accident. Had someone spooked Mercury? Or rigged the jump? Perhaps that someone had followed Mercury to Windy Hill and was now breaking in during major holidays? Even in my feverish state I recognized an insane hypothesis, but everything about Mercury was insane: his intelligence, his strength, his skill. How could I protect him?

I remember when Edward had that operation that involved cauterizing parts of his brain, you showed Marcus a picture of the brain in a medical textbook. "It's like a maze," he said. "Not really," you said, "because people are lost in a maze. More like a busy city with lots of streets and lots of people dashing around, most of them knowing where they're going." Now, as if a town crier were running through the streets of my brain, the question came to me in headlines: How Can I Protect Him?

On the fourth day my fever was gone. Standing in the shower, I felt I had passed through some disaster. On the other side everything was clear. I phoned Helen, and she answered as if people often called at 7:00 a.m. I said I wanted to make sure Claudia hadn't left yet. "Please don't tell her I'm coming," I added.

"You girls," she said.

After days lying in bed, just to step outside made me happy. As I scraped the windows of my car, I took big gulps of the frigid air. Driving to Helen and Claudia's, I kept to the speed limit and stopped neatly at every intersection as if that could make up for my bad behavior. My footsteps were the first leading to their front door. The new snow squeaked underfoot.

"Oh, it's you," said Claudia.

Even at this early hour her face was glowing. How could Rick not notice? She led me not to her part of the house but to the living room, where only six weeks before we had celebrated Thanksgiving. Now she chose an upright wooden chair. I chose another. She didn't turn on the light, and I could just make out her expression of faint boredom. She was interviewing me for a job, a place in her affections, and she didn't expect me to get it. But as soon as I spoke—I don't know how to tell you how sorry I am—her boredom vanished.

"You don't know?" she said scornfully. "I'm the one who doesn't know anything."

In Ann Arbor we used to play a version of truth or dare. How badly could we behave without destroying our friendship? Would we still be friends if one of us burned down a bank, or dated a forty-year-old, or became a Republican, or ate horsemeat, or cheated on an exam? Later, sharing an apartment, we had more serious arguments. She thought the company I worked for did shady deals. I thought she sometimes gave false hope to pet owners. But all these ruptures were minor compared to her fury now. How could I have treated her this way?

I had planned to beg for forgiveness, but I couldn't help fighting back. "You have a grudge against Mercury," I said.

She flung out her hands. "Viv, you're crazy. I don't have a grudge against Mercury. He's Hilary's horse, she pays his fees, end of story." Then she listed my mistakes. I'd been late for lessons. I hadn't noticed a horse was lame. I'd failed to check a delivery. Samson's water bucket was frozen.

"I'm sorry," I said again. Stealthily I tried to invoke her pregnancy. "You seemed so on edge, I didn't want to upset you."

At last she gave a small groan, not so much accepting my apologies as worn down. "If you're going to keep working at the stables," she said, "you have to pay attention to all the horses."

From my first week at Windy Hill, we had run the stables as equals. Now I heard the threat; we were equals only by her choice. I promised everything she wanted. Then I asked humbly about the break-in. She told me the details: the ladder, the hayloft.

"The police said our biggest worry is arson," she said. "If someone drops a cigarette, the barn would catch fire in a second."

She stood up; my interview was over. I hadn't gotten the job, but I hadn't been rejected outright. As I walked back to the car, the snow was silent. I understood Claudia's anger. What I didn't understand was how she, who could find a good word to say about the most spavined, swaybacked, knock-kneed, badly trained horse, could be immune to Mercury. Not just immune, but hostile.

At the stables, on all sides, I saw the effects of my absence. Mercury turned his back on me. Only after I had brought him some alfalfa hay and talked to him for ten minutes did he nudge my shoulder. I fetched a notebook and began to check the horses one by one, making a list of what needed to be done. By the time Matheus and Felipe arrived, I had turned the page.

"The police were here again," Matheus said. Beneath his woolen hat his face was dark with stubble.

"Someone broke in through the hayloft. Did you see any-thing?"

"Not me, not Felipe. Trust me."

"No one thought it was you. Can you do the stalls?"

"No problem."

The phrase lacked his usual cheer. For four years he and I had worked easily side by side. We were all—owners, students, stable girls, employees—in this together, shoveling shit as fast as we could. But that morning everyone was gloomy and ir-ritable. One of our best students burst into tears when I told her to shorten her stirrups. Bridget, who'd been boarding horses at the stables for twenty years, complained that her stall hadn't been mucked out. Normally Claudia would have made a joke, and they would each have seized a fork. Now she said curtly, "You can't expect everything to run like clockwork over the holidays."

"What did I do to deserve that?" said Bridget when Claudia was out of earshot.

"Breathed," said Matheus, who was passing with a load of hay.

No one had connected the second break-in to Mercury, but when I went to get his saddle, it was on a different peg.

YOU USED TO TEASE me about reading my horoscope in maga-zines. Did I really believe that a twelfth of the population was going to have a good Thursday because the moon was ascen-dant in Jupiter? No, but that didn't stop me from enjoying the optimism that came with reading that the day was especially promising for business, or romance. What I do believe in is fate, moments when the people and events in my life line up, like iron filings in the grip of some giant magnet. Fate saved me in the subway, made you talk to me on the train, brought Mercury to Windy Hill. And that afternoon, in the produce aisle of the supermarket, it nudged me once again. I was reaching for a cauliflower when I saw our former student Tiffany standing a few feet away, holding a box of pasta. I wished her a happy new year and asked what she was doing there. The store wasn't near her house.

"Visiting a friend," she said. "Mom texted me to pick up some things."

I offered her a lift home. When we were both in the car with our groceries, she asked after Sir Pericles. I told her he was fine. Then, we were idling at a red light, she said, "Dad's in trouble again. There was a fight in a bar, and when the police came, he had a gun. He wasn't using it or anything."

"Where did he get a gun?"

"I don't know. New Hampshire? That's where he got the last one."

It wasn't even news to her. Guns, police, prison, that was the world she lived in. I found myself asking if she'd like to help exercise the horses. The last thing I needed was another fight with Claudia, but I remembered all the times when I was Tiffany's age and the only thing that made me feel better was riding. Outside the triple-decker we tapped our numbers into each other's phones.

"I'm sorry about your dad," I said.

She picked up her groceries and reached for the door. "Mom says he's the baby of the family. He'll grow up one of these days."

You made the same comment, I remember, when I came home from my eye exam and reported that I still had 20/20 vision.

6

With Claudia's permission, I bought eight fire extinguishers, stationed them at key points in the barn, and summoned everyone for a fire drill. No one smokes anywhere in the buildings or within a hundred feet of them. If you smell smoke, call 911 and get the horses out. Matheus said he'd found a cigarette in the arena. Was it okay to smoke there? No, not okay. Charlie volunteered that a couple of the parents sometimes smoked.

"We'll put up signs," I said, "and make sure everyone knows the rules."

For a few hours I felt better; I was protecting Mercury. Then I thought, Who was I kidding? A burglar wasn't going to obey a No Smoking sign.

The next afternoon Claudia asked if I could take Helen to physiotherapy, while she met with a prospective boarder. It was the first hint she'd given that we were still friends. As I was driving to their house I suddenly wondered if Helen might have guessed about Claudia's pregnancy. What would I say if she asked? But her first question, when she and her walker were safely stowed in the car, was, "How's that horse of yours?"

I told her we were working on spread jumps. Mercury could clear almost anything, but he didn't like extending himself. I was worried about our training schedule: that I was pushing him too hard in some areas, not enough in others.

"Maybe you should consult Garth," she said. "He's giving master classes in New Hampshire for the next couple of months."

Garth was a legendary teacher in our riding circles. At once I was sure he could solve my problems. "That's a great idea," I said. "I'll phone tomorrow."

A truck passed us, spraying grit. Little pieces pinged against the hood as I asked Helen if she had ever thought of competing outside New England.

"I wanted to, but the best-laid plans . . ." She'd been about to qualify for the regionals when she got pregnant. She didn't ride for three months and then miscarried. "It caused a lot of grief with my husband. He couldn't help blaming the horses, and when I started riding again, it was different. I still loved it, but I didn't have that drive. The first time I saw you ride, I knew you did. Of course Claudia's green-eyed about Mercury."

"Green-eyed?" For a moment I didn't recognize the expression.

"Jealous," said Helen. "She thinks all your attention goes to him these days."

Claudia had said the same thing. But now I understood her comment differently. It wasn't just the other horses I was ignoring; it was her. Suddenly her hostility toward Mercury made sense.

"And maybe she's not the only one who's jealous," Helen continued. "She says someone's been breaking into the stables. You need to be careful." Then she told me the old story about the two horses being stolen and the third, her favorite, Snowbird, poisoned.

"Horses bring out the best in people," she said. "And the worst."

After I took her home, I stopped at Paddy's Lunch. We'd talked about going there for years. What I must do, I thought as I sipped a margarita, was make Mercury disappear among the other horses. I would ride only in the early morning; I would groom him secretly; I would buy his vitamins and bandages myself. At the same time I would redouble my efforts to make sure the other horses were taken care of, the bills paid, the barn clean, the students and owners happy. And I must watch over Claudia, be there for her when Rick bolted. She would have ample evidence of my devotion.

While I drank a second margarita, I turned over the paper placemat and wrote a list: "Students, Owners, Parents, Deliverymen, Strangers." Names, or sometimes descriptions—"the hay man, the wood shavings man"—soon filled the mat. Not one of the people I'd listed seemed likely to drive out to the stables at night, drag a ladder over to the hayloft, and clamber inside to visit Mercury. The risks were too great, the rewards too small. The only person crazy enough to do such a thing was drinking margaritas at Paddy's Lunch.

ALMOST EVERY DAY THERE was more snow. I shoveled out my car and drove to the stables, and shoveled some more and directed Matheus to use the snow blower. We cleared the paddocks for our own horses, but most of the owners wanted their horses kept indoors. Claudia exercised them on the lunge line, and I rode as many as I could. It was too cold to train Mercury properly, but I came to the stables half an hour early each day to ride and groom him. And I started going to New Hampshire to watch Garth teach his master classes.

In all the busyness I refused several invitations from Hilary.

Then late one afternoon the farrier canceled, and I called to see if she was free. "Can you come here?" she said.

I hadn't been to her house before. In the kitchen she introduced me to a dainty calico cat called Teacup. Then she showed me around. Each room was painted in warm, surprising colors, the furniture carefully chosen, the lamps and rugs glowing. The whole effect made me want to sit down and never leave. Later, when you visited Jack there, you said the same thing.

"It's my only skill," Hilary said. "I can look at a room and see how to make it nicer."

We settled in the living room, and I told her about our plans for your father's anniversary, how I hoped your mood would lift once the day was passed.

"Anniversaries are hard," she said. "Last Tuesday was Michael's birthday. I suddenly found myself wondering if maybe he was the way he was because of Jessie."

"What do you mean," I asked, "'the way he was'?"

She gazed toward the empty fireplace. "This will sound strange," she said, "but for years the news about my sister was mixed up with my abortion. It was only after I split up with Franklin that I realized she was Michael's sister too. I phoned to ask if he remembered her. He said yes, Jessie was great. She was always smiling, and she made a rumbling sound, like pigeons cooing. When she learned to walk, she came into his room in the morning and pressed her face against his. I asked what happened when she died. 'What do you think happened?' he said. 'She died, and then she was dead.' I asked if he understood she might die. There was a long pause. Then he laughed and said, 'Who ever understands someone's going to die?'"

I thought of you, still waiting for the Simurg. "What do you mean," I asked again, "'the way Michael was'?"

At critical moments a horse sometimes simultaneously shrinks and gathers itself. Hilary sank briefly into the sofa, and reemerged to say that defending Michael was a lifelong habit. Since she was nine or ten, he'd been in trouble. He was hopeless with money, rude to employers, took too many drugs. It wasn't just bad luck that he was forty-four and living in his boyhood bedroom.

I reminded her of what she'd said on Christmas Eve: perhaps his fall wasn't an accident.

"I'm afraid that was your Chianti talking." She tilted her glass mockingly. "The autopsy showed he was high as a kite. But the weird thing was, he seemed to have a premonition. Three days before, he phoned me and talked about this scene in *Anna Karenina*. The hero is racing his beloved mare. They're in the lead. Then, at one of the jumps, he shifts in the saddle, and the mare falls and is killed. Of course in Michael's case it was the other way round."

She went to get more wine. I stared at the oil painting over the mantelpiece, blues running into blues, thinking how strange it would be if I inherited both Michael's horse and his enemies. After the second break-in I had almost told Hilary that someone was interested in Mercury. Now, more than ever, I was glad I hadn't. When she returned, I said I'd entered him for a couple of shows in late March. We would see how he responded to crowds and competition.

Hilary's lips parted, she was about to speak, when the door opened. "Are we ever having dinner?" Diane said.

7

EVERYTHING MIGHT STILL HAVE been all right if Tiffany hadn't taken me up on my offer. I was helping Marcus draw a map of sub-Saharan Africa when she phoned to ask if she could come to the stables on Saturday. Her whispery voice made me picture her alone in a small apartment, crowded with rickety furniture.

"We'd be glad of the help," I said. "Can you be there at seven?"

"I can't get there on my own," she said, even more whispery.

I felt blindingly stupid—did I think she lived in a family of doting chauffeurs? I said I'd pick her up, six thirty sharp. After I hung up, Marcus asked what was wrong.

"I just agreed to do something that's going to make Claudia mad." He studied me with his blue eyes—your blue, not mine—while I described the problem. Tiffany was a little older than him, she loved horses like he loved swimming, but her parents couldn't afford lessons, and now her dad was in prison. "So," I said, "I invited her to ride."

"I think that was a good thing to do, Mom. I'd hate you or Dad to be in prison." There was, at the time, no irony in his comment.

"So what should I say to Claudia?"

"Tell her what you told me. If she's mad, let her tell the girl she can't come."

I held out my phone. He dialed Claudia's number. When she answered, I confessed my invitation and started to apologize. But she was laughing. "I could never resist a horse-crazy teenager," she said. "We'll just have to be sure she doesn't fall."

I thanked her and leaped across the room to hug Marcus. "Do you promise you'll keep giving me advice, even when you grow up and get all confused?"

"My pleasure." He made a little bow. "Why will I get confused?"

"It happens to grown-ups. We want too many things, and it makes our lives complicated."

"Mom, everyone wants too many things. You sounded happy when you spoke to Claudia."

"I was," I said. Only as her anger began to recede did I grasp the toll it had taken.

That Saturday when Tiffany stepped into my headlights, I had a moment of panic—she was not much taller than Trina—but before I could change my mind, she and her backpack were in the car. I asked if she had boots, gloves, food, drink.

"Yes, I made a list."

"And your mom knows where you are?" I persisted.

"Like she gives a crap."

Go back upstairs, I wanted to say. *Go back to sleep.* But there she was, sitting next to me, a small, determined figure. Instead I turned on the radio and pulled out into the street. Neither of us spoke until we were driving up the hill between the empty paddocks. Then she said, "It's so strange not to see any horses."

"They're all inside. That's why we need help exercising them.

How did your dad get a gun in New Hampshire?" I had no idea I was going to ask the question.

"The usual way. He gave someone money to buy it for him."

Inside the barn I headed to the lockers. All sixteen doors were wide open, as if they'd been ransacked. Had they been that way the night before? I couldn't remember. Like so many things at the stables, I passed them dozens of times a day without seeing them. As Tiffany put her possessions away, I looked up and down the corridor. Had that wheelbarrow been there? Had someone left the door of the tack room ajar?

"Is something wrong?" Tiffany said. Like Trina, she was very sensitive to adult moods.

I said I always worried when so many horses were shut in for the night. If one started banging up his stall, the others might panic. But here was Mercury, his usual eager self, and no sign of nocturnal visitors. We left him in the corridor and went to get Sir Pericles. When Tiffany tried to hug him, his lips pulled back. Then, recognizing affection, he nickered. In the arena she at first posted stiffly but soon found her seat. Afterward, as we rubbed down the horses, she asked if I'd ever seen *National Velvet*.

"I bet Mercury could win a big show," she said.

"I do too." I was thinking how odd it was that this girl I hardly knew should be the one, the only one, to guess my heart's desire when Matheus showed up.

As usual Saturday was busy with owners and lessons. Not until lunchtime did I have a chance to ask Claudia about the lockers. She said lost-and-found was overflowing. If the doors were left open, she thought, people would be less likely to forget stuff. Walking back to the arena, I noticed the modest sign above the lockers: "Please leave doors open. Thank you!" Later

I stopped at Mercury's stall and left my own sign. I looped two halter ropes, one brown, one black, around the first bars of the door and the stall. They wouldn't stop a visitor, but they would betray him. Then I took a photograph so I wouldn't spook myself by misremembering.

That night, after you were in bed, I updated my spreadsheet: Tiffany, two new riders, an owner's friend, a student's father. Each evening when I got home I marked down everyone I'd seen at the stables that day. If there was another break-in, I would have a complete list of suspects. I remembered Rick saying, "Get a gun." I remembered summer camp and the thrill of hitting three clay pigeons in a row. The next morning the ropes were as I had left them.

8

I started going to the library to use a computer so you wouldn't stumble on my searches. Rick, Tiffany, Helen, even Michael, each had nudged me in this direction, but nothing would have happened without the Internet. I could look up one thing; I could look up another; I didn't have to admit exactly what I was thinking. Buying a gun in Massachusetts required waiting several weeks for a license which required a background check which required . . . But in New Hampshire things were easier. I schemed, got prices and addresses, and finally—you and Claudia had both grown accustomed to my visiting Garth's classes in New Hampshire—I had a plan.

The forecast that day was for no precipitation, upper twenties, but as I exercised the horses, snow started to fall. Each time I went between the arena and the barn, the flakes were hurtling down thicker, faster. But by the end of the first lesson the snow was dwindling and the clouds were clearing. When Claudia arrived, she said, "Shouldn't you be on the road?"

"I was worrying about the weather." I gazed at her glowing face, hoping she would stop me.

"The forecast is good," she said. "Come back and teach us everything you learn."

"Are you sure?"

"Absolutely. We only have four lessons scheduled today."

I drove away before I lost my nerve. At the bottom of the road, I got out my list of addresses and maps. On the drive north I tried to listen to the radio, tried not to think about what I was planning to do. A few weeks earlier you had mentioned a patient who had a shadow inside her head. That morning I'd have liked a shadow between me and my plan.

The first address turned out to be a busy intersection. The store sat alone in a parking lot. A large sign read "Guns." Another asked, "Are You Ready for Hunting Season?" When the light changed, I kept going.

The second address, seven miles away, was a mall with a liquor store, a shoe store, a diner, and a hair salon. I parked outside the shoe store: a nice, innocent alibi. In the mirror I combed my hair, put on makeup. There was nothing to be done about my clothes, but just before I got out of the car, I remembered my wedding ring. As I slipped it into the zippered pocket of my jacket, I saw how dull the gold had grown, all that shoveling. In my other pocket were the stiff new bills I'd collected from the ATM.

The diner was a daytime cousin of Paddy's Lunch: a narrow, L-shaped room, the windows streaming with condensation. Almost all the tables were full. I took a seat at the counter between two men and ordered a second breakfast. The man on my left was deep in conversation with the woman to his left. When the coffee came, I asked the man on my right for the cream.

"Cold enough for you?" he said. The metal jug looked very small in his fat fingers.

"I'd no idea it could be so cold in New Hampshire."

He edged his stool around to examine the woman who would utter this stupidity. At dinner one night you explained that although some people's eyes look much bigger than others', they actually differ by only a few millimeters. This man's eyes were like small, dull pebbles. He stared at me for several seconds and swiveled back to his food. A few minutes later, he asked for the bill.

Almost immediately another man, much younger, sat down. While he unzipped his jacket, the waitress brought him coffee. I passed back the metal jug. He added a few drops of cream, and when he saw me noticing, said, "I promised my mom to start putting cream in my coffee. She thinks it'll make me less jittery."

"Is it working?"

"Maybe, but I like being jittery. I haven't seen you here before."

It was an observation, not a line. I told him I was from Michigan. I'd come to help my sister with her kids. He said he'd been fishing in the UP. Beautiful country. You could walk all day and not see a soul. As he spoke, I glimpsed the darkness of a missing molar. I asked if he came from around here, and got the answer I wanted: New Hampshire born and bred.

The waitress brought my eggs and his special and flourished the coffeepot. "Any more for you, Chance?"

As she circled on to another customer, I asked if Chance was his real name.

"Wild, isn't it? It's an old family name on my mom's side."

"I'm Jane." His plate was still half full, but he was eating swiftly. "Can I ask you a strange question?" I launched into part two of my story. My sister had asked me to buy her a gun, but I'd no idea how things worked in New Hampshire. Buying a gun in other places, I tried to suggest, was no problem. He asked why she couldn't buy her own gun, and I said the rug rats kept her so busy she could barely buy a gallon of milk.

"Well, it's pretty easy in these parts. All that live-free crap. You just need money and a driver's license."

I said I had both, but my license was for Michigan. If I couldn't find a job here, I might have to go back. Chance's plate was nearly empty. My boss in New York used to claim the key to successful negotiation was knowing when to shut up. I ate my last slice of toast in silence.

"So your sister," he said, "does she know anything about guns?"

Once again I was glad I'd rehearsed. She used to have one. Then she got rid of it because of the kids. But last month a friend of hers was home alone when a man shot her dog and broke into her house. My sister didn't want to feel scared every time there was a noise in the night.

"Maybe she shouldn't live in the country," Chance said.

"She shouldn't, but that's where her husband left her."

The waitress set down our bills, V'd to avoid the damp counter. We both swung round on our stools. For the first time I saw him full face. His eyes were the faded blue of Marcus's bathing suit after six months of chlorine. A faint scar zigzagged his jaw.

"So, Jane, do you by any chance have the money for a purchase on you right now?"

"I do."

He gave a little smile. "So here's what I suggest. We go outside and get in my truck, and you give me the money. Then you watch me walk over to the conveniently located gun shop, and hope that I pass the security check. You can put your wedding ring back on while you wait."

You'll be glad to know I blushed.

We did just what he said. I handed him $600. Alone in his very clean truck, I turned up the heat and thought this was the stupidest thing I'd ever done. What if Chance absconded with my money? Or had me arrested? But he didn't seem the kind of person who leapt to dial 911. I sat there, looking at my watch, looking at the snow, remembering Mercury that morning clearing a five-foot spread.

After nearly thirty minutes, the driver's-side door opened. He climbed in, holding an incongruous brown paper bag. "Here you go," he said. "One Smith and Wesson, M&P Shield, 9mm, plus ammo. I kept the change."

As soon as I took the bag, I felt the weight. At the bottom lay a black gun and a small box. I reached in and lifted out the gun. Over and over in movies, on TV, in the holsters of policemen, I'd seen guns, but I'd never held a handgun. At camp, when we shot clay pigeons, we had used shotguns. Here was an object, unmistakably heavy, that changed everything.

"Let me give you some advice." Beneath his hat only the final curve of his earlobe was visible. "Go to a range and learn to shoot. Never leave a gun loaded. Never leave it anywhere unlocked. Never use it except as a very last resort. If I hear on the news that a woman from Michigan called 'Jane,' with a broken finger, has had some kind of accident with a firearm, I'll be so darned mad you won't know what's hit you. Now beat it. I have to get to work."

I opened the door and jumped down onto the dirty snow. Chance reversed out of the parking slot and headed for the exit. I walked over to my car, with its incriminating Massachusetts plates. I pictured him passing it on his way to the gun shop: one more piece of evidence against "Jane." I put the bag on the passenger seat. Then I realized I couldn't drive around with a gun on the seat beside me. I got out again and put the bag in the trunk, under the jumper cables and the extra horse blanket. All the way to the stables I kept thinking, I am a person who owns a gun, and when I walked into the arena and took a seat in the viewing area, I kept waiting for someone to notice. Surely the woman sitting on the bench next to me would sense my new possession; surely the older man who'd come to watch his daughter ride would guess. But when they talked, it was to exclaim about the weather, to remark on my driving so far, to comment on one horse's steep shoulders, another's gait.

Afterward, when I drove home and saw the Welcome to Massachusetts sign, I thought, Now I'm a criminal. But no police car flashed me down. No motorist cut me off.

9

Do you remember how Trina used to believe five ghosts shared our house? Month after month she drew pictures of Fred, Cowboy, Betty, Green Light, and Skirty Mom, and told us what they were doing. Fred was sweeping the floor; Betty was making pancakes. Then one day, when I asked about them, she frowned and said, "Oh, they don't live here anymore." I thought that might happen with the gun; it would simply disappear. The next morning I woke in the dark, dressed, made my lunch, and drove to the stables, all the time telling myself nothing had changed. I parked in my usual place. As I approached the barn, the security lights came on; a horse neighed. I stopped, I turned, I went back, I opened the trunk of my car.

Yes, things had changed.

In the barn the horses were quiet. The ropes I had looped around the bars of Mercury's stall were untouched. I gave him a quick brush, saddled him, and led him past the other horses, across the yard, and into the arena. I rode him without stirrups for ten minutes. Then we did lateral work, something Garth recommended, which made him flick his ears. He cheered up when we approached the jumps. I reminded him to keep his hindquarters under him, myself to sit up in the saddle.

Riding Mercury, I never looked at my watch. Everything

was here, now, his stride, my seat, his mouth, my hands. He was my way to escape time. I think surgery used to be yours. Perhaps tennis is now. But we never escape for long. Much too soon the sparrows who lived in the rafters began to chirp, calling me to my duties.

The following week I went back to New Hampshire to watch another of Garth's classes. For him the ideal was a rounded frame where the horse's energy appears to arc up from his hindquarters, over his back, and into the rider's softly containing hands. When he mounted even the most ragged animal, it began to move more smoothly. Garth was paying so much attention to the horse, the horse couldn't not pay attention to him. And he was generous with his praise. "Tell her she's done well," he said. "Let him know he's doing good." The channels of communication were always open. "We're all students," he said.

After the class, I followed Chance's advice. I parked as far from the entrance to the shooting range as possible, kept on my sunglasses and hat. In my daily life, apart from Rick, I was surrounded by people—friends, parents, students, you—who didn't own a gun, who spoke with horror of Binghamton and Blacksburg and Fort Hood. But as soon as I stepped through the doors of the range, I became part of another tribe, a tribe for whom gun ownership was the norm. I was ready to describe my imaginary sister and her lonely house, but no one expected an explanation. The only question was why it had taken me so long to join them.

The boy who set me up with a target and hearing protectors asked what I was firing.

"Nice," he said when I handed him the gun. He made me practice pulling the trigger, showed me how to load the magazine. "Don't take the safety off until you're ready to shoot," he advised, "and take your time. You don't get better going bang, bang, bang."

I slipped on the hearing protectors and stared at the target. I'd heard of ranges that used silhouettes of animals or, worse, people, but that first day even the dark circles of the traditional target looked menacing. I raised the gun, sighted along the barrel, and squeezed my finger. A white tear appeared in the outermost circle. I fired again. When at last a bullet pierced the bull's-eye, I found myself exclaiming, "Yes!"

On my second visit to the range I finished my session at the same time as a tall, gray-haired woman. As we headed to the exit she saw me notice the broccoli sticking out of her bag.

"Back to the kitchen sink," she said. "Mustn't keep hubby waiting."

"Does he mind you coming here?"

"I tell him it's cheaper than Keno." She winked. "What about yours?"

I said I hadn't told you, and she said, "Uh-oh. Wife on the rampage."

She was opening the door of a grimy black car when I asked where she kept her gun.

"In the hall closet," she said briskly. "Locked in George's old tackle box. They go on and on about gun safety, but as long as it isn't loaded, what's the problem? Nothing magical about a gun."

As I drove home I thought about her easy words: nothing magical about a gun. You and I, and everyone we knew, thought there was. Guns changed people; they made people do things they'd never normally do. From that first evening, I'd been moving it from place to place. I kept it in a locked box, which I moved from our garage to the back of the filing cabinet at the stables. I hid it in the hayloft for a night and in the back shed for twenty minutes. Now I decided to leave the gun where it was, in the trunk of the car, separate from the ammunition. Two blocks from our house I pulled over between streetlights. I opened the locked box and put the ammunition at the bottom of a bag of clothes destined for Goodwill, the gun at the bottom of another bag full of shoes. I was closing the trunk when a car pulled up.

The police, I thought, my brain already jostling with half a dozen lies.

Then Anne rolled down her window. "Everything okay?"

"Fine. There was a bottle loose in the trunk. It was driving me nuts, rolling around."

I followed her home, trying to breathe as my Pilates instructor urged, from the diaphragm.

Later that evening I made an excuse to go to the stables. When I showed Mercury the gun, he bent to sniff, nostrils flaring.

"I got this because of you," I told him. "Michael couldn't protect you, but I can."

He gave a gentle snort—not something to eat—and turned away. Next month we would compete in our first show. Start small, I told myself. Find out his weak points. Don't ruin him like you did Nutmeg.

10

Claudia claimed I was different. So did the children. We were watching a nature show when Trina pointed at a cheetah bounding across the screen. "That's you, Mom." And Marcus said he wondered if my brain was bigger since I cut my hair. But it wasn't the gun that changed me; it was Mercury. What the gun changed was the balance of power.

Do you remember that Sunday Marcus and Trina came home from their play dates, demanding hot chocolate? We were low on milk, and I drove to the 7-Eleven. The parking lot was empty except for a truck in one corner and a low rider, throbbing with music, in another. As I walked across the dirty snow, I remembered all the evenings in Ann Arbor I'd spent in parked cars, drinking, smoking a joint, always sure that somewhere nearby more sophisticated people were having more fun.

I was retracing my steps, a jug of milk in each hand, when the music stopped and the doors of the low rider opened. Two men, their faces hidden by hoods, got out and started walking toward the store, bracketing me. I could hear their footsteps on the packed ice. I pictured them punching me in the face, kicking me in the kidneys, not knowing I had only the change from $20. Then I remembered: I wasn't at their mercy. I pressed the key ring. The car lights flashed. But before I could dash for the trunk, the man on my left spoke.

"Doing the milk run?" he said.

At home you were settling Nabokov for the night. As I made the hot chocolate, I described my encounter. "I'm getting paranoid," I said, "thinking every guy who drives a rackety car is a thug. I told you we'd become Republicans if we lived in the suburbs."

You looked up from straightening Nabokov's cover. "Women have to be careful," you said. "You never did find out who broke into the stables."

Your eyebrows rose above your glasses, your lips tightened in concern. You understood, I thought: the stables were no longer safe. As I poured the hot chocolate, I imagined showing you the gun, offering it to you on my outstretched palm, the way I had to Mercury. But then all I could hear was you lecturing me, telling me to take it to the police.

A few days later I was alone at the stables at dusk, checking the water buckets, when I heard footsteps. A man's step, but not Matheus's; this person was walking quietly, stealthily. I crouched down in the stall, trying not to rustle the straw. What good did the gun do, shut in the trunk of my car? I was about to make a run for the back door when a voice called, "Claudia."

In the corridor I found Rick wearing a Davy Crockett hat and a down jacket over his suit. He was halted mid-stride, as startled by my presence as I was by his. "Hi," he said. "I was looking for Claudia. She isn't answering her phone."

"She's gone home for the day. Maybe she's taking a nap. How are you?"

He swung his briefcase. "I've seen better days. How's Mercury the magnificent?"

"Great, though he could do with more exercise."

"Well, I'll take my chances and see if she's receiving visitors."

He stood there, his briefcase motionless, waiting for me to say something, but whatever was going to happen next could only be played out between him and Claudia. I walked over and put my arms around him. Through our bulky jackets something passed between us, a little flash. He was trying to leave behind the scared boy from Nebraska, and I was wishing him Godspeed.

I walked him to his car and watched him drive away. In the almost darkness my eyes played tricks. Something moved in the manure pile, someone slipped between the horse trailers. I went to my car, opened the trunk, and reached in among the shoes. I put the gun in the inside pocket of my jacket, ammunition in the other pocket. The two would never touch, but I felt safer. What had I spent $600 for, if not to feel that way?

I finished checking the stalls at top speed. I was almost certain Claudia was at home, almost certain this would be the night she told Rick. Christmas was past; his sons had returned to their lives; her pregnancy could no longer be concealed. Silently I said to Rick what I kept saying to myself. Don't give up on yourself. Don't settle for the second-rate.

At home I helped Trina with math and Marcus with English and fed Nabokov peanuts and made broccoli surprise and apple crisp. After supper I insisted we play Scrabble, and when the children went to bed, I persuaded you to watch a film. Anything to get through these hours.

You were already in bed and I was brushing my teeth when I remembered the gun still in my jacket pocket, and my jacket in its usual place, on the hook nearest the back door. Quickly I rinsed my toothbrush and stepped into the bedroom.

"I've left something—," I started to say.

But, from the bed, you held out your arms. Your first invitation in weeks. How could I refuse?

11

THE NEXT MORNING THE gun was back in the trunk, and Mercury and I were carving out figure eights, when the door of the arena opened. A figure came running toward us. Mercury reared, and Claudia came to a standstill. As I struggled to keep my seat, I thought, Rick's ditched her; she's going to be a single mother. Mercury too seemed to sense bad news; he kept rearing and sidestepping. At last I got him settled, all four hooves on the ground. I jumped down and hurried toward Claudia. She was talking and sobbing, her words echoing in the empty arena.

"He's going to move in with me. We're going to have a daughter."

Tears rose in my own eyes. I wrapped my arms around her.

"I couldn't wait to tell you," she said. "I'm sorry I startled Mercury."

I put him back in his stall and met her in the office. She showed me a photograph of the sonogram. "Our daughter," she said. "Here's her head"—she indicated a dark mass in the galaxy—"and her foot."

"I'm so happy for you."

"And you're floored." She laughed. "You never thought he'd do it. Nor did I. If I had three sons, a circle of friends, a wife, a nice house, I'm not sure I'd give them all up. But that's what

I asked him to do. When I showed him the sonogram, I said, Your daughter needs you. Your sons had you while they were growing up; your daughter deserves the same. Viv, he couldn't stop smiling. All the things I've been afraid of—he'd be scared, or angry—none of them happened. He said I'd been so distant, he was sure I was planning to break up with him."

"I'm so happy," I said again. "Have you told Helen?"

The thought of her alone in her large house gave me a pang, but Claudia said Helen was thrilled: she wasn't planning to move out. With alimony, Rick would need to economize, and there was plenty of room for the three of them, the four of them. "I want to thank you," she added.

"Thank me?"

"Rick said he talked to you the day he came to photograph Mercury. You were very helpful."

Suddenly I had the awful thought: What if he didn't keep his word? What if this was only the start of still more waiting? Hesitantly I asked if he had a plan.

"This is what's so amazing." All her giddiness was abruptly gone. "Amazing and awful. After we talked, last night he drove straight home and told Nan he was moving out. Then he packed a suitcase and went to the Holiday Inn. And he phoned each of his kids."

"He really did it." The impossible was happening with impossible speed.

The snowy fields were starting to glow. Claudia and I were both silent, gazing at this view we knew so well: our paddocks, the land dipping down to the road, the hills fringed with trees rising beyond.

"I'm almost frightened," she said quietly. "I have Rick, you, Helen, the stables. I have a family." She knocked the table. "I have a home."

"You deserve them," I said, "more than anyone I know."

She clasped her hands to her chest as if to hold on to all the things she'd just named. "But that's not how the world works. We don't necessarily get what we deserve. I worry Rick never told Nan how he felt. That from one day to the next her perfect marriage was a train wreck. And it's my fault. He wouldn't have left her without me. Without our daughter."

"Maybe she'll meet someone at her church," I said. "Maybe she'll be remarried in six months." Then I asked if I could tell you about Rick and the baby, and she said yes. She wanted all her close friends to know.

On my way to the tack room I stopped at Mercury's stall. "Everything will be easier now," I told him. Fate, once again, was sending me a message. If Claudia could change, if Rick could change, then I could change. I could become the champion I'd dreamed about being for so many years, and given up on for so many more.

THAT NIGHT AT DINNER I broke the news about Claudia and Rick and the baby. I was happy to have one less secret, happy to celebrate Claudia's happiness. We all clapped and raised our glasses. But later, when the kids were in bed, you and I had an oddly stiff conversation.

"It never occurred to me," you said, "that she wanted children."

I couldn't see your face—you were at the computer—but you sounded as if I were somehow to blame for this misunderstanding. "How can you know what people want when they can't have it?" I said. "She didn't want them in her twenties. Then she wanted them more and more."

I put my hand on your shoulder. You clicked the mouse. "You were like that too, weren't you?" you said.

"Until I met you."

It was a cornerstone of our romance: you had made me want children. Now, even as I squeezed your shoulder, you kept clicking the mouse, opening various folders, filling the screen with spreadsheets.

12

I NEVER DID TELL YOU what happened with Nutmeg. After my first year at Yale I came home for the summer and, to my mother's dismay, got a job at the stables. "How is this going to help your résumé?" she asked. But I had a different résumé in mind. I was going to train Nutmeg and enter him in a three-day event in early August. We didn't have to win first prize, but if we placed, it would be a sign. After I graduated, I'd figure out how to ride full-time.

Claudia was studying in Spain that summer, and I had no one to talk to about my training program. Nutmeg was very flexible, good at dressage, and a bold jumper with plenty of stamina, but he was erratic. The owners of the stables, Elsa and Harry, gave me pointers—several times Elsa warned me not to ride him too hard—but mostly I worked on my own. I read books about champions, watched films, kept notes on each day's training. We won rosettes in a couple of small dressage events; we placed in show jumping, Nutmeg learned to go into a trailer and grew used to crowds. I was training myself too. In the evenings, when it was cooler, I went running. My friends complained they never saw me.

The three-day event was thirty miles from Ann Arbor. The first day Nutmeg and I were on the road by five. Just outside town a rabbit darted in front of the truck. I remember the scene so clearly. I didn't want to hit it, but I didn't want to brake in case Nutmeg lost his footing. I was still hesitating when, at the last second, the rabbit swerved to safety. From then on, everything flowed. I found a place under a tree to park the trailer. Nutmeg wasn't spooked by the journey, and he stood quietly while I braided his mane and brushed his tail. We rode twelfth, and placed first. Riding him into the arena to collect the rosette was one of the great moments of my life. Elsa had said, more than once, that events are won on dressage. Driving back to the stables, I wondered if there was any way I could bring Nutmeg to New Haven.

The next day was the cross-country. I'd worked hard at the precision of dressage, but this was what I loved, galloping at top speed, jumping the different kinds of jumps. It had rained in the night, and the course was sloppy, but Nutmeg's boldness served him well. Mine too. We were both covered in mud as we crossed the finish line with a clear round and no penalties. I rubbed him down, singing his praises. Next day's stadium jumping seemed like child's play. Victory was so close I could taste it.

Back at the stables, Elsa was waiting. "Hurrah for you," she said when I told her about the cross-country, but as I backed Nutmeg out of the trailer, her eyes narrowed. "Stand still," she said. She ran her hands up and down his legs. His near foreleg was hot. Maybe he'd fractured the pastern.

"But he's not lame," I protested. "He cleared every jump."

"Hopefully I'm wrong. Cold-hose his leg tonight, and see how he is in the morning."

I kept protesting. How could this have happened? I had taken the best possible care of him.

Elsa gave a pinched smile. "It's probably been coming on for a while," she said. "You've been training him awfully hard."

I ran cold water over his leg for half an hour, bandaged it, and sprinkled bute into his grain. That night I hardly slept. In the last few weeks Nutmeg had had a couple of off days, but there'd always been a reason; he was stiff from the previous day's training; he'd hit a rail. Now I remembered those days, and I remembered the hill where he'd stumbled in the mud and I had urged him on. Perhaps it was then that he had hurt himself? Or at the last jump, where he'd taken off awkwardly and landed hard.

I was back at the stables at 4:00 a.m. His pastern was cool to the touch. It was nothing, I told myself; a passing tenderness, a little bump. I drove north as if he were made of glass. I mustn't push him, I told myself. Better to be a few seconds slower than to knock down a rail.

But when I led him out of the trailer in broad daylight, he was walking gingerly. I ran cold water over the leg again. I borrowed a bandage. If it hadn't been illegal, so close to the event, I would have given him more bute. I only needed to ride him for ten minutes.

"What's up with your horse?" the woman in the next trailer asked.

"He bumped himself," I said. "He'll be fine."

By 9:00 a.m. there was no doubt: Nutmeg was lame. I tortured myself by watching the jumping—we would have won easily—and spent the rest of the day loitering around the show. I brought Nutmeg back after dark and left a note for Elsa: "I quit." If I saw her, I knew I'd start yelling. Why hadn't she saved me from overtraining Nutmeg? Spelled out the dangers? We'd been so close. I'd rather we'd fallen at a jump, gone down in a blaze of glory, than this pathetic mishap.

The next day I got a job at the photocopy center. I spent the last weeks of August running machines and flirting with students. The next summer I followed Claudia's example and went to Spain. I was in a library in Barcelona when an e-mail came from Elsa. "We put Nutmeg to sleep yesterday," she wrote. The fracture in his pastern had worsened until they'd had no choice. "I'm sure you weren't to blame," she added, which could only mean I was.

For more than a dozen years I kept my failed ambitions in a tightly sealed box, like your box of Robert's letters. But when we moved out of Boston and I started working at Windy Hill, the box began to open. I gave up on becoming a CEO and once again pictured myself training horses, winning competitions.

13

THE WEATHER GREW A little warmer, the days a little longer. I began to train Mercury in earnest. He learned quickly
but was easily bored. I had to vary our routines, to surprise
him with different challenges. More than six weeks had passed
without a break-in, but I didn't believe that the intruder had
lost interest. I wished I could follow Michael's example and
sleep at the stables. On several occasions I came home for dinner and made up an excuse to return: I'd forgotten to check
the office radiator, a horse needed medicine. One evening I
told you I was going to Pilates and drove to the stables. I sat in
my car, holding the gun, watching until I was sure everything
was safe.

The week after Claudia's announcement, I took Mercury to
New Hampshire. I was determined not to repeat my mistakes,
to get the best advice about training him. Garth was just finish-
ing another lesson when we came into the arena. Mercury was
cold from the journey, and jumpy. Horse trailers had always
meant huge changes in his life: Kentucky to Ontario, Ontario
to Massachusetts. Perhaps he thought he was moving again? I
stroked his neck. "I'm right here," I said. At the far end of the
arena we started cantering.

"So this is the horse you've been telling me about."

Garth was walking toward us. I muffed the change of leads, jerked the reins. Mercury, too, was distracted and kept looking at this strange man. And Garth, who normally kept up a stream of advice, said nothing, although I knew he saw every misstep. Then Mercury stumbled, and I pulled myself together. I shifted my grip on the reins, patted his neck.

"Let him go," Garth called. "Circle the arena."

I lost count of how often we passed the mounting block before Garth said, "Now you're ready to listen to each other. Do a figure eight. Nice tight circles."

From then on he directed me and I directed Mercury, until at last he called, "Let's talk about balance and position in the halt." For ten minutes he described how my balance affected Mercury's. "Can you feel it?" he kept saying. "Can you feel the difference?"

I couldn't. And then I could. My commands were flowing into Mercury, and he was moving with a new precision. When Garth told us to stop, I was suddenly aware of the people in the viewing area. We had never had an audience before.

"Get down," he said. "I want to show you something."

In an instant he was in the saddle. "Your hands and your legs are only part of the picture," he said. "What you want is for your whole body, starting at the top, to be in control." Inch by inch he demonstrated how he aligned himself with Mercury. Then he let Mercury walk forward, his hindquarters squarely under him, his stride long and fluid.

"You're almost there," he said, "but getting beyond almost means watching yourself every minute. We all learn to ride in a less than ideal way, on a less than ideal horse."

Sometimes at the end of a lesson a student asks me if she's getting better. She's embarrassed, almost ashamed, but she has to know. Now I couldn't leave without Garth offering some confirmation. "Should I book another lesson?" I said.

He swung himself down from the saddle and stood, one hand resting on Mercury's withers. "If you don't," he said, "I'll hunt you down. People often make their horses sound like the second coming. I've learned to be a tad skeptical. But you underplayed this one. He's a great horse and a quick learner. I don't know what you have in mind, but if you're asking is he worth the trouble, the answer is a hundred percent yes."

"And me," I persisted, "what about me?"

His broad face broke into a smile. "That's always the question. There are no guarantees but yes, I think you've got what it takes. And he likes you; he listens to you. You won't hold him back."

I held out my hand as if to seal a bargain.

As I led Mercury to the exit, a woman asked what prizes he'd won, another wanted to know his age and pedigree.

All the way back to the stables, I kept repeating Garth's words, and as soon as I had Mercury in his stall, I wrote them down. I longed to share them, but who could I tell? You'd listen politely and say "That's nice." Claudia and Hilary were out of the question. Peggy and Anne, like you, wouldn't understand. Helen was too close to Claudia. The only confidante who came to mind was Charlie. Next time we were alone at the stables, I thought, I'd tell her about Garth. Magic, she would say. Cool. We would sit in the office, looking over the schedule of shows. Perhaps she could be my groom.

I was still fizzing with excitement when I met Hilary that evening. The bar was crowded with young people, but we squeezed into a booth. She ordered a cosmopolitan; I did too. Later I regretted the choice, but at first the sweet, icy drink seemed perfect. She was taking her real estate exam next month.

An older agent at the office was coaching her. "She's like you," she said. "Kind and super efficient."

"I wish," I said, pleased that she saw me that way. I told her how we'd marked Edward's anniversary, and she said it sounded beautiful. Maybe she could do something similar for Michael. Her parents had asked several times what she planned to do with the ashes. She was taking Jack to meet them in April.

"He claims he's a much nicer person since he went blind," she said. "Do you think that's true?"

I said I didn't know; I'd met him only after he stopped being your patient. Then, despite my earlier concerns, my firm belief that I should not confide in Hilary, I found myself describing the master class, what a great teacher Garth was, how he'd praised Mercury.

"You took Mercury to New Hampshire?"

"Yes. Garth couldn't get over how well trained he is." Still in the grip of my day, full of enthusiasm and alcohol, I barreled ahead, describing the shows we planned to enter.

When I fell silent, Hilary said, "I thought our arrangement was I pay to board Mercury, you exercise him. I don't want you driving him here and there, putting him at risk."

For once she was not smiling, not even about to smile. If only I had kept quiet. Carefully I explained. Michael had been training Mercury to compete. He had died training him. All his work would be in vain if Mercury just trotted around a field. I would pay the entry costs. We'd share any prize money. The easy road of our friendship was suddenly slick with black ice. Didn't Hilary remember the conversation we'd had in her living room? Then I recalled how, just as I began to explain my plans, Diane had asked about supper.

"Viv, calm down. All I'm saying is I need to figure out what's best for Mercury. Competing is dangerous. A woman I met suggested I lease him to keep down expenses. If you want to compete, why not ride another horse? You've got plenty to choose from."

Both ideas—her leasing Mercury, my riding another horse— were so preposterous that I couldn't speak. Our server came over to ask how we were doing. I held out my glass. Hilary said no thanks and excused herself. In the empty booth, I sat very still, my mind racing. A month before, when you suggested I get my own horse, I'd been furious. Mercury was the only horse I wanted. Now I understood that you and Claudia had been right: Hilary could take him away on the slightest whim. All these months I'd thought I was doing her a favor: training her beloved horse as her beloved brother would have done. But some stranger had turned everything upside down. I'd been riding Mercury for free. I'd been putting him in danger.

I had almost finished my second cosmo when Hilary returned, smiling. She'd run into a woman who was interested in one of her houses.

"Great," I said. I was desperate to get away, to figure out what to do next. I drained my glass, waved my credit card. We parted with kisses, good wishes to you, love to Jack. The four of us must have dinner soon.

As I reversed out of the parking lot, a voice shouted, "Stop! For Christ's sake, stop!"

I stamped on the brake; the car fishtailed to a halt. I was looking over my shoulder, trying to find the owner of the voice, when a man tapped on the window.

"You nearly hit me." He was about my age, bundled up against the cold, his eyes bright with anger. "You could have killed me."

"I'm so sorry. I didn't see you with all the snow."

"You could have killed me," he repeated. And walked away.

I drove home, still shaking. After the crises of the New Year, I had thought I was finally doing everything right. Taking care of the stables, training Mercury, giving more lessons to pay for extra babysitting, keeping you, and Hilary, and Claudia happy. Now I had nearly run over a man, and Hilary had got it into her head that competing was dangerous.

Do you remember when Jack reenacted Roman battle formations with Marcus and Trina's toy animals? There was one called the quincunx in which gaps were left in the lines so that the first warriors could retreat after throwing their javelins. Another, the Cannae, had a weak center—Jack lined up four sheep—and strong flanks: Marcus and Trina arranged their lions and tigers. The sheep collapsed while the big cats circled the enemy. For years Claudia and I had guarded each other's flanks. But not now.

I was so upset I pulled over to reread Garth's words. I sat there holding the piece of paper, reminding myself that nothing terrible had happened. I had taken too much for granted, but I would explain to Hilary. If she needed to lease Mercury, then of course I'd lease him. And when he won a couple of events, she'd begin to understand that together we could fulfill Michael's dreams.

When I got home, I tried to talk to you. Perhaps you were right, I said, about my arrangements with Hilary. We ought to have something in writing.

"That's a good idea," you said. "Then you'll both know where you stand."

"But what if she won't let Mercury compete?"

I was voicing my worst fear, the thing I couldn't bear to con-
template, that would make a mockery of all my hopes and hard
work, and what did you say? You probably don't remember.

"That is her prerogative," you said.

Do you wonder that I felt alone?

14

Two days later I was approaching Mercury's stall when something brought me to a standstill. For a moment I didn't know what it was. My eyes registered the change before my brain. Then I understood. The ropes I'd draped around the bars of his stall the night before now hung from the saddle post.

Someone had been here. Someone had visited Mercury. I looked up and down the corridor: empty. I looked in his stall: empty save for him. I didn't know what to do first: phone the police, phone Claudia, check the building. He settled the matter by whinnying. I ran my hands down his legs but found no bumps, no hot spots.

"Who was here?" I said. "What did they want?"

I hurried back to the car. With the gun in my pocket, I went around the building, testing windows and doors. In the office I made a cup of tea and tried to calm myself. There was no point in calling the police—I'd already done everything they'd do— and there was no point in telling Claudia. She'd only worry. And besides, how could I tell her without mentioning the ropes? My cunning precaution would strike her as evidence, yet more evidence, of my obsession with Mercury. I clasped the gun until I felt calm enough to return to him.

In the arena I swung myself into the saddle, adjusted the stirrups, and walked him forward. We circled only twice before I urged him into a canter. I gave myself over to his drumming hooves, his steady breath, his muscles moving beneath me, his mane flying. Then we turned toward the jumps. The day before I'd set each one an inch higher. Now Mercury cleared them greedily. And with each jump I felt myself not flying, but even better than that, entirely one with him, each of us exerting every bone, every brain cell, to clear the jump, each of us thrilled as we arced through the air.

Give me more, he was saying.

"I will," I said.

This time I was determined. Nothing, nothing I could prevent, would go wrong. Can you understand? I loved you, Marcus, and Trina, but I loved Mercury too. I was going to ride him to victory. After more than a decade I was going to fulfill the promise of my second life.

PART THREE

DONALD

1

What I have recounted so far is my experience of events more or less as I lived through them, and Viv's account of those same months, which she delivered at our kitchen table during several late-night conversations. Like the three blind men, each encountering different parts of an elephant, each believing he grasped the whole, I had believed myself the possessor of the 20/20 vision my progressives promised. That night at the stables, when I saw Viv holding a gun, I realized my vision was almost as limited as Jack's. There is listening and listening; there is also seeing and seeing. I had missed, or misunderstood, almost everything. Which surely means that, despite everything Viv told me, I am still missing a good deal.

Even as I came to a stop outside the emergency room, Hilary was running towards the door. Jack was deep into shock, moaning softly. Then two orderlies were sliding him out of the car, wheeling him through the waiting room and the swing doors beyond, into a curtained cubicle. A nurse began to cut off his jacket. Briefly the sound of scissors ripping through fabric carried me back to that afternoon at my mother's house when, while I opened the box containing the bookcase, she had urged me to let Viv pursue her dreams. Now Hilary held

Jack's hand. "You're at the hospital," she said. "They're cutting off your clothes. You're going to be fine."

But Jack was far from fine. His skin, always pale, shone white as Mercury's mane; his mouth was screwed tight with pain. For nearly three years I had seldom seen him without his dark glasses. Now they were gone—safe, I learned later, in Hilary's bag—and his eyes were the same disconcerting, vehement blue as they had been the last time I examined them.

Dr. Gaitonde appeared, slight and narrow-shouldered. "So Mr. Brennan got in the way of a bullet," she said, bending over him with her stethoscope. How long ago was he shot? Did we know his blood type? Any heart problems or allergies? I introduced myself as Jack's optometrist, and answered as best I could. She typed my answers into a computer terminal.

"Please," said Hilary, "will he be all right?" In her blue dress, lipstick still gleaming, she looked as if she were on her way to a party.

"I can't promise," said the doctor, "but he's young, his heart is strong, I don't think he's lost too much blood. There's every reason to think he'll make a good recovery. As for his shoulder, we won't know until we see the X-rays."

Jack was wheeled away to radiology.

"So who shot Mr. Brennan?" she asked, still typing. "And why?"

A word once let out of its cage, Jack used to say, quoting one of his beloved ancients, cannot be whistled back. I longed to answer Dr. Gaitonde, to tell the truth, but I was reeling from what I'd seen outside Mercury's stall—the incomprehensible spectacle of Viv, my wife, Marcus and Trina's mother, holding a gun, a gun that she had, only moments before, fired at my friend. Even in my muddled state, I grasped that these words, once released, would fly far and wide.

In the next cubicle a woman's voice rose. "I told them the exterminator can't work with a dog in the building."

I was still gazing at the empty linoleum where Jack's gurney had stood when Hilary spoke. "We don't know what happened. After dinner we went to visit my horse at the stables. We were in his stall, and someone shot Jack. We didn't see who. Mercury, the horse, went berserk. All we were thinking about was getting Jack out of the stall. Getting him here."

"My heavens." Dr. Gaitonde's dark eyebrows arched towards her dark hair. "What were you doing there so late?"

"My wife manages the stables," I offered. "They're owned by her best friend." Two sentences, both true. On the other side of the curtain the woman said that a dog was no different from a baby. And would you leave a baby to the exterminators?

"We'll notify the police immediately," said Dr. Gaitonde. Then she held out Jack's wallet and told Hilary to talk to admissions.

IN RECENT YEARS I have spent many hours at the emergency room with my father, but seldom late on a wintry Saturday night. At least half the people there were, like Hilary and me, waiting for news rather than attention, and more than half were drunk, or stoned, or in some uncertain state. While Hilary dealt with Jack's admission, I sat at the end of a row of chairs and dialed the number of our house. My own voice, sounding calm and reasonable, asked me to leave a message.

"I'm at the hospital with Hilary," I said. "They're calling the police. . . ."

Was Viv standing in our study, listening? Had she driven directly to the police station? Was she even now handing over the gun? At last the machine cut off my silence.

Hilary came back, holding two cans of Diet Coke. She offered me one and said she was worried about Mercury. What if the gunman had injured him too? Under cover of opening the can—that comforting little *pftt* sound—I said I'd just phoned Viv. She would check on him.

Hilary sank into the chair beside me. "I can't believe this. One minute we're in a nice restaurant, eating dinner. The next we're in the emergency room."

I repeated the doctor's reassurances: Jack was young and fit; the bullet hadn't touched any major organs. "What we have to worry about is his shoulder."

"And his spirit." She told me then what I had not known before, namely how frightened Jack had been when he understood he was going blind, how, like my childhood neighbor, he hated never knowing who was in a room, or in the street.

"He always seemed so stoic," I said.

"Jack's proud." Her hair swung back and forth as she described how a few months ago a colleague had failed to meet him for lunch. Jack had eaten alone, but as he was leaving the cafeteria, he heard a familiar voice. "The guy had totally forgotten their meeting," Hilary said, "and was eating with friends at another table. That's Jack's life in a microcosm."

Listening to her, gazing at the worn chairs, I glimpsed the edges of outrageous grief. If Jack x'd, then I would y. Where x was lost the use of his arm, or ended up in a wheelchair, or died, and y was burn down the stables, or banish Viv to Patagonia, or rend my garments and put out my eyes. Beside me Hilary checked her phone, although the only news either of us wanted would come through the doors at the end of the emergency room. I could feel her fidgeting beside me; I could feel myself doing the same. If there had been treadmills instead of chairs, we would have been running, furiously, side by side.

"So what on earth happened?" she said, giving up on the phone. "Someone else was at the stables? They tried to shoot us?"

If I told her what I had seen, then my life, my family, would not be over—nothing so simple as that—but changed almost out of recognition, like the flimsy Coke can I had unthinkingly, crumpled in my fist. "Maybe someone"—I was groping from one word to the next—"was trying to rob the stables. There's been a spate of break-ins recently at farms, garages. Lonely places."

On the nearest TV screen the time flashed, and so I can report that I told my second major, premeditated lie at 12:27 a.m. on the morning of Sunday, March 6, 2011. Perhaps that was my second birthday.

WE WAITED, AND HILARY, despite the magazines scattered around the room, waited mostly by talking. I heard the story of her marriage. Deeper into the night she described Jessie, her secret sister. The exterminator woman left. A young man arrived with a broken wrist and three drunken friends. A woman limped in with two small children, the older sobbing from earache. Hilary, happy for the distraction, walked her baby round and round the waiting room. At last Dr. Gaitonde returned. They were going to operate to remove the bullet; it was the only way to stop the bleeding. The shoulder—she shrugged her own—would be dealt with later by her expert colleagues. As she held out the permission forms, with their dire warnings, she added that the police would be here shortly.

Sometime after the doctor left, Hilary said, "I understood about Michael and women, but I never understood about him and horses. To him one horse was worth a hundred people."

Was that really any different, I asked, from people who were mad about tennis or music or climbing Everest? Just because we didn't value the object, that didn't mean the passion was unworthy.

"What about people who collect garden gnomes?" said Hilary. "For Michael, horses justified everything. I think that's why I married Franklin. His fanaticism felt familiar."

Years ago in Edinburgh one of my lecturers pointed out that *fan* comes from *fanatic*, an obvious connection I had never noticed and which I now pointed out to Hilary. Desperate to keep the conversation from turning to Viv, I continued to urge counterexamples. People who were trying to cure cancer, or stop the glaciers melting, surely they weren't fanatics?

"Because they know when to stop," she said. "The first time Michael talked about Mercury, he said, 'Hil, I've fallen in love.' But love became something else."

"I can understand you loving Jack," I said.

It was then that she told me they wanted to have a child. "I know it's crazy," she said. "We've only known each other four months." Her eyelids fluttered, rapid as a moth's wings.

2

AND WHERE WAS VIV during these hours? As soon as we'd carried Jack out of the barn, she ran to Mercury. He was still wild with fear, kicking, screaming, and the other horses were whinnying and banging, their panic magnifying his. At the stables in Ann Arbor a stallion had killed a man by pinning him to a wall. People said the man was to blame—he'd whipped the horse—but she had always kept her distance. Now she was afraid of Mercury, and he was afraid of her. Perhaps he could smell the gun. She stood at the door of his stall, talking to him—No one's going to take you away. You're safe—until at last he lowered his head.

The boy at the shooting range had told her that when the police in his town shot a junkie, the bullet had passed straight through the junkie and hit another man, a teacher, in the throat. "He was a standup guy," the boy had said. "No justice in that." So when she took off Mercury's blanket and saw his dappled coat gleaming, no sign of blood, she gasped with relief. To have shot Jack was unspeakable; to have shot Jack and Mercury was unthinkable. She put his blanket back on, strapping it loosely the way he liked, gave him a handful of oats, locked the door, set the alarm, and then she was in the car, the gun on the seat beside her, not knowing what to do next.

"I kept telling myself," she told me later, "you wouldn't let Jack die."

She sat there, gazing out at the soiled snow. Should she go to the police? If Jack died, she was sure, I would accuse her. If he lived, she could not imagine what I might do. And all her wondering might be beside the point. Perhaps I had already told Hilary. Perhaps she had already lost everything.

At some point she started driving. When she reached the main road she stopped, removed the ammunition from the gun, and threw the magazine as far as she could into the woods. Then, with no conscious plan, only revulsion, she threw the gun. Back in the car, she knew she was not going to the police station that night. She had to see Marcus and Trina. But at the sight of our house, all lit up, she braked. What if I was already there and had barred the door? She pictured herself knocking on doors and windows, calling my name, while I sat on the sofa, my gaze fixed on one of my history books.

But the door opened easily, and inside everything was as she had left it, weirdly quiet. Even Nabokov was asleep. In all the years we had lived in the house, she had never been there alone at night before.

"I saw myself in the bathroom mirror," she told me later, as we sat drinking Scotch at the kitchen table, "and I looked just the same. Like Dinos."

For a moment I couldn't place the name. Then I remembered. When I still lived on Linnaean Street, Dinos had owned the shop where I bought my coffee. A handsome man, always ready for a chat, he had married his pretty manager. The year after Marcus was born, a photograph had appeared by the cash register: "It's a girl." Beaming, Dinos told me that Natalie was named for his grandmother in Thessalonika. She liked the smell of apples, and slept for six hours a night. We no longer lived near the shop, and several months passed before I returned to buy coffee. When I asked if Dinos was around, the boy behind the counter lowered his voice. Natalie had died ten days before; Dinos had been charged with shaking her to death.

I had been shocked to think that someone I knew, someone so genial, could have done such a thing, but in the ongoing emergency of my own life, I had gradually forgotten Dinos. Then last autumn, searching for a birthday present for Viv, I had gone into another shop near Linnaean Street. The saleswoman was flirting with a dark-haired man in a leather jacket. As I studied a row of blouses, she complained that she needed to lose weight.

"Honey," said the man, "you look great, and I'm not just saying that because I haven't seen a woman in nine years."

At once I recognized Dinos, and he, catching my glance, recognized me. Before I could move, he had crossed the small shop and embraced me. He asked after Viv and Marcus; I said he was looking well. He left the shop, and the saleswoman helped me choose a gift.

At home I had described the encounter to Viv. "Here was this person," I said, "who killed his daughter, and he looked just the same."

"But he served his sentence," Viv said. "Shouldn't he be forgiven?" Her hair was still long, and it was easy to picture her as Portia, the role she had played in her high school production of *The Merchant of Venice*.

"I don't know," I said. "I kept feeling it was too easy."

"Nine years in prison isn't my idea of easy."

"Even nine days, but all the time we were talking, I was thinking that if Natalie were alive, she'd be a year older than

Trina, old enough to pick apples. Perhaps that's what bothers me: I'd forgotten her, and he seemed to have too. I don't think forgiveness should involve forgetting. But if I remember Natalie, then I'm not sure I can forgive him."

Viv's gaze had sharpened. "Dinos isn't a criminal," she'd argued. "Just a person who made a terrible mistake, and who has to live with that day after day, knowing he can never ever go back and undo it."

Which was, she told me, staring sorrowfully across the kitchen table, how she now thought of herself.

3

ONE OF THE THINGS Viv and I share—used to share—was a belief in the rational. We both believed in facts and figures, chemical reactions and reasoned argument. But that night the shock of what she'd done, the awfulness of her mistake, the excruciating slowness with which the hours passed, made her afraid she would lose her wits as easily as a set of keys. Thoughts were running wildly through her brain, like when she had the flu, only much worse. She could see, as I had years before when I tried to juggle child care, my hospital duties, and my father's illness, the possibility of them running away altogether. Not knowing what else to do, she began to clean the empty house. Scrubbing, dusting, washing, vacuuming, made her feel a little calmer.

Meanwhile in the emergency room the Saturday-night revelers dwindled. An elderly woman was brought in. The man at the admissions desk asked after her cat. During my stint in ER we had had several regulars, old people living alone, who came in two or three times a month, convinced they were at death's door and, once they were settled in a cubicle, fell happily asleep.

A nurse called, "Ms. Blake." We jumped up, thinking there was news. Two policemen were waiting in the hall. Each wore a wedding ring, and one had a faint scratch on his cheek, the sort of injury a small child might inflict. They asked me to sit down again while they spoke to Hilary. I remember staring at my clasped hands, my own thoughts running wildly: Viv had confessed, the children, Jack's shoulder, my father. For a moment I was back in Edinburgh, my ruddy-faced Sunday-school teacher towering over me. Children, he boomed, when you tell a lie you are hidden from God.

Hilary returned. The policeman with the scratch led me to an alcove off the hall. The two men asked their questions, and my thoughts stopped running. I pictured Trina waving to the whales; I pictured Marcus carefully cutting up a stalk of broccoli for Nabokov.

"My wife, Viv Turner, manages the stables," I said. "I have a key. We wanted to visit Ms. Blake's horse."

The policemen took notes; Ms. Blake had said the same thing. They would check out the stables and return in the morning to speak to Mr. Brennan. Back in the waiting room, I asked Hilary if she would like something else from the vending machines: Coffee? Chocolate? Peanuts?

She shook her head. "What's happening?" she said. "Why is everything taking so long?"

"Shoulders are complicated. The surgeon has to be careful of the muscles and tendons."

"In that case, I hope they take as long as possible. Do you know a girl who works at Windy Hill, Charlie something? She came by my office yesterday."

"Charlie? What did she want?"

Hilary was saying she didn't know, she'd been out, when a nurse, an older man, appeared, calling her name. Once again we jumped up, jostling our chairs. *Please*, I thought. In a soft Irish accent the man said Mr. Brennan was in recovery. We could see him soon, just for a few minutes.

"Thank you," Hilary kept saying. "Thank you so much."

My vision narrowed. I was afraid I would fall to the floor. The nurse guided me into a chair and told me to put my head down. Someone brought me a glass of water. "Sorry," I said when I could speak again. "I don't know what came over me."

"You love Jack." Hilary's hand was warm on my arm. "This has been one of the worst nights of my life." It was then that she told me about her sister, and the grief of losing that first pregnancy.

Half an hour later the nurse returned to lead us along a series of corridors, past darkened rooms, into and out of an elevator, and then at last into a dimly lit room.

"Just three minutes," he said. "Don't expect anything."

Jack. One small word: an entire being.

He lay propped up in the hospital bed, surrounded by the panoply of drips and monitors, his face still pale but no longer waxen, his lips no longer taut with pain. It was he who had told me that the word *panoply* came from the Greek phrase meaning the full armor of the Hoplites. I took his living hand in mine.

Hilary bent to kiss his cheek. "I love you," she said. "Your only job is to get better. Sleep and get better. I'll be back soon."

The nurse ushered us out, promising to phone if anything changed. Then we were standing in the frigid parking lot with no sign of my car. After several minutes of searching near the entrance, Hilary remembered that at some point in the night, I had moved it. We found it in a distant corner, slewed across two spaces. I turned on the engine and scraped the windows. Hilary waited in the passenger seat, eyes closed. Neither of us spoke on the way to Il Giardino, but at the sight of the dark-green awning, I was dismayed. Don't go, I wanted to say. Let me come home with you. Perhaps Hilary felt the same. Awkwardly, across the gearshift, she clung to me. We agreed to talk in the morning. I waited until her car started and she was safely on her way.

I managed three blocks before I pulled over. Once, driving back from the nursing home after seeing my father, I was so overwhelmed that I parked at the 7-Eleven, the one where Viv encountered the young men, and walked the rest of the way home, every step a protest against the atrocious, unbelievable fact: my father was going to die. Now I could scarcely begin to name the feelings that roiled inside me, but one emerged with absolute clarity: I did not want to see Viv. Had she confessed? Was she already in prison? Or was she at the house? I could not deal with one more thing. We had waited. Let her wait. I did a U-turn and drove to the office. Inside I turned up the heat, took off my shoes, wrapped myself in the blanket we kept for emergencies, and, on the small sofa in the waiting room, fell abruptly asleep.

4

Perhaps in some other language there is a word for that state of mind one discovers upon first waking after a terrible event. For barely a fraction of a second everything seems the same. Then there it is, the awful "it," and the world is utterly altered. Or so I felt the morning after my parents announced we were not going back to Edinburgh; the day after I learned of my father's illness. I felt it again that Sunday morning, waking on the office sofa, my cheek against the stubbled cushion. Reaching for my glasses, I hoped for evidence that last night's happenings were a vaporous dream, but everything, from the ficus by Nabokov's table to my own presence, confirmed their reality.

I phoned the hospital. A nurse reported that Mr. Brennan was still asleep.

Marcus texted: *great time bowling. pancakes for b'fast.* I texted back: *lucky you.*

Then I sat looking at the screen of my phone as if it would tell me what to do next. The words I had kept in a cage the night before banged around. I longed to call the police, let them fly. I pictured the man with the scratch on his cheek writing them down. I pictured Viv in a prison jumpsuit, handcuffed, being led by two policemen to a room with a table, a chair, a small barred window.

At last I forced myself to leave the sofa. I washed, brushed my teeth, put away the blanket, plumped the cushions. The windows of my car were still clear, and not until I was behind the wheel did I notice the piece of paper wedged beneath the windscreen wiper: "D, please come home. V." At some point in the night, after cleaning the house, she had driven to the hospital, to Hilary's, and finally to my office. She had not dared to knock.

As I approached St. Catherine's, the bells began to toll. A few months before, at my patient's funeral, I had stood with the rest of the congregation to say, "Forgive me, Father, for I have sinned in thought, word, and deed." If only, I thought now, I could go to confession. But how could I ask for absolution before I knew the size of my crime? I kept driving and stopped instead at the café where Viv and Hilary had met to look at the photographs of Mercury. As I stood in line, listening to the hiss of the steamer, the people around me talking, I felt briefly taken up into ordinary life. All would be well, as my father used to say. All manner of things would be well.

"Dr. Stevenson." The woman ahead of me, her gray eyes familiar, turned to greet me. "Happy Sunday," she said. "We're so thrilled your office is sponsoring science week."

Before I could reply, she had turned back to the counter and was reeling off a complicated combination of caramel and soy milk. What the blazes am I thinking? I thought as I asked for my black coffee. Ordinary life is over. Nothing will ever be well.

I HAD MADE—I COULD make—no preparation for what to say to Viv. I knew I would open the door of our house; then something unimaginable would occur. And that was what happened. I parked my car beside her car. My key, which sometimes stuck, turned smoothly; the door, which often creaked, swung open. Viv was standing by the kitchen table, empty-handed, hair still damp. She wore a blue sweater I liked (used to like) and clean jeans tucked into boots. She took a step towards me.

"Don," she said. "Donald."

Then she too came to a standstill. Less than twenty-four hours earlier, before I took the children to my mother's, we had made French toast and discussed who to invite to Trina's birthday party. Whatever Viv had been through since we parted had passed like an iron over her features. Only her red-rimmed eyes betrayed her wretchedness. As for my own expression, I could feel all the tiny muscles in my face pulling in different directions. She tried again. "How's Jack? He was still asleep when I phoned."

"When I phoned too."

"Did you tell Hilary? The police?"

I stared at the floor, this time the gleaming blond wood of our kitchen rather than the linoleum of the hospital.

"Shall I compare thee to a summer's day?" said Nabokov.

My silence betrayed me. Then I did something that surprised us both. I raised my phone and took a photograph. I needed evidence of the bewildering fact that Viv, as she herself said, looked just the same; she had not sprouted laurel branches, or turned into a swan.

"Did you go to the police?" I said, already knowing she hadn't.

"Not yet," she whispered. "They phoned, but I turned out the lights. And I texted Claudia I had a migraine. I have to see Marcus and Trina first."

I asked what she had done with the gun, and she told me.

What sort of conversation does a man have on the occasion

of his wife accidentally shooting his dear friend with a gun she has purchased secretly, and owns illegally? I am afraid I cannot tell you. I know I made tea; I found the mugs later that day as I set the table for supper. I know we sat at the table and talked. I know Viv did not cry; I think I did. The phone rang several times; each time one of us checked to make sure it was not my mother or Hilary. Viv told me the bare facts of her evening. After walking Samson round the arena until his colic subsided, she had driven home, stopping at China Garden. She was sitting on the sofa, watching TV, reaching for a dumpling, when she realized she couldn't remember setting the alarm.

"I remembered putting Samson back in his stall," she said. "Closing the tack room, and then . . . Finally it seemed easier to drive back and check."

She had been almost glad to find the barn door open. It meant she hadn't been worrying in some OCD way. She decided to take a last look around. If she'd forgotten one thing, perhaps she'd forgotten another. The gun was already in her jacket pocket, the ammunition in the other pocket. She had left the lights on too. As she reached for the switch, she heard voices. At once she knew they came from Mercury's stall. Fate had brought her here, to save him. She slid the magazine into the gun and made her way quietly to the far end of the stalls. She could see Mercury's head, a man beside him. Two other figures.

She took the safety off. That was her worst, her very worst mistake. She meant to shout a warning. *Get away from the horse.* To let the intruders see the gun—but there were three of them. She was afraid. The man raised his hand. Was he injecting Mercury? Poisoning him? She didn't notice her finger tighten around the trigger. The sound was huge. Mercury was screaming, like a human. And the people were screaming like humans too.

"But you had a gun," I said. "Where on earth did you get a gun?"

She told me.

Then she asked what we were doing at the stables, and I understood she still believed she had left the door unlocked. I did not enlighten her, not then.

The conversation was by no means as calm and orderly as this record. We both shouted. Viv screamed. I whispered. For several minutes one or the other of us would refuse to speak. Viv flung a book on the floor; I banged the table. I kept waiting for her to convince me that she would give anything not to have bought a gun. And she did say, over and over, how sorry she was, how terrible she felt. But heavy as lead, sharp as glass, the thought persisted that, given what she saw—three strangers trying to hurt her beloved horse—she still believed, in her heart of hearts, that what she had done made sense. Whereas to me it made no sense at all.

"Do you think the police will let me out on bail?" she said.

AT TWO O'CLOCK, WITH nothing settled, I went upstairs to shower before heading back to the hospital. Viv went to buy groceries. For now we would tell the children Jack had slipped on the snow. So we pulled ourselves together as parents do.

In his room Jack was still unconscious, Hilary beside him. "It's over twelve hours since the operation," she said. "Doesn't that seem a long time for him to be asleep?"

Jack's breathing was steady, his color good, but it did seem a long time. Invoking my doctor's status, I went to make inquiries. After clicking through several screens, the nurse at the desk reported that Mr. Brennan had been awake in the recovery room; he had known who he was, and where.

"Oh, I feel so much better," Hilary said. "Sleep as long as you like, Mr. Brennan." She added that the police had been by again. "They asked if I thought the attack might be connected with the break-ins at the stable. Why didn't Viv tell me they'd had a break-in?"

"Everyone thought it was just kids," I said. "She didn't want to worry you."

"But we're friends," Hilary said. I remembered making the same plea to Jack.

She went to the cafeteria, and I took her place. Jack's face was still, his breathing shallow. Only the pneumatic compression stockings, rippling up and down his legs beneath the blankets, seemed to promise a return to health.

"So," I began, "you and a fat man are standing on a railway bridge, and you see that a train is on the wrong track. If it keeps going, it will collide with another train. Many people will die. You can stop the train by pushing the fat man off the bridge. Should you?"

That spring Jack had posed this philosophical question to the four of us. Marcus had immediately said, "Yes, push him."

"But what if you like him?" said Jack. "Or a family of ten depends on him? Or he's about to discover a cure for cancer?"

"Can't you push something else?" said Trina. "A rock? Or a branch?"

"And what if both trains are filled with horrible people? War criminals and psychopaths?"

"Let them crash," said Marcus.

"But then suppose the trains are full of good people—teachers and ophthalmologists and horse trainers and well-behaved children—and the fat man is good too."

"It's too difficult," Trina exclaimed. "I want to save everyone."

Jack had reached over to pat her arm. "We can do that," he said. "We'll make the engineer switch the points so that the first train goes onto another track and everyone is fine and the fat man diets and becomes a thin man no one would ever ask to stop a train."

"And the horse trainer teaches him to ride," said Viv.

But Trina was not so easily distracted. "Even if one person can save lots of people," she said, "it seems awful for that person. Shouldn't they get to decide if they want to be a savior?"

"There are some very smart people who think so," Jack had said.

Sitting at his bedside, I thought, I am my daughter's father. I don't know who to save, or how to count the costs. And neither Jack, nor my father, is here to help me.

AT HOME MARCUS WAS talking exuberantly about the Museum of Science. They'd seen a skeleton and two kinds of metal; one felt hot and one felt cold, but they were exactly the same temperature. Trina asked how Jack was, and I said still asleep. As soon as we were alone, Viv said, "Shouldn't he be awake by now?"

I repeated what I had said to Hilary: gunshot wounds inflict deep trauma. What mostly kills people is the shock, not the actual wound. Sleep allows the body to recover. "What did you say to Claudia?" I asked.

I saw at once that she had said nothing. "The police will have told her what happened," I said. "That I was there. You can't hide."

Grim-faced, she went to the study. She was gone for so long that I had to summon her to dinner. Somehow we got through the meal. Afterwards, at Trina's request, we watched a movie about elephant migration. Suddenly—neither Viv nor I had been paying attention—Trina was crying. The screen showed a railway line in northern India where several elephants had died. A calf had got stuck on the tracks, and the adult elephants had surrounded it, trying to save it from the oncoming train.

"They love their children like we do," said Viv. "Time for bed."

Waiting at the kitchen table, I remembered the dream Hilary had recounted at Il Giardino about her and Michael walking along the railway line. Please, Jack, I thought. Wake up. Viv returned, poured herself a glass of Scotch, and sat down opposite me.

"The short version," she said, "is that Claudia is totally devastated that Jack's been shot and totally freaked out that he was shot at Windy Hill. She kept saying the baby could have been shot, or I could have, or one of our students. It was even worse than telling Peggy."

I swore, using a word I'd never used before. Why the hell had she told my mother?

"The same reason you made me phone Claudia. Anything else would be too weird."

Of course she was right. This was no longer, if it ever had been, a domestic quarrel; the battle had overflowed the stables, our house. But she had told the two people closest to us a lie. The lie was getting stronger.

"Tell me again," I said, "why you got a gun. You were always so anti gun. We even went on that protest at the State House."

Stumbling, stopping frequently to qualify or explain, she described the chain of events—her fear, Rick and his gun, Tiffany's father, Michael, the second break-in, New Hampshire—that had led her to buy a gun. "I needed to protect Mercury," she kept saying.

I heard the name differently now, not just a messenger god or a shining liquid or the smallest planet but a toxic substance that could cause blindness and death. When I phoned the hospital, the nurse said, "No change."

5

Strange as it had been to sleep on the waiting-room sofa, it was even stranger to occupy our familiar bed, with Viv lying a few inches away. I was conscious of every scrape of fabric, every breath. If I could, I would have slept at the opposite end of the house, the opposite end of the street. Hour after hour I lay awake, clicking away on my nocturnal abacus. I know I slept at last only because I had the sensation of waking. The bed was empty: Where was Viv? Then I understood: she had already left for Windy Hill. What else could she do? And what else could I do but take the children to school and Nabokov to my office? As soon as he was safely in his cage, I broke the news to Merrie. When Jack was my patient, the two of them had enjoyed trading Catholic jokes.

"Oh, my god," she cried. "What kind of person shoots a blind man?"

For several minutes I endured her shock, fury, incredulity, dismay, horror: a carousel of emotions. Finally I retreated to my office and, once again, telephoned the hospital. Mr. Brennan's vital signs were good, the nurse said. The wound was healing well.

"So he's eating and drinking?"

"Not yet. He hasn't woken up."

"You mean," I said, "he's still unconscious?"

"Right," she said. "Asleep, unconscious."

Better? Or worse? I asked patient after patient that morning. My own answer was worse, always worse. Everything was shrouded in darkness, mired in confusion. When Hilary phoned, I tried to reassure her—Jack's body was healing, resting, etcetera—but I could not reassure myself. Then, at lunchtime, my mother phoned.

"Viv was beside herself," she said. "She seems to feel responsible because it happened at Windy Hill."

I reached for my model eye. Silently, while she continued to exclaim, I named the sclera, conjunctiva, cornea, iris, vitreous humor, retina, choroid, optic nerve. My world was in ruins, but this little machine went on working in exactly the same way. "Our main concern is Jack," I said at last. "He still hasn't woken up."

"Oh," said my mother, suddenly understanding.

I promised to let her know as soon as there was news.

Alone with my eyeball, I recalled how Viv, when she first met my parents, had asked if my father minded that my mother was so much more successful. I had been startled—I had never thought of my parents in this way—and told her what I believed at the time: my father had too many interests to devote himself to work. But soon after he moved into the nursing home he had told me another version. "Made your mother crazy," he said. I leaned close to his chair, struggling to understand. His slurred speech was the subject of his last haiku.

My words, once fitted
close and straight as stones,
now scattered on dry ground.

That afternoon at the home I did not catch every detail of his story, but enough to understand the implications. My father had noticed that certain maintenance jobs at the railway were routinely awarded to the highest bidder. One day, at a local restaurant, he had run into the department head, who awarded the contracts, dining with his brother-in-law.

"My bad luck," my father mumbled, "that I recognized his name."

Later my mother had filled in the gaps. He had pursued the matter over hill and dale, first talking to his supervisor and, when nothing changed, moving relentlessly up the hierarchy, oblivious to threats, overt or subtle. Finally he promised to notify local newspapers and radio stations. "After that," she said, "he was never going to get promoted."

"What would you have done," I said, "if your company was involved in something shady?"

"Asked Edward. Remember when I stepped down from that yogurt campaign? It was a big account, but he'd discovered the company had dubious connections. He's never bought the argument that if you don't do it, someone else will. You have to be able to look at yourself in the mirror."

I cannot begin to count how often, in those days and nights, I longed for my father's counsel. Nor how many mirrors I avoided.

6

THE AUTUMN I WAS twelve, still struggling to make friends in America, my mother had urged me to join the Boy Scouts. You'll learn to light fires, she had said, recognize birds. Both were appealing, but almost immediately I discovered I could not bear the scoutmaster's constant refrain to be prepared. I quit after three meetings. Certainly nothing could have prepared me for Jack not waking up, for the awful prospect that he might become one of those people kept alive by machines, his excellent brain generating a barely flickering line. At the hospital that evening I found a note on the bedside table: "Gone to café." I bent over Jack. His beard had come in thick and dark, making him look even paler. The bones in his forehead were sharply visible. Once again I reached for his good hand.

"Jack," I said, "come back to the daylight world. We need you here."

Mindful of his complaint that people often shouted at him, I kept my voice low. I reminded him of how he loved Latin and Greek and swimming, of how his friends and students loved and needed him, of how the world was waiting for his book. "You can write a chapter about what it's like for a blind person to be shot," I said. It was a Jack-like joke.

I was telling him about the research into an artificial retina—

a sheet of electrodes combined with a camera that offered the possibility of vision—when Hilary returned.

"Any sign?" she said.

"Not yet. His breathing seems a little stronger."

She laid her hand on his chest. "I know it's stupid, but I feel that if I leave him for more than a few minutes, something terrible will happen."

I did not say—I did not need to say—that the terrible thing had already happened.

At supper, when Viv asked her standard question, Marcus said he had learned there were numbers that just went on and on. "Whenever you picture the last number, you add one more."

Carefully rearranging the lettuce in her tacos, Viv said she'd learned that Claudia had decided to install a security camera at the stables, and a gate at the bottom of the road.

"So you'll be in a movie," said Trina. "I learned that mice smell like sweet cardboard."

"Why would you want to smell mice?" said Marcus. "What about you, Dad?"

I learned that my best friend might not wake up; that grief and guilt are infinite numbers. Speechless, I stared at my plate.

Trina leaned over to pat my arm. "Dad, it's okay if you didn't learn anything."

She gave me an encouraging smile. Viv offered seconds. In the back-and-forth of plates and food, I managed a question to Marcus about his swimming; a few minutes later I told a feeble story about Nabokov and a patient. After supper Trina insisted on following me to the study. While I read about bullet wounds and comas, the scratching of her pencil—she was working on a portrait of my mother—kept me company. At last Viv took her off to bed.

Once again we sat at the kitchen table, each with our Scotch. "My turn," I said.

I had shielded Hilary from my fears, but I wanted to inflict every last one of them on Viv. I began with what I had just learned about comas. As I spoke, I glanced around the room, taking in the red vase my mother had given us, Trina's paintings on the fridge, the cacti on the windowsill, the print of Edinburgh Castle that Viv and I had bought on our visit there—all the evidence of our shared life, the life that she had sundered.

"So is there anything to be done?" Her voice was barely above a whisper. "Would it help if I went to the hospital?"

"This isn't a fairy tale. You can't just knock three times and say you're sorry." I had no interest in her regrets, was desperate to confide my own. "Remember the night Marcus left his book at the stables?"

She nodded; I hurried on. When I described stepping into the arena, Charlie riding Mercury, Viv let out a wail of pure sorrow.

"You mean," she said, "all the break-ins were Charlie?"

"She and her boyfriend. She's like you. She just wanted to ride Mercury."

"So it was Charlie who set off the alarm at Thanksgiving?"

"Yes. Then one night after the second break-in, you asked her to lock up. She made a copy of the key."

"Oh, my god."

She began to sob with utter abandon. I had been braced for fury, not this outpouring of grief as she understood that Mercury had never been in danger. Everything she had done in the name of saving him had been unnecessary.

Watching her, her face twisted, red, wet with tears, I in turn understood what she had still to grasp: if I had told the truth when I came home that night from Windy Hill, or indeed at any moment during the next few weeks, Jack would not now be lying in a hospital bed. I was not just an accessory to his shooting but an accomplice.

7

IN THE ORRERY OF the past, my wife, my children, my parents, and I had orbited each other in our own devoted system. Nearby, in their own systems, were Jack, Claudia, other chosen friends. Mercury, I had thought, despite his name, was only a random meteor veering into our little cosmos. Charlie was another. Until the night I found her riding Mercury, I knew her only through casual encounters at Windy Hill and Viv's occasional comments. She lived in town, she attended the local high school, she had two younger brothers both keen on baseball, her parents worked in software. They had bought Charlie a horse for her twelfth birthday and been dismayed when she devoted every waking hour to the animal. When it sprained a tendon, they sold it, and she started working at Windy Hill. I thought of her as a child, but at her age Mary, Queen of Scots, had been married for a year.

Four days before the fatal Saturday, Charlie had come by my office. I was typing up notes on my last patient when Merrie appeared. "Charlotte Adams is here. She says she knows you and was hoping to have a word."

"Charlotte Adams?" For a moment the name meant nothing. Then I said she was one of Viv's stable girls and, when Merrie still wore her inquiring expression, added that I'd offered to talk to her about protective glasses.

"Will you be okay on your own?" she said. "I have to pick up the dog."

She was thinking, I knew, of her friend the teacher. Reluctantly I said I would be fine. After she left, I lingered at my desk, trying to imagine what Charlie might want. Whatever it was, I must be on my guard. By agreeing to keep her secret, I had put myself at her mercy as much as, if not more than, she was at mine. Before going out to the waiting room, I pulled on my seldom-worn white coat. Then I recalled how Marcus, at supper one evening, had recorded our conversation on my phone. After three attempts I found the function and turned it on. Whatever passed between us, I would have a record.

In the waiting room Charlie, like many of my patients, was standing beside Nabokov's cage. Only as I came closer did I see that she had opened the door and was urging him to step onto her arm.

"What are you doing?" I stepped over and closed the door, snibbing it tight. Nabokov eyed me askance but for once held his tongue.

"Sorry, Dr. Stevenson. We used to have a parrot. I didn't mean to take liberties." Her manner was conciliatory yet subtly mocking.

In my office I left the door open wide. The chair for patients was across the room, and Charlie sat down, feet together, hands clasped. "Help me," she said. She was wearing a bright red sweater, and I noticed, as I had that night in the arena, how her lips glistened.

"I think I already have."

"And I'm super grateful, but I never get to see Mercury anymore. Viv won't let anyone else near him. It makes me crazy. I'm working all the time, and then I have to ride these old duffers. Viv doesn't understand him. She's pushing him too hard."

I offered the mildest protest: Viv was a very experienced rider.

Charlie smiled enticingly. "My bad for going behind her back. What I want to know is, how can I persuade her to let me ride him in events?"

As she described the competitions she wanted to enter, I recalled how Bonnie's childhood story about the Pekingese had made me lie to Viv. But there was nothing childish about Charlie's ambitions. "I'd be glad," I said slowly, "to see Viv working less hard."

"And she's too old for him."

She saw at once that she'd gone too far. She gazed at her clasped hands, letting the silence expand. "He's Hilary's horse," I said at last. "Besides, aren't you about to go to college?"

"That's right." For an instant her face flared. "He is Hilary's horse." Then she was back on her feet, saying politely that I'd been awesome.

I had watched her leave with a sense of relief, but as I drove home, I kept thinking I had said something wrong. But no, I told myself, it was only the aftermath of my actual wrongdoing of a few weeks earlier. Even in the emergency room, when Hilary mentioned Charlie visiting her office, I had not put two and two together. Only now, in the midst of Viv's grief and my own, did I begin to understand. Charlie was no random meteor; she was a guided missile, as driven as Viv, unhampered by children or moral codes.

BY TUESDAY AFTERNOON, WITH no sign of Jack waking up, I had become convinced that my lie was one more barrier between him and recovery. So much for rational thinking. Despite Marcus, despite Trina, I would go to the police station on my way home. I had just finished checking a patient for glaucoma when my phone rang.

"He's awake," said Hilary. "It's a miracle." And in the background Jack's voice, faint and irascible: "No, it's not."

I said something incoherent, and promised to visit as soon as my appointments were over. Merrie, when I told her, jumped to her feet and hugged me. Nabokov ran up the side of his cage.

My next appointment had not yet arrived, and I stepped into the street. The day was brutally cold, the brick buildings rimed with frost. If during those forty-eight hours I had been asked to push a bell every time the thought that Jack might be going into a coma entered my mind, it would have rung almost without cease. Years ago a patient of mine, a woman in her fifties, described what it was like when she had a stroke. "In my head," she said, "I was talking all the time—What's this pill? I'm thirsty. Hold my hand—but no one heard me. I thought I'd die of frustration." The prospect of Jack similarly imprisoned was more than I could bear. I stood on the corner of the street, arms outstretched, giving thanks to the unnamed god of atheists.

And so an hour later I stepped into not the police station but Jack's hospital room. The news of his accident—"Blind Classics Prof Shot at Stables"—had spread like wildfire, and the windowsill was lined with flowers. The fragrance reminded me of Robert's parents' shop, which all year round had been pungent with freesias and lilies. Hilary greeted me solemnly, her relief too profound for ordinary exuberance.

"Jack," I said. "How are you feeling?" I put my hand on his good arm.

He gave a lopsided smile. "My shoulder hurts. My head

aches. But I can talk, I can pee, and when no one's testing me for something, I can listen to music."

"I can't tell you," I said, "how sorry I am."

"Why are you sorry? You didn't shoot me. Hilary said you drove like the devil to get me here, and kept an eye on everyone in ER, wielding your doctor's sword."

"You mustn't blame yourself." Hilary smiled warmly. "We all three decided to go to the stables. If anyone's to blame, it's me for wanting to see Mercury in the middle of the night. We couldn't know some madman was prowling around."

There was so much goodwill in the room. Now, I thought, was the moment to tell the truth, to explain how Viv had mistaken us for horse thieves, had accidentally squeezed the trigger. But I had barely begun to speak, a lame, throat-clearing phrase about that night at Windy Hill, when Jack embarked on one of his stories: something about a friend stealing his uncle's pistol. He trailed off after a few sentences, and Hilary said he needed to rest. I left, promising to return tomorrow.

In the hospital parking lot I discovered that I did not want to go home. The prospect of celebrating Jack's recovery with Viv was like running full-tilt into a wall. For a few seconds, standing beside the car, I even thought of calling Bonnie. On the far side of the lot an ambulance swung silently through the entrance gates. I got out my phone and dialed Steve's number. He agreed to meet at the Y in half an hour. Once again I texted Viv. Until recently I had almost always phoned; now I welcomed the curtness of the little box. *Jack awake. Late home.*

"Thank God," said Steve when I told him about Jack recovering consciousness. "But I still don't understand who shot him. And why were you at Windy Hill in the middle of the night?"

"Hilary wanted to visit her horse." I slammed my serve into a corner. "As for the rest, I don't have a clue."

"But you were there. You must have seen something."

I aced my next serve too as I said that the stables were poorly lit; we were all focused on Mercury. "One minute Jack was inviting him to their wedding. The next he was on the ground."

Writing this now, I find it hard to believe that no one noticed something lacking from my account of the shooting. I should have been ten times more furious, ten times more bewildered. I can only suppose that my reputation as a dour Scotsman protected me. I was a descendant of those men who in letters home described the first day of the Somme as "trying." "Mustn't grumble," they wrote as the trenches filled with blood.

Steve, the good scientist, explained that people often fail to remember trauma. For reasons not yet fully understood, adrenaline prevented memories from imprinting in the normal way. "And seeing someone shot," he said, "is pretty close to the top of traumatic experiences. So what are Viv and Claudia going to do? Turn Windy Hill into an armed stockade?"

I bent to pick up a tennis ball and said they were taking new security measures. Once again he didn't seem to notice anything amiss. My wife was working at a place where someone had been shot, and I was cool as a cucumber. But such thoughts came later. At the time I was overjoyed: Jack had returned to the daylight world.

I beat Steve that evening by a memorable 7–3. At home supper was over. I slid easily into the household: taking a shower, eating leftovers, talking to Trina and Marcus. Viv caught me alone at the kitchen sink to ask if I had been to the police. When I said no, she thanked me and went to help Marcus with his homework. For the remaining few hours of the day I allowed myself to be happy.

8

THE NEXT MORNING, EVEN before I opened my eyes, I knew the wind was blowing from a different quarter. Viv made breakfast and took the children to school, two things she had not done in several months. When she came home, I was sitting drinking coffee among the breakfast dishes. Her response to disaster was to clean, mine to let everything slide.

She marched in, cheeks glowing from the cold, and, not even waiting to unzip her jacket, said, "I can't stand this, Don. Wondering every day if you're going to the police. The uncertainty is tearing me apart, which I know I deserve, but Marcus's teacher phoned yesterday. He's acting up in class. And Trina threw a book at Ivy."

"I can't stand it either," I said. "I still can't believe you bought a gun."

"To protect Mercury from Charlie."

Her bitterness scorched the table. I lined up the boxes of cereal, each with its gaudy promises, and said that was another thing I couldn't believe. "I lied to you, and that lie almost killed my friend. What happened when you spoke to Claudia?"

"I told her what I believed at the time: I'd left the stables unlocked. You, Hilary, and Jack had a boozy dinner and decided to visit Mercury. She filled in the rest. We'd had these break-ins. By some awful coincidence the burglar also showed up that night. First I'm convinced someone is after Mercury, and it's Charlie. Now Claudia's convinced some killer is after all of us, and it's me."

She was watching me over cereal boxes with an expression of equal parts sorrow and anger. "Yesterday," she continued, "I was driving home when I suddenly thought, I've got a tank of gas, I've got my credit cards, I should just keep going. Head west on 90, or north on 93. But how would I live without the kids? And where would I go? Mom's sofa bed in Ann Arbor? Dad's basement in San Diego? Some dingy motel with plastic glasses and slippery sheets? I'm too old to be a stable rat."

America is the country of reinvention, of moving on, but this possibility—that she might simply flee—had never occurred to me. I was trying, and failing, to imagine a life in which I knew nothing about Viv, had no contact with her, when Nabokov squawked. Why was he sitting here, rather than holding court in the waiting room? I took him a handful of peanuts, and he clucked with pleasure.

Perhaps still thinking of stable rats, Viv said Charlie had been away visiting colleges. She would fire her as soon as she returned.

"Is that really necessary?" Since her visit to my office, a visit I had not mentioned and did not plan to, I had an inchoate dread of crossing Charlie.

"Don, she lied, she stole, she trespassed, she betrayed me." With each crime, Viv toppled a cereal box until they were all four horizontal.

"And how will you explain firing her to Claudia?"

She hesitated, looking now not at me but at her hand where it moved back and forth over the table, crooked finger bobbing.

"I was thinking, if it's okay with you, I'd tell her the truth: how you found Charlie riding, how she begged you not to tell anyone."

Any step towards the truth seemed like a good thing, and I said so. "I behaved badly," I said, "but I couldn't have guessed the cost would be so high."

"Nor could I." We both watched her hand following the grain of the wood. Steve told me once that trees carry the memory of human disasters. The Highland Clearances, Andersonville, the flu epidemic, the Wall Street crash, each can be read in the grain of an oak. When someone cuts down the maple in our garden, will they find evidence of these last few months: our silences, our fights, our lies?

"So you're okay," she said, "with being the one who's blamed?"

I nodded—even a little blame would be a huge relief—and asked again about Charlie. "What will you say to her?"

"Why would you care?"

Steve might not notice anything missing in my response but Viv was watching me closely. Fortunately Nabokov, peanuts gone, intervened. "Hey ho, hey ho," he called. I had an appointment in twenty minutes. Only when I was driving to the office, with him murmuring beside me, did I realize that, once again, I had failed to tell her I was going to the police. Another day would pass without a clear decision.

AT LUNCHTIME JACK WAS sitting up, a tray of beige hospital food on the table before him, his dark glasses back in place. Hilary's chair was empty; she had gone to get coffee.

"Tell me this looks better than it smells," he said.

"I can't. How are you?" When it seemed that Jack might

not wake up, his recovering consciousness was everything. Now other concerns—the state of his shoulder, the state of his psyche—flooded back.

"I'm not sure. The doctor who came this morning has done a course on how not to talk to patients. He mumbles very fast, and when you ask a question he mumbles even faster."

"I'll see what I can find out. How do you feel?"

"As long as I lie still, okay. As soon as I move, definitely not okay. I want to ask you something while Hil's not here."

Involuntarily—did he know about Viv?—I stepped back.

"I keep having flashbacks," he went on. "This excruciating pain, and then Mercury going berserk. I was sure I was going to die. Why would someone shoot me? Who hates me enough to do that? Haven't I already paid my dues? This morning Hilary dropped a book. I almost leaped out of the bed. I think I should break up with her. Not only am I blind, but I have terrible karma. I worry I'll bring it into her household and—"

No wonder, I thought, he and my father, each offering divorce to a woman he loved, had gotten on so well. I interrupted him with his own words. "Remember," I said, "what you told me about Odysseus. How for years and years nothing goes right. He's tested over and over—Circe, the sirens, the Cyclops—and when he finally arrives in Ithaca, he has to disguise himself as a beggar and kill the suitors. You've said yourself that being blind doesn't protect you from anything. What happened at the stables was an accident. It could just as easily have been me who was shot, or Hilary."

"You're sounding like me," Jack said. "Intellectually I do know I'm not being singled out for special persecution. But I'm having a hard time believing it. Or accepting it. Or something."

Sentence by sentence, I had been approaching the bed. Now,

in the blackness of his glasses, I saw my own reflection. "I'll be-lieve it for you," I said, "until you're ready. That's what friends do, have faith for each other. Being shot is a major insult to the body. You can't expect to feel like your old self immediately."

When he still looked unconvinced, I repeated my feeble joke about how he could write about blind people being shot. My comment did serve to nudge his thoughts in a new direction. His next chapter, he said, was going to be about the differences between those born blind and those who go blind later. The French philosopher Diderot had described asking a man who'd been blind since birth if he'd like to be able to see. To his sur-prise, the man had said no. If he could have an extra sense, what he'd like was longer arms.

"You don't miss what you've never had," Jack concluded. "And I'm always going to miss what I've lost."

Before I could reply, we both heard footsteps. "Hilary," he said.

And there she was, carrying two espressos, announcing that Jack could come home tomorrow. His surgery would be next week.

IN THE LOBBY OF the hospital two boys were fencing with plastic swords. Watching them jab and parry, I found myself thinking about something that happened with Robert in the playground of our Edinburgh school. Most of the time we played nicely, but occasionally, for no obvious reason, we boys would gang up, *Lord of the Flies* style, on a classmate. One day Robert was the chosen victim. Several boys seized sticks and drove him towards the far corner of the playground, where a chestnut shielded us from adult view. A few yards from the tree he stopped and, empty-handed, turned to face his pursuers.

"Hit me," he said, "if that's what you want. It won't make you better than me."

"Scaredy-cat," called one boy. "Cowardy custard," called another.

"No," said Robert. "You're the cowardy custards." He raised his hand and counted steadily. "One, two, three, four, five—"

At "five," the ringleader, Angus—he could climb a rope in under a minute—leaped forward and swiped his stick at Robert's legs, bare between shorts and socks. Robert stumbled and cried out, but he kept watching his assailants, looking from one to the other.

Meanwhile I hung back, hoping for adult intervention, vacillating. Siding with Robert would only anger the boys, and we would still be outnumbered. But if I were the one in trouble, I knew he would come to my aid. As another boy flung a stick, I at last pushed through the crowd to stand beside my friend.

Angus stared at the two of us for a moment. "This is boring," he said. And just as suddenly the boys were gone, leaving Robert and me alone beneath the chestnut tree.

"Almost conker time," he said, bending to pick up a spiny green nut.

As I left the hospital I thought that this incident revealed something crucial about each of us. Robert, like my father, had an immediate sense of justice, whereas I tacked back and forth between various arguments—on the one hand, on the other—and sometimes hid from decisions: Exhibit A: Robert, Exhibit B: Ruth, Exhibit C: Jack and Viv. When our family was running smoothly, in that period after she began working at Windy Hill and before my father got so ill, Viv used to tease me about my caution. She seemed to make decisions effortlessly. Let's take the train to Portland. Let's go to the movies. That shirt is perfect. Shooting Jack, although accidental, was the result of a long line of decisions.

Or perhaps there was only one decision—to buy a gun—and everything else followed. Guns aren't magical; they're logical.

Perhaps it was also logical that once I had lied to the police, once she had failed to confess, once Jack had woken up, Viv started arguing that there was no need for either of us to confess. Doing so would not help Jack, and would only damage our children, terribly, irrevocably.

SOMETIMES AS I CLICK the lenses back and forth, asking, "Better? Or worse?" my patients say, "I'm sorry. I'm not sure." Don't be sorry, I tell them. That means we've nearly got the prescription right. But in my own case doubt did not lead to certainty. Hour by hour I sank deeper into indecision. Driving to and from the office, I sometimes pictured Bonnie sitting beside me, listening to my hesitations and deliberations, saying, "Have you considered . . . ?" "Maybe . . ." So when Merrie said she had made an appointment for her daughters, it seemed the answer to my secret longings. Somehow, without either of us mentioning Jack or Viv, she would tell me what to do.

And there she was on Wednesday, wearing a turquoise jacket, standing with two girls beside Nabokov's cage.

"We're talking to the famous Nabokov," she said. "This is Alice." She put her hand on the shoulder of the taller girl. "And Suzie. Girls, say hello to Dr. Stevenson."

They did, bobbing their heads. "Thank you for making Mom better," Alice said.

Nothing was obviously different. Bonnie's face, her hair, her clothes, were all much the same as on previous occasions, but as soon as she said my name, I knew that whatever had made me reach out to her, whatever had made her name chime so sweetly on my inner ear, made me believe that chiming was reciprocated, was gone. She was just another patient, albeit with a more interesting condition. They all three came into my examination room. I explained to the girls about dilating their eyes. The drops didn't hurt—the first one was an anesthetic—but they made everything bright and fuzzy.

"You'll have to wear sunglasses for the next couple of hours," I said.

"Cool," they said in unison.

Half an hour later I returned to the waiting room to find them delighted by their new vision. "We look like Sadie," Suzie said. "The cat," Bonnie explained. One by one I examined their eyes and was glad to be able to pronounce all well.

"When someone asks you to list ten good things about yourself," I said, "you can say, I have an excellent retina."

They giggled, and Bonnie thanked me. Everything was unspoken, yet she too had felt the shift. Her smile was measured, almost businesslike.

"Do up your jacket," she told Alice, and then, turning to me, "I heard about your friend. I hope he's going to be okay."

"He's recovering," I said. "Thank you." How incredulous she would be to learn that her childhood story had played even the smallest part in Jack's injury.

No sooner had she left my office than Merrie appeared. "What great kids," she said. "I'm glad their mom's on the other side of that operation."

All along, I realized, she had known about my feelings.

LATER THAT AFTERNOON HILARY phoned: she was at her wits' end. Twice Jack had shouted at her, and once he'd shouted at Diane for setting a cup of tea down out of reach. "It's like we have this monster in the house," she said. "We never know when he's going to start yelling."

I told her that general anesthetics often affected people's moods for several weeks; the drugs would wear off soon. "You've been wonderful," I added.

"I have," she agreed, "but I'm just not sure how long we can cope with the new Jack. He keeps playing the cripple card over and over."

I did my best to reassure her, promised to visit soon, but I put down the phone with a new dread. Jack had already lost so much. What if he lost Hilary too?

9

U NLIKE SOME LESS FORTUNATE colleagues I have, so far, had little to do with lawyers. After Trina was born, Viv and I went to one to make our wills. Our only disagreement was around the choice of guardian for the children; I wanted my mother; Viv wanted Claudia. After learning of my father's condition, the lawyer suggested we name Claudia with my mother as a backup. Then we had signed DNR forms and promised to honor each other's wishes. That night, I remember, we told ventilator jokes. "What exactly is a ventilator?" Viv had asked.

Apart from this, and the paperwork around buying our house and setting up my business, my only other encounter with the legal system has been jury duty. Twice, since we moved to our town, I have been called. The first time was high summer, and my prospective fellow jurors had opted for shorts and tank tops. In my white button-down and chinos, I felt staid and grumpy. Didn't the judicial system deserve some respect? I thought as the young man to my left dozed and the young woman to my right filed her nails. Shortly after noon a court official announced that all the cases on the docket had been dismissed, and so were we. I drove home in my respectful clothes, baffled. Why had forty-seven people given up their morning to sit in a stuffy room? At supper my father said that often happened in the case of minor offenses: traffic violations, petty thievery, D and D. He had been called for jury duty seven times, and regarded himself as an expert.

"But it's so wasteful," I said. "They show this inspiring film. Then they send us home."

He nodded, or perhaps his Parkinson's nodded, and said he'd thought that the first couple of times. "Then I started to regard it as a mechanism, like the safety procedures on the railway. Superfluous to requirements most of the time but, when something goes wrong, essential."

The second time I was summoned to the superior court. Prospective jurors filled out lengthy questionnaires in one room and were herded into another. Finally the defendant, a boy of sixteen, was led in, shambling, head down, wrists cuffed. He had stabbed another boy to death in the presence of several witnesses and was to be tried as an adult. When my turn came to be interviewed, I told the judge that I detested violence, but I would hate to put a child behind bars. She dismissed me.

That evening I described the scene to my father, who had just moved into the nursing home. "Maybe the boy needed people like me on the jury," I said. "Maybe I should have lied?"

"Bad to lie at any time," he said. "Worse under oath."

Six months later I read in the newspaper that the boy had been sentenced to life without parole. He had been photographed, clutching his teddy bear, on the way to prison.

Now, as I try to understand how Viv changed, I keep thinking about that boy clutching his bear. Would his parents and friends have sworn that he was a good person? Always ready to carry groceries and shovel the sidewalk? That the stabbing was some awful aberration? Or did they know something was amiss, that he carried a knife and might use it? Jack once described the

Greek idea of genius as an external force taking over a person. Had some force entered Viv—the mysterious Fate she sometimes invoked—and made her buy a gun? No, I believed she was entirely responsible for her actions. She had chosen, and she could have chosen otherwise.

During these difficult days I was meticulously attentive to my patients, double- and triple-checking tests, making sure people had no questions, no hidden fears, but when a woman came in reporting that the vision in her right eye had a hole in it—like a doughnut, Doctor—I sent her to Leah.

As for Viv, she went daily to the stables, where she rode Mercury and carried out her duties. Except for our nocturnal talks, she and I were like business partners, managing Marcus and Trina's lives. On the day Jack got out of hospital, I had to pick them up at Windy Hill. It was my first visit since the fatal evening, and as I drove up the hill I remembered the three of us laughing together, how I had pictured more such evenings with Viv there too. The snow was melting, and in the paddocks I spotted Samson, whose colic had caused so much trouble, and a sleek brown horse that might be Mrs. Hardy. No sign of Mercury.

In the barn, hoping to avoid Claudia, I walked briskly towards the office, but as I passed the lockers, the bathroom door opened. When I last saw her in the tack room I had not known she was pregnant. Now, as she came over and kissed my cheek, her condition was unmistakable. She asked about Jack, and I said he was at home, waiting for his second operation.

"I can't help feeling responsible." Her forehead furrowed. "After all, he was shot here."

I had a sudden, unexpected pang of sympathy for Viv. "If anyone should feel responsible," I said, "it's me. Viv told you about our drunken dinner, how I had a key."

"It must have been very drunken for you to drive here at eleven p.m. But nothing like that will happen again. We're having a gate installed at the bottom of the road, and a camera in the barn."

I praised the new measures and, on the pretext of collecting the children, hurried away.

That night Viv described what had happened with Charlie. She had waited until the two of them were alone, mucking out the stalls, to announce that she knew about Charlie riding Mercury. This was her last day at Windy Hill.

"She started waving the shovel, yelling. I just wanted to keep Mercury to myself. I didn't give a fuck what was best for him. I was sure she was going to hit me. She's worked at Windy Hill for three years, and I thought she saw me as an ideal big sister. But actually she thinks I'm a fat old bitch with poor hands and a terrible seat."

"You should have walked away," I said. "Fetched Matheus."

"I should, but it was like staring into the eyes of a snake. I was hypnotized by her anger. She knew exactly how to hurt me. Somehow she'd got it into her head she was going to compete on Mercury."

"She's obsessed with him," I said. A car drove by in the street.

"How can she be obsessed?" Viv's voice rose. "She's ridden him once, maybe twice. She knows nothing about him."

As she continued to rant, as another car drove by, I understood two things: she had no inkling that she and Charlie were peas in a pod, and, despite everything, she still cherished her own ambitions for Mercury.

"For god's sake," I said, pushing back my chair, "Jack nearly died. He may never have full use of his arm again, and he's suffering from PTSD, losing his temper all the time. Doesn't that change things?"

Standing there, looking down at Viv, I heard my own words and knew the answer. Yes, it did. There could be no more excuses. Tomorrow I must go to the police.

"She'll never see him again," Viv said, "if I can help it."

10

I woke the next morning still fully resolved, and when Merrie told me that the police had phoned to ask if I could come to the station to make a statement, I felt only relief. But as I read the notes for my first patient, I pictured Trina drawing her five ghosts. As I flicked lenses back and forth, I remembered the four of us, one hot afternoon last summer, swimming across Walden Pond, with Marcus acting as our personal lifeguard. When I left the office, I headed not directly to the police station but to Hilary's house. The sight of Jack, I thought, would strengthen my resolve.

"I'm so glad you've come," Hilary said. "He's having a bad day." Her hair hung limply around her wan face.

In the living room Jack was sitting on the sofa. With his arm strapped to his chest, he was an oddly misshapen figure. "You find me at a nadir," he said.

"Is there anything I can do?"

"Unless you're a magician, no. My shoulder is excruciating and will be worse after they operate. The painkillers make me stupid rather than pleasantly stoned. I can't work on my book. And the flashbacks are worse."

He kept remembering the shot and gradually other details were coming back: the music in the car, the bumpy road, the stink of horses as we stepped into the barn. And then the hospital. "I remember Hilary," he said, "sitting beside me, talking, and you. I remember a nurse, wiping my face, murmuring, 'Le pauvre aveugle.' "

So I was right. Like my patient imprisoned by her stroke, he had known what was happening.

"Donald," he went on, "I'm scared, not so much of the operation but the anesthesia. What if they put me under, and this time I can't get back? That stupid song keeps running through my head . . . 'Get back to where you once belonged.' "

I promised to talk to the surgeon and the anesthesiologist, to make sure they used different drugs. "I'll tell them to keep you as close to the surface as possible without pain."

"Even pain," Jack said, "is preferable to going too far away."

I left the house furious, yet relieved. My path was clear. But as I pulled into a parking space at the police station, another long-ago memory seized me. One Christmas in Edinburgh a group of us had gone carol singing round the pubs to raise money for charity. When we paused for a drink, a fellow singer, a history student I scarcely knew, confided that she had just come from visiting hours at the prison. More than twenty years earlier, her mother had driven the getaway car for an IRA bank robbery in which a cashier had died. Although she had not known that guns were involved, had never touched a gun, her mother was in jail for life.

"She could get parole," the daughter said, "if she snitched on the others."

"But you wouldn't want her to betray her ideals."

"Wouldn't I?" She gave a bitter smile. "I've seen her once a month through a bulletproof window since I was five years old. All I want is for her to come home."

I was still thinking about that smile when Detective O'Donnell appeared. Dressed in a blue suit, perhaps five months pregnant, she led me to a small office. After asking permission to record our conversation, she told me to give my name, address, and phone number, and recount the events of that Saturday night. I described having dinner with my friends Hilary Blake and Jack Brennan. Afterwards Ms. Blake had wanted to visit the horse she was boarding at Windy Hill. My wife managed the stables, and I had a key. I included all the facts until the moment we pulled Jack out of the stall. Then I remembered Trina crying in the night, and fell silent.

"So," said Detective O'Donnell, "you have no idea who shot Mr. Brennan, or why anyone would want to?"

"No."

"In your opinion, you or Ms. Blake could equally have been the target?"

"Yes."

Glancing down at some papers on her desk, she said that unless the gunman struck again, or they found the weapon, she was afraid they weren't going to solve this one. Then she asked after Jack, and I described his fears and flashbacks. She nodded. Two colleagues, she said, had been shot in the last year. Both had made a full recovery, but each had had nightmares for months afterward.

"The shock of another person trying to kill you," she said, "it's like nothing else." As she spoke, her hand moved to her belly. She was due, I judged, around the same time as Claudia.

I had not told Viv I planned to go the police, and I did not, that evening, confess my failure. Instead I announced that I was worried about the gun. She could not have thrown it far. What if someone else found it? Used it? Then she would have more blood on her hands. I was glad to see my phrasing made her wince.

"I'll look tomorrow," she said. "But please, Don, can't we agree to put this behind us? Marcus and Trina need us, need both of us." Wisely she did not mention her own needs, only gazed at me beseechingly.

"I can't promise anything," I said.

11

THE NEXT DAY I waited until everyone had left the office, texted Viv—*late home*—and typed "Robert Walter Dougherty" into my computer. If Viv could find a gun online, perhaps I could find Robert. The little icons whirled: three pages of results. It was as if someone had applied a defibrillator to my chest. When I could move again, I got up and checked that both office doors were locked. Back at my desk, I had the sudden awful thought: What if he was dead?

But he was not dead, and he was not in Scotland. All along he had been within reach. Robert W. Dougherty, born Edinburgh, Scotland, 1969, BA Williams College, MFA New York University. He now worked in Washington, DC, restoring pictures; his specialty was gilding. He was married and had two children. There were four photographs of him. At first only his fair skin and long eyelashes were familiar but as I kept looking I began to see, hidden among the pixels, the boy I had known.

I wrote to him that evening, first typing the letter and then copying it out by hand.

> *Dear Robert,*
>   *I am at last answering your letters, the letters I*

couldn't bear to read, still can't, but that I keep with all the ones I did read, in a shoebox. As a child the word sorry had a magical power. All you had to do was say it, and you were forgiven. You could get back to the place you'd been before you'd done whatever you'd done. As an adult, "Sorry" seems a very small thing to say, but I am sorry. I was a coward and didn't answer your letters. I couldn't bear to. My mother's decision to stay in the States was the worst thing that had ever happened to me until my father's death last spring. He had Parkinson's for many years.

I did look for you when I came back to Edinburgh to study medicine, but the shop was gone. No one answered your door. I was there for eight years, always on the look-out for you. Now I know we crossed paths mid-Atlantic as you came to Williams. Hard to picture you in that small, neat town, so different from Edinburgh, but you must have enjoyed it; you stayed. I came back here to help take care of my father.

I am writing to you now because I find myself in a try-ing situation—I am speaking what my two children call "Scottish"—and it would mean a great deal to me to have your advice. I'd like to talk to you, even for an hour. Please know that I don't expect you to forgive me.

I also have less selfish reasons for wanting to see you. I would like to know how you are, how your life has turned out so far. You have excellent press on the Web. I include all possible ways of reaching me.

Yours ever,

Donald Stevenson

I addressed the envelope to "Robert W. Dougherty, Personal," c/o the museum that was listed as his main place of work, and drove to the post office. When I arrived home, there was a note on the kitchen table: "Looked for nearly an hour. Couldn't find it."

12

MY MOTHER HAS NOT appeared in these pages for some time, an omission that reflects my behavior. In the days following the accident I avoided her company, and she unwittingly abetted me by canceling her Friday babysitting; Larry's wife was gravely ill. The day after Jack's second operation—he had come round in recovery and stayed awake long past the point of exhaustion— she phoned to ask if we could meet for lunch. "Same place," she said. "My turn to ask a question."

In one of our library books Robert and I had read the story of Tristan and Iseult. Iseult's husband, King Mark, suspects her of infidelity, and decides to test her with hot irons. When Iseult learns that the test will be held in a meadow by the river, she sends a message to Tristan; he must be waiting on the bank, disguised as a beggar. On the appointed day she arrives by boat. The beggar is summoned to carry her ashore. King Mark asks his question, and she says, My lord, I swear no man save you, and that beggar, has ever held me in his arms. Then she plucks the irons out of the fire, walks eight paces, drops them, and holds up her hands, pale and unmarked, for all to see.

"But Iseult lied," I said. "Why didn't the irons burn her?"

"What she says is true," Robert argued.

My father, when consulted, said we were both right. Iseult had told the truth with intent to deceive, which many people would call lying. But King Mark, he went on, was a bad man, trying to hurt his wife. Desperate measures, like hot irons, require desperate remedies.

As I walked down Main Street that day to meet my mother, I wished I knew how my father would counter Viv's arguments. "Why would you want to hurt your family?" she had said last night. "Hasn't there already been enough hurting?"

At the bar, with its glowing bottles and TV screens, I chose a corner table and ordered a Bloody Mary. I was taking the first sip when my mother appeared. "That looks good," she said, and kissed my cheek. We each ordered the same sandwich as last time. I told her Jack was awake, talking and eating.

"Wonderful. And how is he doing in other ways?"

I moved my hand from side to side. "Being shot has shaken his worldview."

"Understandably. Sometimes I try to imagine what it's like being Jack: buying a sandwich, crossing the street, walking into a roomful of strangers. Just the courage it takes to get through a day seems unbelievable. Let me tell you why I wanted to see you. Jean has pneumonia, and Larry has asked the doctors to honor her DNR form. But yesterday she was struggling so hard to breathe. It was horrible. I feel like we're killing her."

"The pneumonia is killing her," I said. "It used to be called the old man's friend—and maybe that's no bad thing."

She leaned back in her seat, arms folded. "Would you say that if this was Edward?"

"No, but that's my problem. You know, once at the nursing home I tried to kill him."

"What do you mean, 'tried to kill him'?"

Neither of us paid any attention to the sandwiches our server set before us.

"I took one of his pillows and stood by the bed, trying to get up the courage to hold it over his face."

"Oh." She smiled gently. "I thought you meant drugs, or some secret doctor's trick. I can't tell you the number of times I stood in his room, clutching a pillow and wishing I had the guts to use it. He made me promise, over and over, to help him when things got desperate, but I couldn't. I always wanted one more day with him."

"We're a fine pair," I said. "So what does Larry think?"

As we began to eat, she said Larry was stalwart in wanting to abide by Jean's wishes, but last night had been too much even for him. Briefly my own dilemmas receded. "Get her doctor to give her morphine," I said. "She'll look like she's still struggling, but her spirit will be far away. Isn't that what you want?"

"Devoutly. I thought I'd got everything under control, but I keep waking up in a panic. Graham says I'm reliving Edward's death."

"Graham?"

"My therapist. I needed someone to talk to about Edward, to help me keep my balance. Haven't you ever talked to anyone?"

You, I thought. My father. Jack. "No," I said.

She smiled again. "You're Edward's son through and through. Speaking of balance, how are you and Viv doing? She left a cryptic message the other day. I phoned back, but she never replied."

Once again I moved my hand from side to side. "So-so."

My mother looked at me closely. "For you, that's like saying World War III has broken out. Would you care to elaborate?"

I shook my head and reminded her about Marcus's swim meet. She typed the details into her phone. But as we got up to leave, she said, "What if the doctor won't give her morphine?"

I promised to intervene. "Jean shouldn't have to suffer another minute," I said. Unlike the rest of us, I thought.

13

I POUNCED ON THE MAIL at home and at the office; I held my breath as I opened my e-mail; between patients, I checked my phone. Nothing, nothing, nothing. Stupidly I had not thought to use express or certified mail but had reverted to my youthful confidence in the postal system, when letter after letter had flown safely across the Atlantic. I was about to write again when at 4:45 on the day after I met my mother, Merrie announced I had a phone call.

"Good afternoon," I said, "Dr. Stevenson speaking."

"Good afternoon. Robert Dougherty speaking."

I must have responded in some way.

"No need to go overboard," said Robert. "You still sound amazingly Scottish."

"I was in Edinburgh for nearly eight years as a student."

"And I have one of those mid-Atlantic accents, neither fish nor fowl. I don't recognize my own voice."

At first I didn't recognize him either, but sentence by sentence, he sounded more familiar. "Where are you now?" I said.

"Like you, at my place of work. My assistant just left for the day. In a few minutes I have to pick up the hellions, aka Nora and Tom."

That we each had a boy and a girl pleased me deeply. "If I come to DC," I said, "can you spare me an hour?"

"Or two. When do you want to come?"

I said as soon as possible, and he said Thursday. He knew the perfect place to meet.

I do not know how long I sat there after I put down the phone, staring at my model eye, the dark pupil staring back.

A FEW HOURS LATER my mother summoned me. As I drove to the nursing home, I recalled all the late-night trips to visit my father, fear so high in my throat I could barely breathe. He had talked to me about death, directly, only once. One October afternoon, when I was planting tulip bulbs under his supervision, he announced that he was not afraid of dying.

"I'll miss all of you," he said. "I'll miss the tulips, but I'm not afraid."

"Perhaps"—I wedged a bulb into a hole—"you'll change your mind."

"Probably. The selfish limpet will make one last effort to cling to the rock. I respect the limpet, but it shouldn't be allowed to banish my saner self. I don't want you and Peggy wasting your lives at my bedside. Please remember that."

Jean, according to my mother, shared his view. Push me out of a window, she had said. Don't waste your drugs and sympathy on me.

At the nursing home the attendant directed me to her room. "Poor dear," she said. "She's listening to the angels."

From the top of the stairs, I saw two girls sitting on the floor, halfway down the carpeted corridor. As I approached, their heart-shaped faces turned towards me. A Scrabble board lay between them.

"Sorry," one of them said. "Are we in the way?"

"Not at all. Are you visiting your grandmother?"

The same girl spoke again. "She's dying, but there's nothing we can do. We've said good-bye and we love you. Our mom said it was okay to play. Before she got sick, Gran loved Scrabble."

"I'm sure she'd be happy you're playing," I said.

They turned back to the board. The room I stepped into was identical to my father's, even down to the Matisse collage on the wall. The lamp on the chest of drawers cast a soft light over the bed and the figures around it. Larry and my mother rose to meet me. My mother kissed my cheek.

"Thanks for coming so quickly," she said. "This is Rosemary, Jean and Larry's daughter."

An older version of the girls smiled and offered her hand. I said I had just met her daughters; they seemed very composed.

She nodded. "They wanted to come, and I didn't have a sitter. People used to die at home all the time."

Jean was propped up on several pillows. Her eyes were closed, her mouth open, her breathing stertorous. She wore an elegant white nightdress, the neck and sleeves lined with lace. As I searched for her pulse, she took another faltering, noisy breath.

"Let's hope," my mother said in a low voice, "she's dreaming of the green fields of her youth."

"Should we call the doctor?" Larry said. "Is she in pain?"

I said truthfully that I didn't think so. "She's already far, far away. All you can do is keep her company. In practical terms, she's beyond help."

"We thought so," said Larry, "but we wanted to be sure. You've released us. Now we'll try to release her."

He stood up and, moving to the end of the bed, began to

rub Jean's feet. My mother took one of her hands and began to gently stroke it; on the other side of the bed Rosemary did the same. Then she began to sing, her voice clear and sweet:

> *The water is wide, I cannot get o'er.*
> *And neither have I wings to fly.*
> *Build me a boat that can carry two*
> *And both shall row, my love and I.*

When the song ended, I went to the bathroom, rinsed a washcloth in warm water, and came back to wipe Jean's face. Rosemary had begun another song, one I didn't know, when Jean grunted, choked, choked again, and, after a long, shuddering moment, fell silent.

"She's gone," said Larry. His hands did not stop moving over her feet.

"Finish the song," said my mother.

Rosemary did. Then she went to fetch her daughters. The three of them came in, hand in hand, the girls' eyes wide. Without being asked, they stepped forward. The smaller girl patted her grandmother's hand. Her sister said, "Thank you for taking care of us when we were little."

My mother's face was wet with tears, and I put my arm around her. "I'm not crying for Jean," she said. "It was just so beautiful."

We were all silent, letting that word hold sway. Then Larry said, speaking to the five of us gathered around the bed, and also to some larger presence, "Thank you. Most of the last few years were the exact opposite of what Jean wanted, but tonight was exactly what she wanted."

Writing this now, I notice what I failed to at the time: I had begun to like Larry. No one could take my father's place, but my mother had chosen a man of substance and generosity. As I moved towards my final accounting with Viv, the knowledge that my mother had a worthy companion was a comfort. If my family went aground, she would sail on.

14

Ever since my first reluctant journey across the Atlantic, I have liked flying. Not so much leaving one place and arriving at another, but that sense of being lifted, however briefly, into some parallel universe. I envy the select group of people who have made love at thirty thousand feet. Now, on the 8:00 a.m. flight to Washington, I wanted only to arrive. At no point in our conversation had Robert seemed in danger of being swept away by emotion, but why should he? I was the one who had broken our friendship. What had he thought when, day after day, the postman had passed by empty-handed? Our affection had never been put into words. We were chums, pals, on the same team for rounders and cricket. We signed our letters "love," but the question "How do you feel?" referred only to the physical: Are you hungry? Are you tired?

I had visited Washington twice, thirty years before with my parents and two years before with Viv and the children. They had been too young for most of the sights, although Marcus enjoyed the Air and Space Museum; we all four rubbed the shard of moon rock for luck. The oldest thing you'll ever touch, Viv had said. As the plane came in to land, I recognized the tall white obelisk of the Washington Monument and the dome of the Capitol. Robert's city. Fifteen minutes later I was on the Metro. We crossed the shining Potomac and headed underground. With nearly two hours to wait, I decided to go one more stop and visit the Archives Museum. In Marcus and Trina's restless company it had been hard to do anything besides count eagles in the Rotunda. Now the idea of seeing the documents that both marked and created America's independence from Britain, on the day of my reunion with Robert, seemed suddenly fitting.

An escalator carried me out of the gloomy Metro into the pleasant spring day. In front of the giant pillared building, as if waiting for me, were two large seated statues. "What is past is prologue," one announced. "Study the past," commanded the other. Only a few other people were there at that early hour, and soon I was climbing the wide marble steps and weaving through the lines of ropes into the Rotunda. The documents were, as I recalled, dimly lit and faded, the Constitution in its four large cases guarded by two flags. Marcus had said that in an emergency the cases descended into a lead-lined vault, but I saw no sign of any mechanism. I went over to the earliest document, the Charter of Freedom, and began to work my way around the semicircle. Peering closely at the Declaration of Independence, I could make out only a few words: "We, therefore," "united States of America," "Free and Independent." Somewhere on these four pages were the words Marcus had quoted at supper, months ago, about that very un-Scottish concept: the pursuit of happiness.

Examining the Bill of Rights, I struggled to decipher the amendment that allowed gun ownership. Later I looked it up. "A well regulated militia, being necessary to the security of a free State, the right of the people to keep and bear arms, shall not be infringed." Poring over the sacred document, I could barely distinguish *militia* and *infringed*.

By dint of stopping for coffee, I was only twenty minutes early at our designated meeting place: the Freer Gallery of Art. Inside, I followed a corridor around two sides of a courtyard to the Peacock Room. My first thought was how modest it was in size; my second how poorly lit. The three tall windows were shuttered, and the decorative lights shed a subdued glow on the blue-green ceiling and walls. The walls themselves were lined with thin gold shelves, holding numerous bowls and vases. Over the fireplace was a large gold-framed picture of a woman wearing a kimono. Facing her, painted directly on the wall, were two golden peacocks. I sat down on the single bench at the end nearest the door, my back to the shuttered windows. Each minute was a huge boulder I must roll up an enormous hill and push over the edge. I did this fourteen times.

My mother claims she can tell almost everything about a job candidate from how he or she enters the room. I kept my eyes fixed on the doorway, enduring with each set of footsteps the crest of hope, the dash of disappointment. If I saw Robert enter, I would know whether there was any chance of him forgiving me. He walked in lightly, casually. Indeed I had dismissed the footsteps as those of a woman when he appeared in the doorway. He halted, and I, moving to stand, froze.

"Donald Stevenson," he said. "As I live and breathe."

Then he was laughing, stepping towards me, kissing me on both cheeks. Once I straightened, we were exactly the same height. If we had turned back to back, a tea tray could have balanced level on our two heads. He was wearing a gray shirt of which only the collar showed above a navy blue sweater, black jeans, and black boots. His brown hair was neatly combed. He looked elegant in a way I had not expected.

"Thank you for meeting me," I said, or tried to say.

He laughed again. "My pleasure. How long have you been here?"

"My plane got in soon after nine."

"I meant here, in the Peacock Room?"

"Fourteen minutes."

"Still precise to a fault. So you've had a chance to look round?"

I said no, and he said we must look at the shutters. "They open them at noon. I wanted you to see the room change."

The three sets of shutters were painted the same blue-green as the walls, and each was decorated with a golden peacock, although in the dim light, peering across the rail that contained visitors, it was not easy to make out the details. This art history lesson was not—not remotely—how I had imagined our first meeting as adults, but if Robert had come to my office, I would surely have shown him my model eye and various machines. He made us stand in front of the sideboard as the attendant folded back the shutters. The intricate lattice of the ceiling and the lush dark hair of the woman in the painting were suddenly vivid.

"Do you see the butler's door?" Robert gestured at the leaded glass door on our left. "The whole design for the room grew out of that scalloped pattern."

He described how the English industrialist Leyland had commissioned the American artist Whistler to decorate a room in his London house to display his Chinese pottery. Whistler had created the Peacock Room and presented a bill for two thousand guineas. Leyland, protesting the excessive decoration, had paid him a thousand pounds, at which point a defiant Whistler had painted the two fighting peacocks over the sideboard: Art and Money. The peacock on the left, Art, with its little white tuft, was Whistler, who had a white forelock. On the right

Money sported ruffled neck feathers and a glittering glass eye; Leyland often wore ruffled shirts.

"Whistler never saw the room again," Robert said. "Then Leyland died, and the new owner of the house sold it to Freer, who had it shipped to his house in Detroit. After World War I it was moved to the Smithsonian. I couldn't think of a better place to meet you," he concluded, "than a room that began life on one side of the Atlantic and ended up on the other."

"A movable room," I said, struck by the poetry of the idea.

"We can pretend we're in London, or Detroit, or Washington. They only open the shutters once a month. Let's sit down, and you can tell me about your 'trying' situation."

For a few seconds I was tempted to invent some minor crisis. Why spoil our reunion? Then, recalling the torment and indecision of the last fortnight, I launched into an account of the events leading up to that night at Windy Hill. Robert did not interrupt, nor did his expression change as I described my friendship with Jack, Viv's obsession with Mercury, Charlie's secret riding, but when I said Viv had gone to New Hampshire and bought a gun, he shifted abruptly.

"You're married to a woman who solves problems by buying a gun?"

"It was news to me too."

A couple had stationed themselves in front of us. Robert lowered his voice. "Before you tell me anything else," he said, "I have to tell you I am not remotely impartial on this topic. My first year here I was mugged twice. The first time was kids on a spree. Hopefully they had a good night out on my fifty dollars. But the second time the guy shoved a gun in my chest. His pupils were big as a cat's. I was sure I was going to die a hundred yards from home."

I pictured Robert alone on a deserted street, as terrified as I had been when the bullet whistled into Mercury's stall. "But you didn't," I said.

"An ambulance drove by, and the siren distracted him. He grabbed my wallet, spat at me, and loped off down the street. The police found me sitting on the pavement. They said there wasn't a prayer of catching him. The next day I packed my suitcases and rang the travel agent. All I wanted was to get back to Edinburgh."

The right of the people, I thought, to keep and bear arms.

But to fly the same day cost a fortune. He had booked a flight for the following week, and by then he'd decided to stay until the end of his contract. "I found a therapist," he said, "and I talked and talked about the squalid fact that I'd have done almost anything to stay alive. So when you tell me your wife bought a gun, I am not in sympathy."

"It was partly my fault," I said. "She thought she had to protect Mercury."

"You sound like you're defending her."

"No, no, I'm as horrified as you are, but I am married to her. I feel obligated to try to understand."

Behind us the guard was pointing out details of the fighting peacocks. "In some odd way," Robert said, "this country doesn't care about children once they're out of the womb. Education, welfare, health care, they're always under siege. And if the lack of those three doesn't do kids in, then the adults, the people supposedly in charge of keeping them safe, give them guns."

I have paraphrased his speech as best I can. It was one I knew well, one that my parents, my friends, my colleagues, had uttered at various times: Hey ho, America and her guns. At the time I barely listened. I kept my eyes fixed on the blue vase beneath Art and Money and described that night at the stables.

"So let me get this straight," Robert said. "Your wife accidentally shot your best friend. He's blind, and you're the only person who saw what happened? Christ. When you said you needed advice, I assumed it was something simple: an affair? bankruptcy?"

A woman sat down beside me and opened a notebook to a page filled with neat cursive. I remembered Robert and I at our wooden desks, practicing joined-up writing. "What should I do?" I said.

"If it was an accident, why didn't she go to the police?"

"She was scared, she panicked, she wanted to talk to me, then we got caught up in the children, waiting for Jack to recover consciousness—"

"And you didn't go either."

I said nothing. My silence seemed shameful, inexplicable. I could only offer more. At last Robert broke it by asking if I still loved Viv.

"I'm not sure," I said, "if the person I love still exists."

"Does she love you?"

I had tried, for several months, not to ask this question. "It's hard to tell. She's so focused on Mercury. I'm useful—I earn money, cook meals, help with the children—but otherwise, I think, I'm pretty much irrelevant."

Robert put his hand, briefly, on my arm. "Tell me about Jack," he said, and I did: Jack the brilliant scholar who had denied his blindness for years, Jack in the midst of his tricky recovery.

"He sounds remarkable. So if Viv were here, how would she plead her case?"

"She would say that Mercury is a horse in a million, that together they can win competitions. She can be a great equestrian." I stared at Art and Money. "She would say she gave up a lot so that I could take care of my father, that he and the children have always come first, that she got a gun because I lied to her and she was sure Mercury was in danger. She never meant to use it. She saw three strangers trying to hurt her beloved horse, and her finger slipped."

Robert stood up and motioned towards the door. In the corridor, he said, "At first I was surprised you'd become an ophthalmologist. Then it seemed just right that you would work on a small, precise organ. Those model airplanes were good training for both of us."

He was speaking casually, over his shoulder, but something about his phrasing caught my attention. "Did you know, before my letter, that I was a doctor?"

"I googled you. Years ago."

"And you didn't contact me?" In my surprise I came to a halt.

Then it was his turn to be startled. "Do you mean," he said, stopping and turning to face me, "you only just found out I was here?"

I nodded. "I looked for you in Edinburgh. I didn't think of the Web until I was desperate. I'm sorry I didn't answer your letters. When I realized we weren't coming home, I didn't know what to say."

He led the way to a glass door, and we stepped into the courtyard. In the center a fountain rose, glittering and calm, surrounded by a low privet hedge. We sat down at one of the wrought-iron tables. "I wrote to you," he said, "suggesting we start a flying fund. No more models. We would save up for real planes, to visit each other. I'd saved nearly forty pounds when I gave up."

The possibility that we could have remained friends, seen each other in the summer, written and spoken on the phone, broke over me like a flood tide.

"But maybe," he continued, "it was just as well you stopped writing. Maybe we both needed to be where we were, doing whatever we were doing."

"Do you really think that?" I asked when I could speak again.

"I think the world is everything that is the case, as Wittgenstein so unhelpfully said. When I told my parents that I wanted to study in the States, they assumed it was because of you, and in a way it was. Thanks to you, America was always on my radar. I'm very sorry about your father. I remember when we played trains, he used to make up amazing journeys."

The courtyard suddenly brightened. A gust of wind tossed water from the fountain onto the privet leaves. I asked about his wife. Marguerite was French. She worked at the embassy and understood the painstaking nature of restoration. "See that green." He pointed to the privet. "In the fifteenth century that was a hugely expensive color. Artists used it only when patrons requested it. Then green got cheaper, and suddenly there were all these nature painters."

Now that we were outside, he gestured freely. I might have passed him in the street without recognizing his face, but I would have recognized the way his hands accompanied his words, and although they were presently encased in neat black boots, I am sure I would have recognized his bony feet. Whatever came next, I was glad to have these hours.

Much that we talked about has nothing to do with this story. At some point Robert phoned his office to say he was taking off the rest of the day. We abandoned my problems and walked to another museum to eat delicious food off cafeteria trays. We exchanged news of our parents—his were flourishing in Fife—and of people we had known. We reminisced about an outing to the open-air swimming pool at Portobello, when we had dared each other to jump off the highest diving board.

"We were eight years old," Robert said, "and the board must have been thirty feet high. I remember you could see the Castle from the top. I can't believe no one stopped us."

I remarked that there weren't so many rules back then.

"That's still true in Britain compared to here," he said. "But I do like the States. It's the country of second chances." He paired his knife and fork neatly on the edge of his plate as if one of our mothers, his or mine, might be about to reprimand his table manners.

"I wish I felt that way," I said. "Perhaps it's because I never really decided to be here. First my parents brought me. Then my father's illness brought me back."

"And now?"

"Now I could never do to my children what was done to me."

"They'll grow up," he said. "You'll have a second life and a third, like the Peacock Room."

I thought of Viv, fainting on the subway platform. I thought of my lies. "I think my second life has already begun," I said.

We returned once more to the Peacock Room. A man in a blue shirt was lecturing a tour about the painting over the fireplace. Christina Spartali's father had refused to buy it because it wasn't enough of a portrait. As the tour straggled out, Robert asked if I remembered that sonnet, "My mistress' eyes are nothing like the sun."

"Who would ever say Spartali's name now," he said, "if not for Whistler? I have to pick up the kids in an hour. How can I help?"

"What do you think I should do?" I said. "There's no one I trust more."

Once again he circled the room, pausing at what I presume were favorite vases, before he led the way back to the courtyard. It had begun to rain. We sat at a different table under the arcade. I felt very calm. The rain fell on the sidewalk in big warm splotches.

"I think," Robert said at last, "you have several choices, none of them simple. You can beg Viv to go to the police. You can tell Jack and let it be his decision. You can consult a minister or a rabbi or a Zen master and do whatever they advise. You can walk away. But if you want to know what *I* think you should do, I think you should go to the police."

Night after night, I had stood in the doorway of Trina or Marcus's room, weighing their well-being against my need to look in the mirror. Now, listening to Robert, all the equations fell away. Going to the police was the only right thing to do. I could not shift the burden of decision onto Viv, or Jack, or even my children.

"So?" he said.

"The police," I said.

The rain fell softly within a few inches of our feet. "Will you tell Viv first?"

Again I knew the answer. "Yes. This doesn't have to do with my feelings for her."

"And Jack?" Robert's eyes were closer to gray than I remembered. Or perhaps I had misremembered.

"And Jack what?"

"Do you think he'll be able to forgive you?"

All along I'd been thinking that Viv was the one who had hurt Jack. Now, with Robert's question, I began to understand that I too, by my silence, by my lies, had hurt him. I held out my hand to catch the rain. "I don't know," I said. "I'm not sure anyone will forgive me: Jack, Viv, my mother, my children."

"I bet they will," said Robert. "Eventually. And then you have to forgive yourself. In your letter you wrote that sorry is a very small thing to say, but what else do we have?"

We went back into the museum, walked past the Peacock Room and out into the street. As I apologized for monopolizing the conversation, Robert's hair grew dark with rain. Mine too, I assume.

"I hope we can meet again," I said, suddenly awkward.

"Sure," he said. "Give me a heads-up when you're next in DC, and I'll do the same if work brings me to Boston. Do you know the way to the Metro?"

I did. We embraced, kissed each other's cheeks. He wished me luck and walked off with his quick, easy stride into the rain.

15

WE WERE PAST DAYLIGHT savings, and the sun was just setting behind downtown Boston as I left the airport. I found myself thinking again of the woman who'd driven the IRA getaway car, the yearning on her daughter's face as she sang "Deck the Halls." Which matters more: ideals or people? When Diane posed the hypothetical question about the Rembrandt and the grandmother, I had felt certain I knew the answer. But I had lost that certainty. Now, thanks to Robert, I had it back. There might be different versions of reality, but there were indisputable facts: a gun, a bullet, Jack's pain, the laws of Massachusetts. I arrived home to find the children playing Ping-Pong and Viv scrubbing the kitchen floor, a latter-day penitent in her yellow rubber gloves.

An hour later, sitting at the kitchen table, the air still smelling faintly of Murphy Oil Soap, I described my day. "How great," Viv said. "After all these years you found Robert." Her smile was so bright, I blinked. I had forgotten what she looked like when she was not struggling to contain, or conceal, her feelings.

"I needed his advice," I said.

The brightness vanished. "And?"

I told her my decision. "I'm sorry," I added.

I had been ready to justify myself, to explain my reasoning, but she gave a small, curt nod. "For what it's worth"—her gaze was surprisingly neutral—"I'm amazed you waited this long."

Quietly she stood up and left the room. I heard the study door close. Later, in a notebook on the desk, I read the list she wrote that night.

> *Saddle pad for M.*
> *Talk to Claudia, kids, Peggy.*
> *Speak to Francesca re lawyer.*
> *Police.*

My jaw clenched when I read this for the first time, and still does when I reread it. The human brain often juxtaposes the sublime and the trivial. On the beach at Gloucester, in the midst of lamenting my father, I was momentarily distracted by what I thought was a seal. But that the arrangements of our lives came after a saddle pad for Mercury made me want to break things.

That night at the kitchen table, though, the night after my day with Robert, I had no idea what she was writing. I sat there, looking at the print of Edinburgh Castle, wondering if I should go after her, tell her that, whatever came next, we would face it together. Instead I went over to Nabokov's cage. He was sitting on his perch, one claw drawn up, his head tucked to one side. I opened the door and reached in to stroke him.

"Tell me I'm doing the right thing," I said.

"Now is the winter of our discount tents," he said in my father's voice. Then, giving me a bright, attentive look, he reached out and pecked my wedding ring.

In bed I did not read but turned out the light and lay there, my head full of thoughts about Robert and the movable room. Around the feet of the Money peacock the ground was strewn with little gold coins. The blue vase on the sideboard was from the Song dynasty, eleventh or early twelfth century. How had it survived nearly eight hundred years when I could barely survive forty? I was in that state between waking and sleeping, neither fully inhabiting my body nor entirely absent, when I heard footsteps. The mattress dipped. There were hands on my chest, my stomach, lower. One part of me drew back, watching; one part plunged into doing. Then Viv and I were making the beast with two backs: rocking, pushing, almost fighting. We cried out, and for a few seconds we were both free of the net of time. When I opened my eyes again, she was gone. Only a lingering warmth testified to her presence.

16

My confession, after all my agonizing, was surprisingly easy. At lunchtime—Viv had asked me to wait until noon—I drove to the police station; there was a parking space; Detective O'Donnell was on duty. Seated once again in her small office, I offered neither apology nor excuse. There was something I hadn't told her. I had seen who shot Jack Brennan. My wife had accidentally fired the gun. Detective O'Donnell offered no reproaches. She thanked me and asked for details: Where did Viv get the gun? New Hampshire. Where was it now? She'd thrown it into the woods. Where was she? At Windy Hill. Did she know I was here? She did. The whole momentous conversation took less than ten minutes.

"What will happen?" I said.

"We'll talk to Ms. Turner, and hopefully recover the weapon. It'll be up to the DA exactly what she's charged with."

"And me?" I said. "Will I be charged with concealing a crime, withholding information?"

"In the circumstances—Mr. Brennan is recovering, the assailant is your wife—I very much doubt it. And you have children, don't you?"

As I rose to leave, I asked if she could wait until tomorrow evening to speak to Jack. "I want to be the one to tell him," I said.

She eyed me curiously; I was sure she was going to refuse. Then she said, "It's quite irregular, but I don't see why not."

All afternoon as I met with my patients, I was thinking, Is Viv being arrested now? Or now? Is she being taken away in handcuffs? I was waiting at the school gates when finally a text came: *talked to police tell u later*. In the supermarket I allowed Trina and Marcus each to choose three treats.

"Is something wrong?" Trina asked.

I was in the kitchen, unpacking the groceries, when there was a knock at the door. "Hello," called my mother. Viv had phoned to ask her to babysit. She needed me at the stables. The code of the new security gate was the year of her birth.

Only now, writing this, do I realize that I could have ignored her summons, gone to Paddy's Lunch and enjoyed a solitary beer. At the time I seemed to have no more choice than one of my father's trains. It was just growing dark, and the road outside town was still lined with snow. I listened to the CD Hilary had played as we drove to the stables. In all the turmoil, I had never once thought to call my sister. Without our father, we had less and less in common. On the barn door was a note: "In the arena." The windows shone as they had the night I came to retrieve Marcus's book. When I stepped inside, Viv and Mercury were at the far end. I sat down in the viewing area.

As they approached, I saw the dark shine of his eyes, the muscles rippling in his shoulders and haunches, his tail flying like a flag carried into battle. I had never seen Viv ride him before. Now she was offering me her most persuasive argument: Mercury in motion. After circling twice, she approached the row of jumps. I watched, and then I shut my eyes and listened. Gradually I began to separate out the sounds. The thud of hooves, the snort of breath, Viv's comments when they were close: "Good boy." "Pay attention." The way Mercury's pace slowed as he neared a jump. The brief silence while he was in the air and, when he landed, the rhythm different again until he hit his stride.

I opened my eyes to see him galloping towards the highest jump. He and Viv leaned forward, hurling themselves into the air. Mercury drew his hindquarters under him. His forelegs reached for the ground. During one of our early dinners Jack had described the Centaurides, beings half horse, half woman, the two halves not fighting, like Dr. Jekyll and Mr. Hyde, but in harmony. This was Viv's ultimate version of the beast with two backs. This was what she had risked our lives for.

And with that thought, the spell was broken. I was on my feet.

"Wait," called Viv.

In a moment she and Mercury were beside me. I could feel his warmth, hear his breathing. "What happened with the police?" I said.

Her face, looking down at me, was shadowed by her helmet. "I told them everything, except Chance's name, and I took them to where I'd thrown the gun. One of the policemen went back and forth with a metal detector. He found the ammunition but not the gun. They'll try again when the snow's gone. Then I went to the station and made a statement."

"But you're not under arrest."

"Not yet." Her voice was calm, almost gentle, as she described how sometime this spring the district attorney would decide the charges. Then Viv would appear before a judge, who would decide her sentence: probably six months to a year.

As she spoke, Mercury swung his head; his bit jingled. Did he sense her grief? Or mine?

. . .

SURELY IT WAS NO coincidence that that night the Simurg finally came. I was walking beside the Firth of Forth on a summer's day, bright but not warm, when suddenly the air overhead was thick with wingbeats. Before I understood what was happening, a pair of claws encircled me. The Simurg clasped me to its feathery breast. Slowly we rose into the air until I was looking down at the Hawes Inn and the houses of South Queensferry, the gray water of the Firth and then the city of Edinburgh, with its castle and its church spires, the city my parents, Robert, and I had left far behind. When the Simurg set me down at the country railway station, the willow herb was in full purple bloom. My father was standing at one end of the platform, waiting.

The next morning at breakfast I described the dream to Trina and Marcus.

"Did the bird talk?" Trina said.

"It must have been huge," said Marcus.

"It was, but I wasn't frightened. I don't remember either of us talking. There was no need."

I did not tell them about my father, how he had smiled as I approached and how, just as he was about to speak, my eyes had opened.

17

T~HAT AFTERNOON~ I ~BOUGHT~ a bottle of wine and drove to Jack's apartment. As I climbed the stairs, I was keenly aware of how far I was from forgiving Viv. In the city of my brain, there was no road, no route, from the hot, crowded street of anger to the courtyard of calm. And yet here I was, seeking forgiveness. The door was ajar, but for a few moments I stood, staring at the welcome mat, knowing I might never stand here again. I recalled the story of Iseult's clever lie, and my father's response. Would Jack understand how desperate I had been?

He was seated on the sofa, a braille book open on his lap. He raised his head when I came in, and I knew he saw the shadow of my approach. "Thanks for coming," he said. "What did you bring?"

"A merlot."

"Do you mind doing the honors? I can truthfully claim to be hors de combat."

His kitchen was unusually tidy, a single plate, bowl, and cup on the draining board. Hilary had not given up on him yet. Since I spoke to Detective O'Donnell, I had been consumed with the need to tell Jack, to confess, but I had no speech planned. My only thought was to offer the cliché—I have something to tell you—and stumble forward. In the living room, I set down our glasses.

"So," I said, "does facial vision work with one arm incapacitated?"

"Not really. When I saw my surgeon last week, he said it'll probably be six months before I can raise my arm above my shoulder. Cheers," he added incongruously.

"Cheers." Stalling again, I asked about his book. Had he had time to work on it?

His knuckles whitened around his wineglass. "No. Either I feel like crap, or I'm fighting with Hilary. I do want to write something about the blind and trauma. How do we process terrible events without sight? You know how blind people sometimes rock or nod: like Ray Charles, or Stevie Wonder." He moved his own head cautiously. "People used to think it was a sign of mental feebleness—the blind idiot—but it turns out that motion is a way of compensating for lack of visual stimulation."

"I've never seen you rocking."

"That's because I went blind as an adult, not because I'm not tempted. The point is, seeing isn't only about seeing. It's also a way to deal with pent-up feelings." He raised his wineglass. "How are things at Windy Hill?"

I watched as he tipped his glass, swallowed. "Why are you fighting with Hilary?"

"Because, to quote her, I'm surly and self-pitying. She doesn't mind taking care of me, but she can't bear me being such a gloomy son of a bitch. I don't blame her. I came back from the operation, but I didn't come back to the person I used to be. I can't stop being angry."

I felt as I had that cloudy afternoon at Portobello Pool, standing alone on the diving board, the dark water far below me, Robert swimming in the deep end, looking up at me, his expression indecipherable, the cold wind turning my arms and legs to gooseflesh, and the sure knowledge that one step forward would change everything. "I have something to tell you," I said. "It was Viv who shot you."

"Viv?" His voice was absolutely flat, his face absolutely still.

"Yes." Now I was hurtling down towards the frigid water, not knowing if I would touch bottom, let alone ever reach the surface again. "It was an accident. She didn't mean to shoot you. Or anyone. She thought we were burglars. That we were trying to hurt Mercury. She pulled the trigger by mistake."

"Viv?"

"I'm sorry, and I'm sorry I—"

"You're fucking sorry? I nearly died."

He was on his feet, overturning the coffee table, tumbling my glass to the floor, dropping his own. He swore at Viv, swore at me, called down the gods. "But where did she get a gun? And why would she shoot me? And if it was an accident, why wouldn't you tell me? You saw how I was suffering day after day."

Beneath the hail of furious words I sat bolt upright, terrified and relieved. Suddenly he swayed. "I'm going to be sick," he said.

I jumped up and led him to the kitchen. I stood beside him as he heaved into the sink. "Do you feel better?" I said at last.

"My arm is killing me."

I got him settled back on the sofa and brought two painkillers from the bathroom cabinet and a glass of water. "Drink slowly," I cautioned.

He rested his head against the sofa. I went to the kitchen and cleaned the sink. Then I fetched water and salt. Kneeling at his feet, I attacked the wine stains.

"Did you get it all?" he said very quietly.

"Almost."

"Tell me again. What the hell was Viv doing with a gun?"

Still kneeling, I told him the story. "She was obsessed with Mercury," I said. "She thought he could win all these competitions. That he was her last great chance. Then"—I hesitated and hurried on—"there were these break-ins at Windy Hill, and she got a gun to protect him. She never meant to use it. She should have gone to the police immediately. So should I. But when they came to the emergency room, I didn't say anything. And then . . ." I faltered on the dark shores. "Then it was easier to keep saying nothing."

"To lie."

"To lie. It was wrong, and it was stupid. We wanted to protect the children. But it didn't work. Marcus started acting up at school. Trina started having nightmares. As for me . . ."

How to explain that I had wanted to save everyone? I scrubbed at a wine stain near the table. "It was partly my fault," I went on, "that Viv got a gun. After my father died, I was very remote. She said it was like I was wearing an astronaut's suit. Even after all she's done, I hate to think of her in prison."

Jack took a deep breath, and another as I described the role I had played, inadvertently, in her decisions. Now I understand why Viv told me about sleeping with her colleague. I wanted him to know every last bad, terrible thing I had done.

Finally he interrupted. "For Christ's sake, Donald, I'm not your father confessor. Deal with your own shit."

We were both silent. In the kitchen the tap was dripping at long intervals: a solitary ping, ping, ping. In a low voice, he began to recite:

Animula vagula blandula,
Hospes comesque corporis . . .

Later I looked up Emperor Hadrian's famous poem and found forty-three translations. Here is one from 1625:

> *Minion soul, poor wanton thing*
> *The body's guest, my dearest darling.*
> *To what places art thou going?*
> *Naked miserable trembling,*
> *Reaving me of all the joy*
> *Which by thee I did enjoy.*

Even at the time, the Latin only vaguely familiar, I understood that Jack was trying to comfort himself. As he lapsed back into silence, I remembered his remarks at the swimming pool about anger and pain, how the former was only an attempt to hide from the latter. I knelt there on his wine-stained carpet, doing my best not to hide.

Seated in a corner of the sofa, his dark glasses aiming straight ahead, he began to speak. Some parts of his story I knew already: the drunk father falling in and out of jobs, the moves from one cheap apartment to the next, the teachers who encouraged him.

"I didn't care," he said, "if people knew I did drugs, or shoplifted, but I didn't want anyone to know about my going to the library. One night—I must have been eight or nine—Dad came and sat on the edge of my bed and made shadow animals: a wolf, a squirrel, a rabbit. All the time he was doing it, I could hear my mother calling, 'Colm, Colm Christopher, get your lazy ass out here.' My father just laughed. He'd been fired again. We had no electricity for a month, but it was spring. We had a gas stove. We joked about our cold showers.

"My bad sister escaped into religion. My good sister found

her own way to the library. The police picked me up half a dozen times but always let me go with a warning. I went to the community college for a year and then to U Mass. My only religion was avoiding my family. I remember standing in my dorm room, holding my letter from Boston University, thinking, Now I'm free. I'm nobody's son, nobody's brother. I moved to Boston, started on my PhD. Then one night I was in a bar with my friend Hector. We were arguing about the Roman emperors, and I brought my beer bottle down on his head.

"When he came to a few minutes later, he had no idea what had happened. I told him, and he was amazed. Why would you hit me? he said. It didn't seem to occur to him to call the police. I walked him home, and then I walked along Commonwealth Ave all the way to Boston Common. I swore on the monument to the first black regiment in the Civil War that nothing like this was going to happen again. I wasn't going to be my father's son."

I knelt there, saying nothing. As long as Jack kept talking, there was hope.

"But there was one small problem," he continued. "I couldn't fucking see. I denied it long and hard. I went to movies, rode a bike, swam and hiked, made a fool of myself in nightclubs. My denial worked until it didn't. One day when Marie-Claire was out, her ex-boyfriend rang the bell. He'd come to pick up his stuff. He went around the living room and the bedroom, made half a dozen trips to his car. When Marie-Claire came home, I told her about her ex's visit. She went nuts. What else had he stolen? I said I didn't know. But you were here, she said. You saw what happened. Not really, I said.

"At first she didn't believe me. Then she stood across the room. What am I holding up? What am I holding up now?

When she got it—I was a fake sighted person—she threw me out. I came back and begged her, twice. The second time was when I tore the sink out of the wall.

"I finished my PhD, got my job, and one day I wandered into an optician's and let someone, you, examine my eyes. You said two bad Latin words—retinitis pigmentosa—and offered the small consolation that there was nothing I, or anyone, could have done; it was hereditary. When I reached my mom in one of her lucid moments, she said, Oh, yes, Colm was blind as a bat. Dad wasn't just a feckless Irishman; he was a feckless, blind Irishman. Glasses were expensive, and he was always a prescription or two behind. My entire adult life I'd been determined to be the opposite of him, and here I was."

I remembered Hilary in the emergency room, telling me that they wanted to have a child. But it was none of my business and never would be.

"I liked your reserve," Jack went on, "and I admired your relationship with your father. You were so devoted. After he died, I worried you'd go off the rails, but I never imagined anything like this. I can understand you lying to the police at the hospital, wanting to talk to Viv first. But that you kept on lying, even when you saw my despair, saw that I felt singled out by the universe, seems like cruel and unusual punishment."

He was quoting, I realized, another part of the faded Bill of Rights I had not been able to read. "I wasn't trying to hurt you," I said. "It just took me a while to figure out the right thing to do."

He sighed, a long, slow sigh. The fingers of his good hand clenched and unclenched. "That's my whole point," he said. "You weren't thinking about me."

I wanted to protest; for days, he had occupied most of my

waking thoughts. But before I could speak, he said, "Did you know that Hilary's decided to sell Mercury?"

Dumbstruck, I stared at the photograph of Moonshine and Michael. The irony that now, when it was much too late, Mercury could have belonged to Viv was piercing. "No, I didn't."

"I thought you'd be thrilled to see the last of him."

"I'm just wondering," I said slowly, "what this will mean to Viv."

"Why should it mean anything?" His face was stony. "A guy named Adams came by Hilary's office. He offered fifteen. She got him up to eighteen and the promise, in writing, that she can visit Mercury whenever she wants. If he decides to sell, he'll come to her first."

"Adams?" This time I recognized Charlie's last name immediately. Once again, with a single sentence—"He's Hilary's horse"—I had changed everything.

"Stop kneeling there like some goddamn martyr," Jack said, "and pour me another glass of wine."

I fetched a tumbler and poured him the remains of the bottle. "Hilary loves you," I said. "Find a good psychiatrist. The black moods aren't you. They're caused by the chemistry—"

He held up his hand. "Don't," he said, his voice almost kind. "You and Viv, between you, you've caused me so much physical pain, so much mental distress. In a way I can understand what Viv did. It was a mistake of passion. But you lied to me day after day. Even when you were helping me, you were lying. All that crap about Odysseus, about our friendship. It seems so cold-blooded." He raised his glass, drank deeply.

I know many of the tricks our vision can play, that our eyes can persuade us one arrow is longer than its identical twin, that a book is simultaneously opening and closing, that pink is blue or yellow is green, but I had not understood that my claim to have imagined what it would be like to lose Jack hid the deep conviction that I wouldn't. Once again I had been deceiving myself. Perhaps, eventually, as Robert had said, he would forgive me, but for now he was lost to me. I stood beside the sofa in the well-lit room—I had turned on the lights to scrub the carpet—and let my eyes rest on my friend. I would see him across the street, at the gym, but I would no longer have his permission to gaze at him, no longer walk by his side. I had not saved everyone. Indeed it was not clear if I had saved anyone.

"One of the first things Viv told me about Mercury," I said, "was that he was hot-blooded. It's the cold-blooded horses that do all the work, go into battle, plow—"

Again he cut me off. "I see where you're going with this. You're the humble, hardworking Dobbins. I understand you found yourself between a rock and a hard place, but in the end you hurt both of us, Viv and me."

"Are you saying I should have kept lying? That that would have been better?" Only a moment before he had said the opposite, that my continuing to lie was the worst offense of all.

"I don't know," said Jack. "I don't f'ing know. Ask me again in a year. If you'd been stronger, you wouldn't have lied in the first place, but once you did, maybe you should have kept going. Maybe that would have been kinder, less self-indulgent. Now Viv's going to prison. I've lost one more person. Your kids are thrown into this maelstrom. How exactly is the world a better place because you finally deigned to tell me the truth?"

I had thought I knew the answer—that it was, as my father had argued, always better to tell the truth, that to live as a liar would ruin my life, and those of the people I loved—but in the face of Jack's weary question, the certainty I had found with

Robert was gone. I was deep in the cold, dark water, the day-light of forgiveness far above. I picked up my jacket and walked out of the room.

As I stepped into the street a man strolled by, whistling a bright, complicated tune. In my Edinburgh childhood I often heard men whistling, but as an adult in America I seldom do. Now I stood listening until the stranger carried his melody out of earshot.

18

THAT EVENING WE TOLD the children, or to be precise, Viv did. "I did something bad," she said, "something terribly wrong. It was an accident, but it's going to make things hard for all of us for a while."

When she finished, Marcus said, "So Jack was in the hospital because of you."

Trina began to cry. Poachers shot elephants, she said. We were no better than poachers.

"I was only trying to protect Mercury," Viv said. Then, seeing my face, she stopped.

We went to the Mexican restaurant, and she and I took turns reciting stories from our family lore. Viv described teaching Marcus to swim; she'd let go of him for a moment, and he was halfway across the pool. I described the time a neighbor's cat got stuck up our maple tree and Trina had coaxed it into a basket. We talked about visiting the Brooklyn Zoo, and our long-postponed family trip to Edinburgh

"Your mom—," I started to say.

"Please, Dad." Trina scowled at me over her untouched plate. "Don't start talking American."

After they were in bed, Viv told me she had hired a lawyer. Hopefully she could get one or two of the charges dropped.

"So there's no chance of a fine, or probation, or a suspended sentence?" I was throwing out all the terms I knew.

She shook her head. "Even if the judge accepts that the shooting was an accident, there are mandatory sentences for buying a gun illegally, bringing it into Massachusetts. The thing that will count the most is the victim impact statement. If Jack were to forgive me—"

"I'm afraid that's not very likely," I said, and told her about our conversation.

I had imagined, over and over the prison clothes, the handcuffs, the bars, the narrow bed but now, listening to Viv, looking at her, her fair skin and blue eyes, her long neck and elegant collarbones, her strong hands and crooked finger, her lean hips and small feet, none of this was remotely imaginable.

"Will you wait for me?" she said.

No life is without suffering, my father used to say, but I hope never again to see on another person's face what I saw on Viv's when I told her that Hilary was selling Mercury, and that Charlie was buying him.

19

My story is almost over, or at least I have set down the parts I want and feel able to tell. I never believed I was great or awesome, but I had my secret vanity. I was my father's son; I believed myself to be a person of integrity. In the aftermath of that night at Windy Hill, I lost that belief. I lied out of (1) cowardice, (2) love of my children, (3) loyalty to Viv, (4) some essential flaw of character, (5) none, or all, of the above. I finally told the truth because I believed it was the right thing to do, morally and legally, but also because of my secret vanity. I do not fully understand my own behavior, so perhaps it is scarcely surprising that I do not understand Viv's. Why did she buy a gun, load it, fire it? I will never entirely know. We live in a country where such things are possible. In the time I have taken to write these pages, many others have done more or less what she did, often with fatal results.

Three weeks ago Viv appeared before the judge, a saturnine man in his forties. My mother, Larry, Claudia and her three-week-old son, Viv's friend Lucy, and I were present. Hilary sat watching us from across the room. I was glad she and Jack were still together. Viv was charged with five violations: purchasing a weapon illegally, carrying it illegally, shooting someone, etcetera, etcetera. The victim impact statement was one long howl of pain, a pain that Hilary corroborated in piercing detail. Viv received a sentence of a year, beginning after Labor Day, when the children would be safely back in school. With good behavior, it might be reduced to nine months. We will be able to visit her once a week.

I used to compare our family, in those years when everything worked, to the orrery in Edinburgh. We each had our preoccupations, and yet we were all orbiting the same sun. But after my father died, after Viv met Mercury and bought a gun and I lied about Charlie's riding, after she shot Jack, after we both spoke to the police and I confessed to Jack, the orbits in our orrery were vastly altered. We were still busy with school, work, meals, music and swimming lessons, homework, play dates, movies, but for Viv and me, and for the children too, I presume, everything changed as the people closest to us learned what had happened that night at Windy Hill. Viv told Claudia and our neighbors. I told my mother, Merrie, Steve, and Marcus and Trina's teachers. Our orbits wavered. The sun was often eclipsed. Our main priority, Viv and I agreed, was our beloved children. How could we help them to emerge from this relatively unscathed?

I do not know what occurred between her and Claudia, but Viv continued to work at the stables, to take care of the horses, give lessons, manage the accounts. The day after she spoke to Claudia, Helen phoned to say she was an idiot, but if there was any horse that would make her, Helen, pick up a gun, it was Mercury. Steve, when I told him, said, "Fuck me gently with a chain saw. Donald, you never fail to surprise me." Merrie didn't speak to me for two days. Then she told me that the father of her youngest daughter was in prison for armed robbery. If all the guns in America ended up in the Gulf of Mexico, she would crawl from here to Lourdes in gratitude.

As for my mother, for the third time we met at the bar. I walked there after work and ordered our Bloody Marys. I felt, as I had when I stood on Jack's doorstep, that my life was about to change in momentous and irrevocable ways. She arrived in excellent spirits, her fair hair gleaming against her dark coat, her blue eyes bright. She had landed a new account with a big pharmaceutical company. Congratulations, I said, and before she could offer further distractions, launched into my increasingly practiced story.

My mother exclaimed, swore, asked for clarification. When I finished, she said, "What an ungodly mess. I can't believe Viv would do this to Jack. To you and the children. What on earth was she thinking?"

I drank and let her anger wash over me. All around us on the TV screens football players, hockey players, basketball players, were flashing by. Viv had aspired to be among these star athletes. At the bar three men leaped to their feet, flinging up their arms in triumph.

When my mother finally stopped exclaiming, I said, "I lied too."

"Yes," she said. "That's not like you, Donald."

She was looking at me steadily, and I knew she understood how the Simurg had nearly carried me away and how, day by day, I was seeking to make amends. Like Jack, I wanted to get back to the person I believed myself to be. I told her how I had finally found Robert and how we had met in the Peacock Room.

"I'm so glad," she said. "I still remember the phone call with his mother when I realized he didn't know we were staying in the States."

"If you had to do it over again," I said, "would you decide to stay here?"

"Edward asked me that just before he went to the nursing home. I told him I didn't know. When he got too ill to travel, I wished his cousins were nearby, but the doctors here are terrific. We had opportunities we would never have had in Edinburgh."

As she raised her glass, I noticed something was missing: her wedding ring. When had she removed it? I wondered. Yesterday? The day after Jean died?

"What I do regret," she went on, "is not realizing how one thing would lead to another. I really did think we were coming here for two years. Then I got this amazing job offer, and we decided to stay until you and Fran finished school. But by that time Edward had his garden, and he was walking in the Adirondacks, and I had a great team . . ."

She trailed off, looked down at her bare hands, and met my gaze again. "I would have done anything for you and Fran, but I had to live my own life. I've always been grateful that you were less selfish. You came back when we needed you. Edward often said—we both did—how lucky we were to have you in our lives."

My mother raised her glass and turned to look at the nearest TV screen, giving me my privacy. I sat there, silently repeating her words. In the midst of many mistakes, I had done one good thing.

"So," she said gently, "will you wait for Viv?"

I was no closer to answering the question than I had been when Viv asked it. "I don't know," I said.

Now she was watching me, trying to read in my face what I could not, or would not, say. "You'll take good care of the children," she persisted, "run the household, but when she gets out of prison, will you go on being married?"

"I don't know," I said again. "I need to figure that out."

" 'Figure,' " said my mother. "That makes it sound like you're going to measure and calculate. Find the right prescription. But this is about your feelings, Donald. Maybe you should talk to someone like Graham?"

"Would you like another drink?" I said. "Do you and Larry have summer plans?"

But a few nights after our conversation, I started writing this account. I wanted to understand what had happened: how Viv had changed, how I had changed, how we had failed each other not in sickness or in health but in the hard task of leading our daily lives. If I imagine anyone reading these pages, then it is my father. Or perhaps the Simurg, with a pair of reading glasses balanced on his beak.

On a Monday morning in April, with Viv's appearance before the judge still three months away, I walked Marcus and Trina to school, returned home, started the car, and went into the house to fetch Nabokov. When I emerged, his cage in one hand, my briefcase in the other, a police car was parked in the driveway. An older man in uniform approached.

"Mr. Stevenson?" His long, good-natured face made it easy to picture him ignoring insults, quelling bad behavior.

I acknowledged my name. Meanwhile Nabokov, perhaps mistaking his uniform for that of a train conductor, began to recite a railway timetable. "The train for Inverness will depart at eleven oh six precisely."

The policeman asked if Ms. Turner was at home. I said she had already left for Windy Hill. "Might I ask what this is about?"

"We found the weapon." It had, he told me, been retrieved from the woods two days before. Tests confirmed that the powder marks matched the bullet taken from Jack's shoulder.

Two cardinals were flitting around the porch; under the maple tree the first crocuses were in bloom. While I set Nabokov's cage on the roof of my car, the policeman walked back to his car. He returned, holding a ziplock bag of the kind I had just used for Marcus and Trina's sandwiches. There was the gun, the small black gun, that Viv had accidentally fired at Jack; that she might, if her aim had shifted an inch or two, have fired at me. He held it out for my inspection. It was much smaller than the one he carried at his waist. I stared, fascinated.

"I've never held a real gun," I said.

I can no longer recall exactly how I asked the question, what words I used, but after a moment's calculation he reached into the bag and, pointing the gun at the ground, handed it to me. It fitted my hand with the ease of a good tool. I stood there, holding it carefully, feeling the solid weight of it. The last time I had held a gun of any kind was as a schoolboy in Edinburgh, playing cowboys with Robert in the local park. But this was not a toy. This was an extremely efficient machine that had changed my life in almost every way.

"Do you mind," I said, "if I pull the trigger?"

Again the policeman made some kind of calculation, taking in my clean shirt, my dark trousers, my freshly polished shoes. "Don't point it at me," he said, and stepped over to stand beside Nabokov.

I raised the gun, aimed at the vivid male cardinal, and—it took surprisingly little effort—pulled the trigger.

ACKNOWLEDGMENTS

First the books, then the people. A number of books kept me company, guided and informed me in the writing of *Mercury*. I am happy to say that Enid Bagnold's *National Velvet* remains as wonderful as the day it was published in 1935. More recently Laura Hillenbrand's *Seabiscuit,* Jane Smiley's *Horse Heaven,* and John Jermiah Sullivan's *Blood Horses* gave me great pleasure and suggested ways to think and write about horses. I am also indebted to *The Nature of Horses* by Stephen Budiansky; *How to Think Like a Horse* by Cherry Hill; *The Horse in Human History* by Pita Kelekna; *The Eighty-Dollar Champion* by Elizabeth Letts; *Horse Sense* by John Mettler; and *Chosen by a Horse* by Susan Richards.

Keeping African Grey Parrots by David Aldington helped me to think about Nabokov.

I am grateful to the authors of several lucid and inspiring books about the experience of going blind at a young age. Three in particular enabled me to empathize more deeply: *Touching the Rock* by John M. Hull; *Cockeyed: A Memoir* by Ryan Knighton; and *Planet of the Blind* by Stephen Kuusisto. I read *All About Your Eyes* by the physicians at the Duke University Eye Center too many times for comfort. Rosemary Mahoney's *For the Benefit of Those Who See: Dispatches from the World of the Blind* gracefully combines insight and erudition; I am grateful for both. Lastly I want to thank the librarian at the Perkins School for the Blind who patiently answered my many questions.

And there were my lovely human guides. Many years ago in Scotland Chrissie Bulman taught me to ride on a gelding named Ginger. I never thanked them; I do now. My friend Gail Boyajian allowed me to accompany her to the stables and answered many, many questions. I am grateful for her enthusiasm and her friendship. Abby Travis, a stellar rider and a terrific writer, shared with me her encyclopedic knowledge of horses and her many insights into the world of riding. She generously commented on the manuscript. Christina Maranci took me to Bobbie's Ranch.

John McDonough kindly met with me on several occasions and answered innumerable questions about police procedures. He also asked his own extremely helpful questions which encouraged me to think about my characters in new ways.

Needless to say I am to blame for any remaining errors in the book.

I am grateful to my colleagues and students at Emerson College and the Iowa Writers' Workshop, and to the Radcliffe Institute of Advanced Study at Harvard University where portions of this book were written.

I am delighted to offer my heartfelt thanks yet again to my amazing agent, Amanda Urban, and my brilliant editor, Jennifer Barth. Together they helped me to write the story I wanted to tell. I count myself hugely fortunate to have Jane Beirn as an ally. And my deep gratitude to the many other talented people at HarperCollins who helped to bring this book into the world: Amy Baker, Robin Bilardello, Jonathan Burnham, Stephanie Cooper, Lydia Weaver, Erin Wicks.

ACKNOWLEDGMENTS

My friends and family are instrumental in my writing; they give me a home in the world. I thank Kathleen Hill for the continuous gift of her friendship. Susan Brison kept me company on good days and bad ones. Her comments on the novel were inspiring and invaluable. My gratitude to Eric Garnick for his reading of the manuscript and for his gorgeous novelistic paintings; he brings beauty into my life every day. The incident on page 251 is based on a story he told me about his friend Rick Schettler. I am running out of ways to thank Andrea Barrett. Her fierce advice, her keen insight, and her rigorous empathy helped to make this first a book, then a better book.

None of this would have been possible without Merril Sylvester.

ABOUT THE AUTHOR

Margot Livesey is the *New York Times* bestselling author of the novels *The Flight of Gemma Hardy, The House on Fortune Street, Banishing Verona, Eva Moves the Furniture, The Missing World, Criminals*, and *Homework*. Her work has appeared in the *New Yorker, Vogue*, and the *Atlantic*, and she is the recipient of grants from both the National Endowment for the Arts and the Guggenheim Foundation. *The House on Fortune Street* won the 2009 L.L. Winship/PEN New England Award. Livesey was born in Scotland and grew up on the edge of the Highlands. She lives in the Boston area and is a professor of fiction at the Iowa Writers' Workshop.

A NOTE ON THE TYPE

THE TEXT OF THIS book is set in Bembo. Bembo is a 1929 old-style serif typeface most commonly used for body text. It is based on a design cut by Francesco Griffo for printer Aldus Manutius around 1495, and named for Manutius's first publication with it, a small 1496 book by the poet and cleric Pietro Bembo.